THE LAWYER AND THE ASTRONAUT

Jerry Lucas

Published in the United States of America

ISBN 978-1-962730-16-7 (SC)

Jerry Lucas Publishing
222 West 6th Street
Suite 400, San Pedro, CA, 90731
www.stellarliterary.com

Ordering Information and Rights Permission:

Quantity sales. Special discounts might be available on quantity purchases by corporations, associations, and others. For details, contact the publisher at the address above.

For Book Rights Adaptation and other Rights Permission. Call us at toll-free 1-888-945-8513 or send us an email at admin@stellarliterary.com.

Contents

Dedicated to Adriana, my super-hot wife and girlfriend.

1

Josh didn't like his boss. As far as he was concerned, he and his boss were two different people, almost from different planets. Josh was a technologist. His boss was a political hack. Josh was creative and alive. His boss was mundane and half dead.

So, when he walked into his boss's office on that morning, he knew why his boss had asked for this meeting. He knew before his boss said anything. His boss was sitting at his desk and had an accompanying entourage of three other people. One was from the personnel department, one was from the legal department, and one was Josh's boss's boss. Josh was wearing jeans and a short-sleeved shirt. These other guys were wearing expensive suits. Josh's hair was unkempt. His boss had probably recently been to an expensive hair stylist. Just seeing him made Josh sick. Josh's boss was a stupid, ignorant, non-productive know-nothing who somehow had the power.

In twenty minutes, it was over, and Josh was unemployed again. He was a little shaken as he left the office and packed up his things. When he got home, he plopped himself down on his bed, and did some thinking. Part of him was relieved. He was free now. He didn't have to get up tomorrow morning and go to the job he hated. But another part of him was facing an uncomfortable truth. This was the third job in four years that he had been fired from. He was a smart guy. He knew that. But maybe his ex-wife was right about him. He could not hold a job. He was not a reliable provider for his family.

For a while, he looked for some work. He sent out thirty resumes and letters to prospective employers, but got nowhere. Then one day, things changed. He came across an advertisement for something interesting. A job description title read:

WANTED: PARTICIPANTS IN MANNED
INTERPLANETARY PROBE MISSIONS

The accompanying article gave more information. The main requirements would be a knowledge of general science, and a proficiency with mathematics.

The candidate would spend some time on an alien planet, and report on his findings.

Josh thought about this. He needed a job, for sure. He was living on his life savings right now, and that was about to run out. But spending time on an alien planet? What would that be like? Would he have to fight for his life against savage beasts? Would he freeze to death or die of heat exhaustion in some strange climate? Would he starve to death from a lack of food? Even worse, what if the planet was populated by intelligent beings who would promptly execute him as an alien invader?

For the next few days, Josh made follow-up calls to jobs that he had already applied for. He got nowhere. Josh reasoned that he wasn't very interested in those jobs anyway. What really got his heart throbbing was exploring outer space. The risks be damned, he wanted to go to outer space. So, he applied for the job. He waited anxiously, each day checking for some response.

Finally, he received what he had been waiting for. It was a letter, requesting him to appear at a government office for an interview. He tucked the response letter into his jacket pocket, forgot about all his other job applications, and nervously sat around until his appointed day.

On the day of his interview, he had the normal jitters. He worried about what clothes to wear, and how to get himself there on time. He rehearsed some questions that he thought they might ask him, like why he got fired so many times. He was scared of that question. He wasn't sure how to answer it.

He showed up in casual dress, his hair neatly combed, and his palms sweaty. A pleasant female secretary showed him into a large conference room. He had gotten here too early. He sat and waited.

In a few minutes, the secretary returned, handed him some sheets of paper, and said, "This is your test. You have to remove all electronic devices and hand them over to me. You have one hour to complete the test."

Josh obediently handed over his electronics. "Thank you, Josh. Your time starts now." And she left Josh alone in the room.

Josh looked over the test. There were sections on physics, chemistry, mathematics, astronomy, and celestial navigation. Most of the questions seemed relatively straightforward, and Josh tried to speed through the easier questions, in an effort to finish within the time limit. But then there were the harder ones. Not questions exactly, problems. There were problems in orbital dynamics, a difficult subject. Then there were problems in navigation, for example, "Suppose you are in a space ship and you take sightings on three stars, how do you figure out where you are." The problem actually named three stars for him, and gave sighting angles. Josh knew this stuff, but he didn't have that much time to crank through the mathematics without his calculator or handheld computer. Then there was chemistry: balancing chemical equations without the use of a periodic table, and calculating rates of decay for certain radioactive elements. As Josh worked through the tougher questions, his opinion of the test changed. Josh said to himself, "God, this is hard", and faced the realization that he wouldn't complete the fifty questions in time. Regrettably, he was right. He was in the middle of question 47 when the secretary came in to collect his paper. There were three questions that he didn't get to at all. He handed in his paper, and the secretary returned his electronics. She left the room without saying a word, leaving Josh to wonder what was going on.

He sat for what seemed like a long time, when finally, a middle-aged man entered the room. He was dressed casually, and smiled pleasantly at Josh.

"Hello, Josh" he said, as he sat down at the large desk, opposite from Josh. "My name is Larry."

"Hi," said Josh, wondering how he did on the test, but afraid to ask.

"So, tell me, Josh. What interests you about this job?"

"Unlike other jobs that I've had, space travel fires my passion. It's something I can get excited about."

"And what about your other jobs? You didn't find those interesting?"

"No, not at all," said Josh. "I never had a job that I liked. I was just working to pay the bills, not working to accomplish something."

"I see", said Larry. "That might explain your rather poor job history. "

"Yes," said Josh. "I performed poorly because of a lack of interest. My job performance is not a reflection of my abilities or my personality traits."

"Okay, then, let's move on. I'm going to point out some of the negatives of this job. First, there is a very good chance that you will be killed. You have to survive space travel in a small craft. Then you have to spend time on an alien planet in an alien environment. Lots of bad stuff could happen to you."

"I realize that," said Josh.

"Then there is the time that you would be gone. This could be a few years or it could be thousands of years. It depends on where you are sent. Our planet may not even be recognizable to you if you are gone for a long time. Coming back could be a real adjustment. In fact, coming back may be a tougher adjustment than arriving at the alien planet."

"I guess if I am gone for thousands of years, I would not age by thousands of years? Because of relativity and time dilation?"

"Yes, of course. But say you were gone for thousands of years by the time as measured here. Your own clock on the ship would still move by hundreds of years. So, for a trip that long, you would be put into a deep freeze to stop you from aging. You would be woken up automatically when you approach the destination. Same thing on the way back. And select family members, like your wife or your children – this is up to you. They could also be put in a deep freeze during the time that you are gone. But I don't know if you would want to do this to them. My personal advice is to let them live out their normal lives. They would never see you again, but that is less burdensome than having to adjust to a new life thousands of years in the future."

"What about money?" Josh asked. "If I'm gone for that long, all that I have now will become worthless."

"A trust will be set up in your name. Of course, there is risk of some kind of financial collapse, which could well happen over thousands of years. But the likelihood is that you will return a rich man. Another option is you could designate a beneficiary to receive your salary until they die, or until you return."

Josh was quiet. He couldn't think of more questions.

Then Larry spoke. "I guess I need to back up and explain this program to you. No one knows what life will be like in several thousand years or a million years. But, given enough time, catastrophes can and will happen. We could get hit with a stray comet or asteroid, for example. Now we do have systems in place to defend against those things, but they are not foolproof. A nuclear or biological war could develop, and our entire race could be wiped out. Overpopulation could cut into our food supply. Our sun could go nova, wiping out our whole planetary system, although we don't expect this for millions of years. Or a supernova in a neighboring star system could happen, and wipe us out.

"Now I am not trying to frighten us to death of these things that probably won't even happen. But it does make sense to plan for our own survival in the worst case. The idea is to colonize other habitable planets. It is the principle of diversification. If our race is scattered among many planets, a disaster that hits one of the planets won't wipe us out. So then comes the matter of figuring out which planets are habitable. That's where you come in. Your job is to do reconnaissance. Tell us about the environment on the planet where we send you. Is it livable?"

"Can't an unmanned probe tell us the same things?" asked Josh.

"An unmanned probe tells us a lot. We can learn about the climate and see if there is any possibility of life. We can learn about natural resources on the planet. We can also learn about energy sources, such as petrochemicals, hydroelectric, wind power, ocean waves, radioactive materials for nuclear energy, for example. We can learn about the presence of heavy metals, necessary for a technology and tool making. But there is much that we can only learn by a manned expedition. For example, the kinds of life forms that live on the planet, and how they interact. How many different species of intelligent life forms are there? Are the life forms able to communicate, and can they build tools? How advanced are their technologies and how rapidly are the technologies developing? Are any of the life forms warlike? Is the planet vulnerable to extreme weather events such as ice ages?

"Of course, the ultimate bottom line is to figure out if the planet can be colonized. This is complicated, since we are really talking about the planet a few thousand years into the future. If the planet's technology is primitive, then things won't change much in a few thousand years. But, with an advanced technology, new inventions and scientific breakthroughs can happen at a startling rate. This is another area where you come in. How advanced is their technology, and how quickly might it evolve over a few thousand years?"

Josh didn't say anything, so Larry finally said, "Do you have any questions for me?"

"Just one," Josh said. "How did I do on the test?"

"Well, you passed," Larry said. "I guess you figured that out by now."

"I didn't finish all the questions."

"No one finishes all the questions. It's a tough test with a tough time limit.

"Well, next you'll be talking with Peter. We call him the flight director, because he organizes all the trips. Good luck with whatever happens." Larry smiled, shook Josh's hand, and left the room.

In a short while, Peter entered the room. He introduced himself, shook Josh's hand, and took a seat.

"Well, I guess Larry already prepared you for the worst case, that you may be gone for one thousand years or more."

"Yes, he did," Josh said, as he nervously gulped.

"You may have heard stories that the universe is full of life, and full of planets that can support life. That is simply not true. The planets that are habitable are very rare and widely scattered. The planet that we have in mind for you is 500 light years away. The good news is we have a very good propulsion system that will take you there at 80% of light speed."

"How is that possible?" asked Josh.

"Well, we use first a solar sail, which constantly orients itself to receive radiation pressure from the light of the nearest star. It propels a spaceship similar to a sailboat with a large sail being pushed by the wind. On top of that, we use a hydrogen scoop. That is a scoop at the front of the spacecraft to suck in hydrogen molecules. Then, similar to an old-fashioned jet engine, the stream of hydrogen molecules is compressed and shot out the rear to drive the ship forward. Contrary to what many people think, deep space is not a vacuum. Hydrogen molecules exist and are quite plentiful. Anyways, the solar sail combined with the hydrogen scoop gets you to travel most of your trip at 80% of light speed. Of course, we cannot use any kind of fuel, solid or liquid, for an interplanetary flight.

"Now the numbers. To travel the 500 light years at 80% of light speed will take about 625 years as measured on Earth's clock. Because of relativistic time dilation, this corresponds to 375 years of ship time. So for you to travel back and forth to the planet will mean that you will be gone for 1250 years, not counting the time you spend on the planet itself. As Larry explained, you will be put in a deep freeze during your journey, so you will not age at all while on the space ship, even though the ship's clock will advance 375 years for each one-way trip.

"Now as for the planet in question," Peter began, as he pulled out a miniature video projector, and clicked to make an image of the planet appear on the opposite wall. "As you can see, the planet is very much like our Earth. There are large oceans and lakes with liquid water. There are polar ice caps that change with the seasons. Spectroscopic analysis shows that the planet's temperature range is very similar to that on Earth, and the atmosphere is pretty much an exact duplicate of the Earth's. There is also evidence of geologic activity. That is important because it shows an active carbon cycle, which moderates temperature swings. The planet's day and year are amazingly similar to Earth's. Infrared analysis shows us heat signatures which are suggestive of animal life. If there is animal life on the planet, we do not believe that it is technologically advanced. We see no evidence of radio transmissions, for example. We also see no evidence of roads and bridges. None of this means much, of course. If we think about it, we can certainly imagine advanced life forms with no need for roads, bridges, radio communication, or even electricity. But our best educated guess at this point is that there are animal life forms that live in a very primitive state.

"The planet, its sun, and its whole planetary system are much younger than ours. Our Earth is 4.6 billion years old, give or take. This planet, to our best guess, is about 200 million years younger than Earth. If life develops on it in a way parallel to the Earth, then it is several million years behind us."

After a long pause, Peter said, "Well, Josh, where are you so far? Does this sound like something you may want to try?"

"I honestly don't know," Josh said. "I'm a little overwhelmed right now."

"That's understandable," said Peter. "I know it's not an easy decision. Tell you what. Give it some time, slosh it around in your head, and let's meet again in two weeks. You will probably come up with more questions by then."

"Okay," said Josh. He shook hands with Peter, and then slowly stumbled out of the room, his head spinning.

On his way home, there was one thought that stuck in Josh's brain. Here was a planet with conditions very similar to Earth, but millions of years younger. What if the planet's life forms evolved in a way to mimic the Earth? Then, Josh would visit an image of the Earth as it existed millions of years ago. After that, Josh would return to Earth twelve hundred years into the future. Josh's mind was flooded with possibilities. He knew then that he would have to accept the job.

2

When Josh got home, he noticed he had a video message on his phone. It was from Laura, one of his former coworkers. He wondered why he hadn't heard it when it arrived. Probably she had sent it while Josh was taking his test, and his electronic gear had been taken away. Laura was a nice young lady. Josh liked her. He thought it would have been nice to date her, but the company did not allow such behavior among its workers. In her message, Laura said she wanted to meet for lunch.

John messaged her back. She responded and they talked over the video link.

"How have you been doing, Josh? Nobody has heard from you since you left and we're all wondering about you."

"I'm basically fine," Josh said. "A lot has been going on with me. Anyways, sure, let's meet for lunch. Maybe tomorrow around noon?"

"Sure," she said. "What about that nice Italian place over near the office?"

"Sounds good," Josh said. "See you then."

The next day, Josh came to the restaurant. Laura was already there waiting for him.

"How are you?" she said, as Josh was sitting down.

"Well, my answer to that is long and complicated, so why don't we start with you. How are you doing?"

"Well, you remember Doug, the creep that laid you off a while ago. Well, he just laid me off yesterday."

"My God! Why?"

"I don't know. He never liked me, and, when I fell behind schedule on one of my projects, he figured that was his chance to dump me."

"Man, what a jerk."

"Yeah. The worst boss I ever had."

"So, what are you going to do now? Are you looking for another job?"

"Doug just canned me yesterday. I haven't done anything yet. I absolutely hate looking for work. My parents are really poor. I don't think they will help me. And I wouldn't think of asking my ex-husband. I can't stand the guy. I don't know what to do."

She started to cry. At first just a quiet sob, but soon it became an uncontrolled gushing torrent. Josh slowly took her hand, and held it. Eventually, she stopped crying, but Josh kept holding her hand. They just sat together, silently, for several minutes.

Finally, Josh spoke. "For what it's worth, my humble opinion is that the best thing to do is nothing. Just let this mess blow over. Give it a few weeks. Then you can start looking for work."

"Josh, I only have three weeks of severance pay. After that I'm broke. I don't have any savings to speak of. I've been living paycheck to paycheck for years."

Josh couldn't think of what to say to that. So, he just kept quiet, ate some food, and went through an awkward silence.

Finally, Laura spoke up. "I'm sorry, Josh. I'm just in a rotten mood right now. And I really don't know what to do."

"Well," said Josh. "Let me do a little brainstorming with you. First, it will be easier for you to get a job than me. I mean, my employment record is terrible. Every place I go, I'm let go in a year or less. On top of that, I'm no good at job interviewing. I think you would do a lot better at landing a decent job. But, having said that, there are ways to make honest money without having a conventional job. For example, you could start your own company."

"Start my own company? How could I do that without any money?"

"Well, you start out very small, obviously. You get a small business startup loan, as soon as you start showing some profits. And you do something that you're passionate about."

"Hmm," said Laura. "I need to think about that. Sounds difficult."

"You could always write a book. Write a good whodunit about your former boss getting murdered."

She laughed at that.

"Or," Josh continued, "There are lots of jobs that require very little training to do, and pay really well, like realtor, for example. You could probably do okay selling houses, or at least as good as most people."

"You are certainly helping me to look at the positive side of this mess, Josh", she said. "A career change won't be easy but it's something to think about. But what about you, Josh? What have you been doing?"

"After Doug canned me, I started frantically looking for work. I sent out thirty resumes, made a bunch of phone calls, met with a couple of headhunters. It all went nowhere. I didn't get one response back, no letters, no emails, no phone calls, zip."

"That isn't very encouraging," Laura commented.

"I suppose not, but you have to remember that no one will hire me. My job record is awful. I suspect that you will find something, if you choose to job-search."

"Maybe," she said, appearing not too convinced. "But what about this business about 'long and complicated' that you mentioned earlier? Sending out thirty resumes and getting no responses is not a complicated thing."

"Well, you'll probably think I'm crazy, but here goes."

And Josh went on to tell her about the manned interplanetary probe business. He told her everything. He just blurted it all out. He was sure that he was boring her, or maybe even disgusting her, but he was wrong. She listened intently, and asked some good questions, almost making Josh rethink his whole opinion. When Josh finished talking, their one-hour lunch had expanded to four hours.

As they left the restaurant, they kissed. The next day, they met at a park, took a three-mile walk, then sat by a waterfall, and ate a picnic lunch. They did not talk at all about Josh's adventure, or about Laura's job hunting. They talked about meaningless things – favorite movies, past experiences, their old college lives, some of their common friends, the music that they each liked, and so forth.

On the day after that, they met in Laura's apartment, and she cooked him a dinner of lasagna and some veggies. They talked some more. They could not run out of things to talk about. In a way, Josh didn't want to leave Laura. They were each finding a love, and love was a rare thing to be cherished. But outer space was all that Josh had right now. He probably could not get another good job. If he could work at all, it would be sweeping floors at a grocery store or something. Worse still, he would probably get fired from that job too.

He kept seeing Laura every day, and they shared happy times together. When it was four days before he was to meet again with Peter, he and Laura were sitting at a picnic bench, having lunch by their favorite waterfall.

"Laura," Josh said, "You mean the world to me. You're the only person in the world who cares about me, or so it seems. The last thing in the world I want to do is leave you and disappear off in space. But I'm afraid I have to. There's nothing for me here. For whatever reason, I can't seem to hold a job."

Laura stared at the ground. Josh thought she was going to cry. "Maybe you can change, Josh. Lots of people do."

"You never know, but I doubt it. Every job I've had, I've hated. I hate somebody else telling me what I have to do and how I have to do it."

"What about your speech that you gave me a while ago with all those ideas? Like writing a book, or starting a company?"

"Laura, I think my real calling is going to outer space. It's the one activity that gets me excited. Another job doesn't do anything for me. I don't want to start my own company. I don't have enough money for that, and I can't find it interesting. There is really nothing for me but the space travel job. But I don't want to leave you."

"And I will miss you terribly, Josh. I don't know how I can live without you, now that we have been spending time together. I wish I could see you again, even if it's in twelve hundred years."

"Actually," Josh said slowly. "There is a way. The government allows me to pick one family member to go in a deep freeze here on Earth for the time that I am gone, then get woken up when I get back."

"Yeah, but that's family members, not girlfriends."

"Laura, I know it's just been a short time, but I have come to love you more than I've ever loved anyone before. Will you marry me?"

She sat still for a second, as the idea began to register that she and Josh would be together, as they are now, but 1200 years in the future. But they would be together.

She threw her arms around him. "Oh, yes, yes, yes," she cried out. "I will be your wife. I will wait one thousand years for you. Yes."

3

"Hello, Peter. My name is Josh. I think you remember me from a few weeks ago. My wife, Laura is with me today. We have some more questions. Laura is especially concerned about getting frozen for so many years."

"Sure, I remember you, Josh. As I recall, you did quite well on your test."

Josh blushed a little at this.

"And it's very nice to meet you, Laura. My name is Peter, and people around here refer to me as the flight director.

"So let's talk about getting frozen. The science of cryogenics, a fancy word for freezing people over a long time period, was first pioneered around the year 2000. A few very rich people with incurable diseases tried it out, thinking that they could wake up years in the future, when a cure for their disease would exist. Their attempts met with very limited success, but we appreciate their exploratory efforts.

"So let's talk about how to do this safely. First, you have to realize that you can't simply throw someone in a freezer and expect them to live. Their blood will turn to ice, and the ice will burst their veins and arteries. This is exactly similar to pipes freezing in winter and bursting. Ice takes up more volume than water, and, unless it is expelled quickly, it will rupture the walls containing it.

"It's not just blood that will turn to ice. Your body contains a lot of water. Your cells are suspended in the water. The water will freeze, and your cells will be destroyed. Besides that, there are your vital internal organs that will be damaged by a prolonged exposure to cold.

"The modern solution to these problems is to fill your body up with a type of anti-freeze. The anti-freeze effectively lowers the freezing point of the liquids in your body, so nothing will freeze. Your body functions will still stop, so you will not age at all while you are frozen. But no damage will be done to your internal system."

"What if it doesn't work?" asked Laura.

"When you are frozen, you will be lying face-up in a pod, and securely fastened in. A lab worker will be accompanying you to make sure all the proper safety measures are taken. The lab worker will remain at your side until you are safely frozen, and your body is behaving as expected."

"What about this anti-freeze, as you call it?"

"Right. So, before you are frozen, you have to drink five quarts of special gel in two hours. That is the stuff that will protect your body from internal damage. This is not an easy thing to do. The gel does not taste particularly good, and you have to drink it pretty quickly. Five quarts is 20 full glasses, and I recommend drinking a glass every five minutes. That works out to one hour and forty minutes to drink the five quarts.

"When you wake up, first you will thaw out, and then the gel will be expelled through your urine, and you are one hundred percent back to normal.

"Now, for you, Laura, the logistics are fairly straightforward. You drink the gel, you lie down in the pod, the lab worker straps you in, and starts the process up. In the meantime, Josh will be off in outer space. When Josh returns, we will wake you up. You thaw out, and pee out the gel. Sounds simple, right?"

"Sort of," said Laura nervously. "For starters, what if Josh never makes it back?"

"Well, it is a dangerous mission that Josh is undertaking, we aren't going to gloss over that. But we have every expectation that he will make it back safely. Now, Josh's expected flight time is 625 years each way, as measured on our clocks here on Earth. That means he should return in 1250 years. He will spend some time on the planet, maybe a month or so. If he is not back in 1350 years, he will be one hundred years late. In that case, a timer will go off in the control center, and we will have to assume that Josh did not survive. We hope and pray that that does not happen, of course. Anyways, the good news is that you will then rejoin society as a very rich young lady."

"Has anyone ever been put to sleep for this long?" asked Laura.

"No," said Peter. "Our advanced technology has only existed for a few hundred years, so, obviously, we could not have tried to put someone to sleep for over a thousand years. But there is nothing in the technology that is time-dependent. We have every reason to expect you to be woken up successfully and feeling fine in twelve hundred years."

"What about nuclear war?"

"You will be kept in a bunker two hundred feet underground. No nuclear bomb could ever reach you there. Of course, if there is a war, you will have to emerge from your sleep into a post-war world. Sorry, but there is nothing we can do about that.

"I would also add that the computer systems, which will be supporting you, are on their own private network. They are not connected to the grid, so they cannot be hacked. You also have dual processors. So if one processor crashes or goes down, the other processor will take over. Then the first processor will become the backup, and the second processor the master. 'Dual termination' is the computer science word that describes this situation."

"What about a massive power failure?"

"You have your own generator in the bunker. A power failure will not affect you."

Laura was quiet for a while.

The Peter spoke. "While you're thinking of more questions, we can discuss Josh's procedures."

Josh nodded his head stiffly.

"Josh will start out just as Laura. He will enter the spacecraft, consume his five quats of gel in two hours or less, and then lie down in his pod. He won't have a lab assistant. He will give voice commands to the ship's computer to fasten him in, and start the freezing process. The ship's computer is pre-programmed to fly to the target planet, as soon as Josh is strapped in place. Josh will sleep peacefully during the flight. When the ship goes into orbit about the target planet, Josh will be woken up. He should then pee out his gel, and use voice commands to pilot the ship, and tell it where to land. Josh will then have to do two things. He will have to tell the ship to release the rover, and then tell the ship to activate its protective bubble."

"What is the rover?" said Josh.

"The rover is like a small jet plane that Josh can use to travel around on the planet. It uses nuclear energy to get around. The rover can act as a submarine and go underwater, even to the bottom of the ocean, but it cannot exceed three thousand feet of depth. The rover can also travel on land, but it is not very fast. "

"How do I eat?" asked Josh.

"The rover is equipped with a huge supply of food, and a 3-D printer, which can cook pretty much anything. Josh merely has to tell the rover what he wants to eat, and the rover will prepare it for him."

"The rover sounds pretty amazing," said Josh.

"Yes, we are very proud of the rover. The rover also captures video footage of everything it sees on the planet, and sends it to Earth real time via laser link. We have a receiving station in Arecibo, Puerto Rico, and a second one in Canarvan, Australia. Both will receive messages from the rover."

"And what information do I need to gather when I am on the planet?"

"Good question. Rest assured, you will be busy. This trip will not be a vacation at the beach. You should take ice core samples from polar regions, then seabed samples from the ocean. You should capture climate and meteorological data. Of course, you should capture all data possible from wildlife. And capture a lot of videos about topography."

"And then when I am ready to leave?"

"You fly the rover back to the ship. Then you go into the ship through the door in the ship's protective bubble. Then you tell the ship to remove the protective bubble. Then you tell the ship to capture the rover. When all that is done, you drink five quarts of gel, strap yourself into the pod, and tell the ship to return to Earth. The ship will wake you up when you are close to the Earth. Then you can pee out your gel, and land the ship by voice commands."

"What if the rover is damaged on the planet?"

"The rover can do minor repairs on itself. The rover will ask for your help if needed, and give you directions for what to do. If the rover is damaged beyond all repair, then your hope for getting back to the main ship is your rocket belt. With the rocket belt, you can fly at about thirty miles per hour, and the battery in the rocket belt is rated to last one thousand miles. You will have one extra rocket belt, in case the first one goes bad."

"What about damage to the main ship?"

"Again, the main ship can do many self-repairs. The ship also carries along a team of twelve robots that are trained to do repairs on the ship. By the way, the robots also monitor the condition of the ship during the long flights to the planet and back. If the ship is damaged beyond repair, then that is the nightmare scenario. Then you are marooned on the planet. A rescue attempt will take hundreds of years to reach you. Just hope as we do that such a thing does not happen."

Neither Josh nor Laura spoke, so Peter started again to speak. "One other thing that must be considered," he said, "is your return to Earth in the distant future. The Earth will be a much different place, and we can't even begin to predict the changes that will happen. But food, transportation, housing, health care, and general way of life will all change radically.

"So, I recommend strongly that you see an occupational therapist at that time. You also will need a financial planner, so you can spend and invest your money wisely to retain your wealth.

"Now, Laura, as Josh's wife and beneficiary, you do have the option of living out your life on Earth, and receiving Josh's salary for as long as you live. When you die, Josh's salary will start being deposited in his trust account."

"I don't want to do that," Laura said. "I want to be alive to see Josh when he returns."

Peter nodded. "You two are very lucky to be so much in love. I'm not sure many people these days would make that choice."

Josh and Laura both nodded. There seemed like nothing else to say. Peter finally spoke.

"So, where are we? Do you guys want to do this?"

Josh and Laura both nodded. Josh's nod was more enthusiastic than Laura's.

"Well, then, how about we set an estimated time of Josh's departure at a week from today? That will give you both a little time to say your goodbyes and get your affairs in order."

Josh glanced at Laura. She looked at him and quietly said, "okay."

"Okay," Josh said. "A week from today."

4

The ship was smaller than what Josh expected. For something that could travel 80% of light speed, Josh thought the ship would have to be huge. Of course, Josh soon realized that the ship did not carry liquid fuel. It couldn't for a long flight through deep space. So, all that was really needed were a nuclear reactor, solar sails, a computer, a backup computer, a sleeping pod, a freezer to store the gel, the rover, the inflatable protective bubble, and a supply of food.

All told, the ship was about as big as a small commuter jet, with seats for the pilot and ten or so passengers, with a baggage compartment. In this case the baggage compartment, or basement, was for storing the rover and the protective bubble.

Josh turned to Laura. "Don't worry," he said, noticing her nervousness. "I'll be fine, I'll come back fine, you'll be fine, and we'll have a nice life together on the other side."

Laura nodded, choking back some tears. "I know," she said. "And I love you."

"I love you too, Laura. More than anything in the world or the universe."

She smiled at that. They held each other for what seemed like forever in a long tender embrace. Then they kissed and kissed again.

"Well, I guess I have to go now," Josh said. Laura nodded and patted his cheek goodbye.

Josh walked across the tarmac, carrying his backpack that held his personal things. A security official accompanied him as he climbed into the ship. He found the freezer where his gel was stored. There were several very large five-quart jugs there. Josh took one of them, filled up a glass, and drank. The security official asked if Josh was okay, and Josh said yes. The security official then left the ship, leaving Josh alone.

The gel did not taste particularly good, and Josh understood that drinking five quarts in two hours would be a bit of a challenge. But he kept drinking, holding to the pace of one glass every five minutes. It seemed unusual to be drinking so much and not needing to pee, but Josh understood that the gel was being absorbed by his body.

After close to two hours, Josh had consumed five quarts of the ill-tasting gel. He lay down in the pod, and gave his first command.

"Strap me in, freeze me, and set a course for our target planet."

The computer understood everything. The straps wound around Josh's body. The glass door on the pod slid shut. He could feel the ship start to elevate. His pod started to fill up with foggy cold nitrogen gas. At first, Josh felt no sense of cold at all. He reasoned that it was a dry cold and it wouldn't seep into his body very much.

After a few minutes, he started shivering. At about the same time, he started feeling sleepy, like he was about to pass out. Then he was gone.

Laura was watching from outside. She had been patiently standing there for two hours, waiting. Finally, the ship rose vertically from the ground. It was not going fast. It was just a slow, gradual rise. It kept going up until it was a small dot in the sky. Then Laura couldn't make it out any more.

Accompanied by the security official, she walked to the shuttle bus, and they rode to the bunker, where Laura would lie frozen for over 1200 years. She tried to stay calm, but could not. She felt her heart beating faster than normal, and her palms getting sweaty. She thought of all the people and places that she would miss. She thought of the beautiful few weeks she had with Josh, and she said a silent prayer that she would see Josh again, and that all would be well.

The bus reached the bunker entrance. The security guard left, and directed Laura to a female worker. She was a distinguished looking woman, maybe in her fifties, wearing a navy-blue suit. Laura thought she looked a lot like Jackie Kennedy, the famous first lady from hundreds of years ago. Laura remembered seeing pictures of her and her husband, President Kennedy, in history books and television documentaries.

"You must be Laura," Mrs. Kennedy said. Laura nodded, feeling very nervous.

"Please follow me," Mrs. Kennedy said, leading the way to an elevator. They took a very long elevator ride. They went into a dark room. Mrs. Kennedy flipped on a light switch. Laura could see the device that she was supposed to climb into. Laura walked over to the freezer and removed an enormous five-quart jug of gel. She filled up a glass with gel and started to drink, while sitting down at the large conference table. Mrs. Kennedy sat next to her.

"How are you doing?" Mrs. Kennedy asked.

"I'm a little nervous," Laura admitted shyly.

"Well, I guess that's understandable, because you are embarking on a great adventure. But the good news is we are one hundred percent sure this will turn out well. So don't worry. The science will work perfectly for you, without a hitch."

"I guess so," said Laura, sounding partially convinced. She took another slug of the gel. "What's in this stuff? It tastes awful."

"It will save your life, Laura. It will allow you to sleep for twelve hundred years, and not age at all, then come awake in a new life."

Laura kept drinking. She looked down at the enormous five-quart jug. God, there was a lot of this stuff to drink.

"So, tell me, Laura. What kind of work do you do?" asked Mrs. Kennedy.

"Well, right now I'm sleeping for a living. I don't have another job."

"What kind of job did you have?"

"I was a software engineer. I hated it."

"Really? That sounds like a great job."

"I liked writing code, and I was good at it. But my boss was an asshole and fired me."

"Bummer," commented Mrs. Kennedy, shaking her head.

They both smiled. Laura kept drinking the gel. She had probably drunk over one quart by now.

"Part of me is nervous, but part of me is thinking about a new life in a new world when I wake up. Right now, I'm out of a job, and I don't have much to look forward to, except being with Josh."

"Josh is your husband?"

"Yes."

"Did you ever think about going back to school?"

"Sure. I thought about that, and I thought about a lot of other things. Like maybe writing a book, or gambling for a living."

"Gambling? Really? You're joking, right."

"Yeah, of course I am. But I'm actually not half bad at poker."

"Ever play in any poker tournaments?"

"Once I entered the world championships in Las Vegas. I didn't do too bad. I finished about in the middle."

"Did you lose a lot of money?"

"Only my entry fee. So, it wasn't too bad."

"Well, that's still quite something to get to play in the world championships of poker."

"Yes, it was interesting. Being a woman, I had a slight advantage. Poker is dominated by snotty men with big pot bellies and bald spots. Those kinds of guys seem to underestimate the women."

Mrs. Kennedy smiled at that. "Well, what about your husband, Josh? Is he on an interplanetary mission?"

"Yes, exactly. I have to do this so I can be with him again. I love him very much."

"And Josh I'm sure knowing that he is very lucky to have you. I'm sure he loves you too."

"Yes, we are very much in love."

"Well, you know the saying that has stayed with us since ancient times. If your husband loves you, then you are better off than half the women in the world."

"Sounds a bit cynical, but there is some truth in it." Laura looked at her jug of gel, and picked it up to test its weight. It seemed to be about half full now.

"How did you and Josh meet?"

"We worked at the same company together. In fact, we were in the same department, working for the same boss. We liked each other, but romance in the workplace is tricky, to put it mildly."

"Yes, that is certainly true. When two people in the office are dating, everyone knows about it, and everyone talks about it. It can get really ugly."

"Sounds like you have some personal experience with this. Hope I don't sound too nosy."

"No, not at all," said Mrs. Kennedy. "No, I never got involved with any fellow workers, and I'm very glad that I didn't. I saw several careers get ruined by people who did.

"So, you knew Josh at work, but nothing happened. How did you two finally get together?"

"The boss laid Josh off, then a few weeks later, he laid me off. I sent a message to Josh, and invited him to lunch. By then, he was thinking about this space exploration stuff. Anyways, we had a real nice lunch together that lasted four hours. Then we started seeing each other every day. Josh was wonderful to me. I felt awful being out of work with almost no savings. Josh was there for me when I needed him. I'm so happy that we are together now."

"And you don't mind being frozen for twelve hundred years?"

"No. There is nothing for me here in this world. I am out of work, and I will have a lot of trouble finding another job. My boss will never give me a good recommendation."

"And Josh?"

"Same thing. He is very smart, but the boss hated him. What I can't understand is why he hired Josh in the first place. The two of them never did get along." Laura's jug was practically empty. She decided to finish it off with three more large slugs.

"I guess I'm ready," Laura said.

"You did very well," said Mrs. Kennedy, smiling. "A little over an hour and a half."

"You have been very kind to me. I don't feel nervous any more. But I never did catch your name."

"It's Jackie," Mrs. Kennedy said. "Short for Jacqueline. Um-m, why are you looking at me like that?"

"Sorry," Laura said. "No reason. I was just lost in thought."

Feeling suddenly calm, Laura climbed into the pod. Jackie tightened her straps, closed the lid, and pushed a button somewhere. The foggy nitrogen gas started filling up the pod.

5

Josh woke up to the sound of soft music. The ship's computer told him that they were in orbit about the target planet. It also explained that they were decelerating at the rate of 1g. That meant that Josh could walk around in the ship's cabin, and it would feel exactly like walking on Earth.

Josh's body was thawing out, and he was shaking off his sleepiness. His first job now was to pee as much as he could to get rid of the gel in his system. But he could not resist looking through the ship's windows at the planet below.

They were on the night-time side of the planet, so everything was dark. But there were no lights anywhere, which told Josh a lot. If the planet was inhabited, the inhabitants either could see in the dark, or they did not have the technology to create a light source. He also could not see a moon, as he looked full circle around the ship's windows. Either the planet had no moon, or it was in a new-moon phase. If the moon was new, then it would have to be on the sunny side of the planet. Perhaps he could find it when the ship circled around in its orbit.

In the meantime, he had to pee. He went to the restroom, and spent several minutes there. But five quarts is a lot of liquid, and he knew that he would have to keep this up for quite a while to get rid of all the gel that was still in his system. He took another look out the ship's windows. The planet was still in the dark. So he came back to pee again.

After a few more repetitions, the gel was finally gone. He checked the ship's windows, and he saw one edge of the planet in sunshine. Soon he could make out some topographic detail. He was over a large ocean. On his right, which he called east, he could see a coastal mountain range, and land. From the ship's altitude while in orbit, it was not possible to make out any detail of the land. He could make out a range of mountains, and some lakes, but he couldn't tell if he was looking at forests, grasslands, or deserts. Everything merged into a light tan color as it reflected the morning sunlight.

As they flew over the landmass, Josh had another decision to make. Where would he land the ship? Obviously, the prime concern was safety.

He could not let the ship be damaged, because the ship was his way back home. Of course he would deploy the protective bubble to protect the ship, but the bubble could not protect the ship from everything. Enormous wild beasts could pose a problem, although he couldn't imagine why a wild beast would attack his ship. Phenomena of nature were bigger threats -- tornadoes, hurricanes, avalanches, tsunamis, volcanic eruptions, maybe even earthquakes. He had to assume that weather and climate patterns were similar to Earth's. Maybe this was a wild assumption, but it was all he had to go on. So, what were his choices?

The first possibility was a remote island in the ocean. That would probably be safe from wild beasts, but maybe not. A big objection, however, was that most islands were created by volcanoes. With a volcano sitting on an island, Josh would have no way of knowing if the volcano was about to erupt. He could take soil samples from inside the volcano's caldera, but he would have to send them to Earth to get them analyzed. Forget it. Maybe the risk of a volcanic eruption was a small one, but potentially catastrophic. Josh decided it was not worth taking that risk.

What about an island without a volcano? What about an atoll, for example? It is a possibility. But atolls were still formed from volcanoes. Sometimes a shield volcano emitting lava at a slow but steady rate will form an atoll at its peak. Sometimes a volcano will sink underwater, forming a circular atoll around its caldera. In either case, there are still volcanoes in the picture.

What about barrier islands, like Padre Island in Texas, the Outer Banks off Cape Hatteras in North Carolina, or Fire Island off the south coast of Long Island, New York? Yes, another possibility. The problem is that these things are always getting hit by hurricanes. Fire Island on Earth would be the safest because it is outside of the tropics, but the hurricane risk is still there, albeit small. The key would be to find a barrier island where the surrounding ocean water was cold. The cold water would stop an advancing hurricane.

Another possibility is the middle of a large, sandy desert. On Earth, a perfect spot might be the Great Salt Lake Desert in Utah. It has lots of smooth sand to make smooth takeoffs and landings, and is safe from savage beasts. That would be a perfect spot. It was just a question of finding such a place.

Then there are ice sheets and glaciers. A large block of stable ice, like Greenland or Antarctica on Earth, could be safe to land and take off from, while posing little or no danger from wild beasts. The ice sheet in question would have to be stable. If the ship were to sit on top of an ice sheet, could the heat from the ship's body melt the surrounding ice and create a crevasse or sinkhole? That would be the danger.

So what is the bottom line? First, stay away from the tropics. Second, look for a large sandy desert in the middle latitudes unoccupied by wild beasts. Third, look for a large stable ice sheet in the arctic regions. Islands were out of the question.

"Computer," Josh said.

"What can I help you with?"

"I'm trying to find the best place to land the ship. The only consideration is I want it to be safe. I mean safe from wild beasts and safe from any adverse weather. I've thought about remote islands in the ocean, but I ruled them out because they probably all carry some risk of volcanic eruption."

"Yes," said the computer.

"Next, I thought about a flat sandy spot in the middle of a large desert. It would be too far away for wild beasts to get to it, and it would be nice and flat so the ship could make a safe landing."

"Wild prehistoric birds might be able to reach the ship, but the risk is very small. And we don't completely understand the capabilities of the wildlife here. We can't rule out the possibility that dangerous beasts could travel many miles across a desert."

"Then I thought about the polar regions," said Josh. "The idea would be to find a large, flat, stable ice sheet where the ship could safely land, and be safe from wild beasts. Again, we don't know the capabilities of the wildlife, and if some animal could travel several miles across a sheet of ice. Then, there are other concerns. I understand that our planet has approximately the same orbital inclination of the Earth. That means that the polar region we choose would lie in darkness for some months out of the year. The rover might have to return to the ship in the dark. Then there is the issue of the heat from the ship melting the ice below it, and creating crevasses or sinkholes. So the ship would have to be monitored regularly."

"Yes," said the computer. "But first, let me put your mind at ease on the darkness issue. The rover can fly by instrument flight rules, homing in on beacons sent periodically by the ship. As far as animals traversing an ice sheet, I assess this risk to be very small. An animal's food source at this latitude would certainly be a nearby ocean. The animal would have no incentive whatever for journeying across a large ice field. Lastly, there is the issue of heat from the ship melting the ice. It is because of this melting ice danger that inhabitants of the Earth's polar regions build their houses on stilts. Amazingly, the ship has a set of stilts that it can rest atop, and then have no fear of melting the ice.

"But there is another problem with ice that is not so easily solved. Ice is in constant motion, similar to the geologic plates on the Earth. One day the ice could be smooth, and a few days later it could be littered with a collection of ice boulders that could endanger the ship."

"Well," Josh said. "Can you think of anything that I might have forgotten?"

"Have you thought about other islands, for example barrier islands or islands in lakes?"

"Yes," said Josh. "Barrier islands are a problem because they are frequently hit by hurricanes. They are also basically sandbars that keep shifting. I know it is not a likely thing, but the sandbar could shift and leave our ship in the ocean. The other danger with barrier islands is that they are close to the mainland, and unwanted beasts could come from the mainland and vandalize the ship. So I am keeping them in mind, but the big thing is we would need a barrier island where the surrounding ocean water is cold. The cold water would act as some protection against hurricanes.

"As far as islands in the middle of lakes, I have not thought about them very much. Weather events would be the biggest danger. If we found such an island, it might be covered with forests. The ship might have trouble finding a place to land. If the island was covered by grassland or desert, it would face a big risk of massive destruction from big storms or even tsunamis. What do you think?"

"I agree with much of your analysis. I think the best choice is a flat, sandy area in the middle of a large desert. But the key word is flat. In a desert that is covered with dunes, we have to remember that dunes do not stand still. They move with the winds. The ship, parked in such an area near large dunes, could easily get engulfed and swallowed up by a huge dune. The second-best choice is in the middle of a large, stable ice sheet. This also carries risks, especially from crevasses and fissures that could develop. The heat from the ship could melt layers of ice on the surface of the ice sheet, creating unstable situations. In the worst case, a crevice or sinkhole could form, and the ship could disappear into one of those things."

"So I guess let's start by looking for a flat, sandy spot in a desert," said Josh. "Assuming a global climate pattern that is similar to Earth's, we should look for deserts in the latitude ranges of 20 to 35 degrees in both the northern and southern hemispheres."

"I agree," said the computer. "Now, just to orient ourselves, the ship is facing the sunny side of the planet right now. We can call the direction up as north, down as south, to the right as east, and to the left as west. As luck would have it, when we are oriented in this way, the planet rotates in the same sense as Earth, proceeding from east to west. So let's move to a lower altitude so we get a clear view of the topography, and start to look in the northern hemisphere."

"Okay," said Josh.

The ship descended to ten thousand feet above the planet's surface, and began the long, boring, arduous task of finding the best place to land.

6

The ship landed in a very good place. It was a flat desert landscape, surrounded by rocky hills which circled the area a few miles off. Josh reasoned that the hills would act as a sturdy windbreak, and a good protection against wild beasts. The ground was sandy with scattered vegetation, mostly small scrubby bushes. There were no trees.

The search for this spot took a very long time. It was tough to measure it in days, because the ship always followed the sunny side of the planet, keeping pace with its diurnal rotation. The ship explored the entire planet, including the equatorial regions, the polar regions, the arid zones, the oceans, and the temperate forests. Plant life was abundant, and actually quite Earth-like. So far, Josh had not seen any animal life.

When the ship was firmly on the ground, Josh obeyed his instructions, telling the ship to deploy the rover, and to encase the ship in its protective bubble. While the ship was doing these things, the ship's computer said that it had a present for Josh, and directed him to the 3-D printer. There was a 16-inch globe of the planet, showing fantastic topographic detail. Josh was overwhelmed. It was not only highly useful, but extremely beautiful. Josh sat and studied it for several minutes. He was about to ask the obvious question "Where are we", but there was no need. There was a well-defined point on the globe's surface that was labeled "ship's position."

"Note the latitude and longitude of the ship," said the computer. "We are at 32 degrees south latitude, and zero degrees longitude. Set your computerized watch so one day corresponds to 24 hours, like on Earth. The real day here is about 26 hours as we would measure it, but your watch should be calibrated to a 24 hour day. We arbitrarily set ourselves at zero degrees of longitude. That means at 12 noon, the sun will be at its zenith, and directly to the north. As you wander around the planet, and do not change your watch, you can calculate longitude by what time of day the sun is at its zenith.

"Latitude is something else. You have to know the sun's latitude first. You get this by assuming the sun's movement here roughly corresponds to the sun's movement on the Earth. So on June twenty-first, the sun is at 23 degrees

29

north, and on September 21, the sun is at zero degrees, and on December 21, the sun is at 23 degrees south. Right now, based on where we see the sun, we are saying today is October 15. The position of the sun right now is about 10 degrees south. Since we are at 32 degrees south, the sun will appear to us at 22 degrees from the vertical at high noon. So, to sum up, if you want to know your latitude, measure the elevation of the sun at high noon, then take the difference between that and where the sun's position is at your time of year."

"Okay, I think I got it," Josh said. "It was good of you to go over this with me. But the rover should do all this for me, right?"

"Yes, of course. But it's always good to know how it's done."

"Thank you for everything, and goodbye for now, Mr. Computer," Josh said. "Be careful while I'm gone because I need to have you around. And thanks again."

"You're welcome, Josh. Good luck with your ventures on the planet."

"Thanks," Josh answered. He slung his backpack unto his shoulders. "Well, I guess I might as well go," he said.

He opened the exit door, and stepped outside into the sunlight. It seemed funny calling it "sunlight", as the sun was a different star hundreds of light years away. But his new sun seemed pretty close to the same thing. It was yellowish and its apparent size was about the same as Earth's sun. Josh's first steps onto the sandy soil were relaxed. He was not wearing a bulky space suit like the first visitors to the moon or to Mars. He was wearing blue jeans, a tee shirt, and tennis shoes. It almost seemed comical comparing himself to Armstrong on the moon or Nielson on Mars with all their flowery quotes like "One small step for man," or something like that. Josh couldn't remember that ancient history.

The sky was a cloudless blue. There was no wind. The temperature was comfortable, probably in the sixties Fahrenheit. The air was breathable, in fact it seemed the same as Earth's air. The only living things were the plants.

Josh walked over to the rover. He stepped inside, and powered on the computer.

"Hello, Mr. Computer," he said. "My name is Josh."

"Hello, Josh," a female voice answered. "And I am definitely not a mister, I am a miss."

"Sorry," Josh said. "I won't make that mistake again. Anyways, it's nice to meet you."

"Nice to meet you too," said the computer. "How can I help you?"

Josh had already decided that his first action would be to collect data around the polar region. Right now, the north pole was in darkness, so this would mean a trip to the south pole or thereabouts. Right now, his latitude was about thirty degrees south of the planet's equator. He was trying to figure out how the rover could navigate.

"Can you tell which direction is south?" asked Josh. "I want to go close to the south pole."

"I have downloaded a lot of data from the computer on your main ship. I know exactly how to get to the south pole."

"So, let's go," said Josh. "When we get close, I will want to be looking around for interesting features to collect data on. Then I might ask you to slow down, fly lower, or land."

"Okay, Josh. I want to stay slower than the speed of sound, which I calculate is about the same as on Earth. So I will go about six hundred miles per hour. At that rate, we should reach the south polar region in about five hours. I hope you brought a good book to read."

"I'm fine," said Josh.

The rover took off vertically, and spent the first several minutes moving higher until it reached its cruising altitude. Then it accelerated, banking slightly to adjust its course, and it was on its way south.

"So, I don't know what to call you. 'Miss Computer'? That sounds a little weird. How about if I just shorten it to 'Missy'?"

"Missy is fine."

"Okay, Missy. Can you fly and play chess at the same time?"

"Sure. Want to have a game?" Suddenly, a chess board with pieces appeared as an image on Josh's computer screen. "Just use your finger to drag and drop pieces to move them."

"Okay, let's have a game."

"Your move, Josh. You can have white."

Josh moved his queen pawn up two squares. Missy did the same. Then Josh moved his queen bishop pawn up two squares to go into a Queen's Gambit opening. A few moves later, they were in a Semi-Slav Defense. Josh moved his queen bishop out to the g5 square to pin Missy's king knight. Missy took Josh's queen bishop pawn with her queen pawn. This was a very double-edged move. Josh could exploit the pin on Missy's knight by moving his king pawn to the e5 square, attacking it while it was pinned. But Missy was setting up a dangerous pawn mass on the queen side.

As the game progressed, Josh castled on the king side, Missy on the queen side. Josh's attack on Missy's knight turned into a complicated mess when Missy counterattacked Josh's bishop. In the end, Josh got Missy's knight and Missy got Josh's bishop, but Josh came out a pawn to the good. Missy's pawns on the queenside were very dangerous, and it appeared that Josh would have to sacrifice a piece to prevent Missy from queening one of her pawns. In that case, Missy would have a big material edge and certainly win the game. But Josh was lucky. With Missy's king on the queen side, deprived of pawn protection, Josh invaded with a bishop and knight to check Missy's king endlessly. The game ended in a draw by the perpetual check rule.

Josh breathed a sigh of relief. He did not want to lose that game. He was a pretty good chess player, and could beat most computers, except for the computers with special software high-tuned to play chess. Missy was not high-tuned to play chess, but she played a very tough, aggressive game. Josh was lucky to come out of it with a draw.

"Nice game, Missy," he finally said. "You are an exceptional player. I was lucky to get a draw against you."

"You are pretty good yourself, Josh. That was an exciting game. Most humans don't stand a chance against me. You are one of the few that did okay. Congratulations."

"Thanks, Missy. So where are we? Are we getting close to the south pole yet?" As Josh looked out the window, he saw mostly clouds. Occasional breaks in the clouds revealed thick forests, probably pine or spruce, or some variant of those trees.

"We are at latitude 59 degrees south. Soon the forest will break up and we will see only tundra, and, after that, the polar ice cap."

Josh was physically and mentally exhausted after the chess game with Missy. He laid his head down in his seat, and closed his eyes.

"Wake up, Josh. We are in the polar region, and there is abundant animal life."

Josh opened his eyes, and felt very groggy. The rover seemed to be holding its position, waiting for Josh to wake up. Finally Josh propped himself up, and took a look out the window. My goodness, Missy wasn't kidding. There were birds, hundreds of them, some standing on rocky islands, some on a tall cliff on the shore. Some had huge wingspans, like albatrosses, but most were similar to shore birds on Earth, like cormorants, seagulls, and ravens. In fact, some of the birds looked exactly like their counterparts on Earth. Then there were groups of animals lying on a sandy beach. They were seals or sea lions, or at least very similar to those animals of Earth. Beyond the beach were the crystal-clear blue waters of some ocean or bay. Wow, Josh thought. My first glimpse of animal life.

"Where are we, Missy, and how cold is it outside?"

"We are right up against the northern edge of the ice cap. We are at eighty degrees south latitude. The outside temperature is seventeen degrees Fahrenheit. It is sunny with no wind."

"I can see there is no safe place to land, everything is so rocky and jagged. Can you let me down the rope ladder so I can take some pictures?"

"Sure," said Missy. "But first you need a heavy coat and some sturdy shoes."

Josh got dressed up in his winter wear, then headed to the cockpit, opened the hatch, and gingerly stepped onto the shaky rope ladder. He was about thirty feet above some jagged rocks, and Josh was extra careful with his steps on the flimsy rope ladder. It seemed an eternity, but Josh eventually touched down on some pointy rocks. He made sure he had his footing, then carefully climbed down to the beach.

He started taking numerous pictures of the large animals lying on the beach, then took more pictures of all the birds, some of them in midflight. Amazingly, none of the animals or birds showed any fear of Josh. Josh supposed that was because they had no previous contact with humans. To them, Josh was just another species of animal enjoying the beach.

Josh sat on the beach in the midst of the animals. For a few minutes, he blanked out his worries, and just enjoyed a peaceful harmony with his surroundings. It was too cold to be the Garden of Eden, but, in its own way, it was a paradise.

Josh glanced back up at the rover, then started his long, journey up the rocky cliff. At the top, he reached out and grabbed the rope ladder, and hoisted a boot into its bottom rung. Soon, he was back on board the rover with Missy.

"That was amazing," Josh said. "A real wonder. Thanks for helping me down to enjoy it."

"No problem, Josh. And remember, I am here to obey your commands."

"Okay, Missy. Next, I'd like to head a little out to sea, take some seabed core samples, test the chemical composition of the water, and its temperature."

"Sure, Josh. I can do that. Let's fly about a mile off shore so we don't disturb the animals here, then we can submerge and do our work."

"While we are doing that, I would like to download these photographs to you to be sent to Earth."

"You got it, Josh."

The rover flew for a bit over the sea, then eased down onto the water's surface. Slowly, it submerged. Josh took in all the sights of the underworld. Small fish darted around in the increasing inky darkness. The rover captured data about the chemical composition of the water, its depth and pressure, and its temperature. After several minutes, the rover touched down on the seabed floor. Then, one of its arms came out and dug a hole to capture a core of mud from the floor. It pulled the mud up to an analyzing device on the side of the rover. The analyzing device captured its data, then forwarded it to Missy, who sent it off to Earth. Then the core of mud was unceremoniously dropped on top of the seabed floor.

"Okay," Missy said. "What's next?"

"We go up over the ice cap, find a spot to land, and take some ice core samples."

"Fine with me," said Missy.

The rover gently rose out of the depths until it reached the surface. Then it rose vertically into the air, creating some gentle ripples on the water below. Then it was back to the beach, and then onward toward the south pole. This time, Josh stared out the window in fascination as the rover sped south. At first, there was a mass of bare, black, rocky cliffs, covered in part by snow. Then the snow cover increased until Josh couldn't make out much of the black rock any more. Finally, there was only snow and ice.

"It looks like we have entered the south polar ice cap," Josh observed.

"Yes," said Missy. "I am looking for a place to land, but it won't be easy. The ice is a collection of jumbled blocks."

"Well, we have to keep looking, unfortunately," said Josh. "I absolutely need some ice core samples from here. It contains valuable history of the planet's climate."

"We might be able to land over there," Missy said. "It looks a little tight, but I think the rover can squeeze in, and have enough room to take core samples."

Josh didn't see what Missy was talking about. The rover banked and flew in low toward Missy's selected spot. Then it stopped, hovered over the spot for a few seconds, then carefully descended. When it touched down, the ice gave way a little, and Josh was nervous that they would fall into a crevasse. After a few anxious moments, the ice held, and the rover's arms extended to capture the core samples. It took five core samples in all, loaded them into the analyzer, and then the analyzer forwarded the data to Missy, who promptly sent it to Earth. The whole process took maybe thirty minutes, and left Josh quite impressed with the rover's abilities. Josh thought about stepping outside and walking around on the ice, but quickly decided not to. The best thing to do right now was to get the rover out of there and eliminate any chance of falling into a crevasse.

"What next?" Missy asked, as the rover rose vertically off the ice.

"The main thing now is the search for animal life. And we still have a lot of topography to explore. There's tundra, forest, grassland, jungle, desert, ocean, lakes and rivers, and probably more that I'm not thinking of right now. I suggest we make our way back north and do a low flyover of the tundra, looking for any signs of animal life. What do you think, Missy?"

"I agree with you. Why don't you try to sleep for a few hours. I'll fly us to the tundra and do a little initial exploring. I'll wake you if there's anything interesting."

"Sounds great," said Josh, leaning his head back on the seat. "Thanks for everything, Missy."

"You're welcome, Josh. Good night."

7

"Wake up, Josh. I think we have something."

Josh opened his eyes and looked out the window. My God! Thousands of animals were grazing on the tundra. They were some kind of deer, but big, more like elk or moose. Some had horns and some did not. They were munching on the grasses, without a care in the world.

"Can you let me down on the rope ladder?" Josh said.

"Of course. But first I'm collecting a little data. Outside temperature, size of the herd, whatever I can get of the soil from here." "I can take a soil sample, Missy. Easier for me than for you, I would think."

"Okay. Come into the cockpit area. There is a bin labeled 'soil samples. Take a vial from there and fill it up and bring it back up the rope ladder. The rover can do this itself, obviously, but I suspect the tundra is too marshy to support its weight."

Josh took one of the vials and climbed down the rope ladder. The ground felt spongy and a little damp. As he looked around, he could see several areas of standing water. Flocks of bugs circulated around the pools of standing water. Josh took his soil sample, and stuck the vial in his pocket. Then he maneuvered around the scene, taking many pictures. He cautiously moved closer to the herd. They eyed him, not out of fear or suspicion, but out of curiosity. They did not move away from Josh as Josh approached them.

The air was full of bugs. The bugs congregated around the pools of water, but they were really everywhere. He didn't know what they were. Maybe they were some type of mosquito, but Josh could not be sure of that. Some of the bugs landed on the sides of the animals and stuck there. Josh took pictures of them, using his zoom lens. Josh swatted away some of the bugs that were tormenting the animals. Then he noticed that many of the animals were accompanied by birds that sat on top of them and consumed the bugs.

Josh wanted to spend some time sitting among the animals and relaxing, enjoying the peaceful scene. But he couldn't. The bugs were eating him alive. He signaled Missy that he was coming back. Then he stepped into the rope ladder and climbed into the ship, handing over the soil sample to the analyzer.

"How did you enjoy that, Josh?" Missy asked.

"Beautiful animals, beautiful scene, but there were too many bugs." Josh shrugged resignedly. "I guess that's life on the tundra. It's the same back on Earth."

"Yes," said Missy. "But what about the animal life so far? What are your thoughts?"

"The animal life is fantastic, Missy. The animals coexist peacefully and have no fear of me. And they are beautiful. These animals on the tundra look like elk with gigantic horns, or moose. They are all so big. Big, calm, and peaceful, content with their lives.

"I wonder about one thing though, Missy, and I would like to get your thoughts."

"Any way I can help, Josh."

"I'm thinking we are on a planet that is very Earth-like. I would think life would evolve in a similar way to how it evolved on Earth."

"Sounds reasonable," said Missy. "Although there are differences. For one, this planet does not have a moon. So the tides won't be the same as on Earth, and life in the tide pools would not develop in the same way as on Earth. That may not mean much, but the life in the tide pools is what ultimately led to amphibian life on Earth."

"I suppose so," said Josh. "But couldn't that tide pool kind of life also develop on the banks of rivers, for example? The river banks would swell or recede, depending on the weather conditions, and would emulate tide pools."

"I suppose so," said Missy. "It's an interesting idea."

"Well, I guess what I'm really getting at," Josh said, "is this planet is 200 million years younger than Earth, but very similar to Earth, with a few differences, as you point out. But the atmosphere is very similar, the gravity is similar, the length of the day is similar, the orbital inclination is similar, and the climate and weather have got to be similar. So life should evolve along a somewhat parallel path to the Earth. Right?"

"Possibly, Josh. Remember the Earth has been subjected to several mass extinctions, notably the Devonian, the Permian, and the Triassic, all occurring over 200 million years ago. Those things certainly affect the evolution of life."

"And what caused those extinctions?"

"Good question. Nobody really knows. There are a number of theories. One of the more interesting has to do with the movement of the sun through the Milky Way Galaxy. Every now and then, meaning several millions of years, the sun enters a region of space called the Oort Cloud. The Oort Cloud contains a large collection of comets and other debris. When the sun enters the Oort cloud, it can deflect matter out of the Oort Cloud, and some of that may fall into the solar system and crash into the Earth. That, of course, is devastating. When the Earth's atmosphere captures another body, such as a comet or asteroid, that body will eventually strike the Earth's surface at about seven miles per second, and the resulting explosion would be equivalent to several hydrogen bomb blasts."

"And one of those impacts could cause a mass extinction?"

"Some people think so. The most famous such impact was a comet or asteroid that struck the Earth about 65 million years ago somewhere near the Yucatan Peninsula in Mexico. The time of the impact roughly coincides with the disappearance of the dinosaurs. So lots of people have taken off on the idea that that impact caused a mass extinction that killed the dinosaurs."

"What do you think, Missy?"

"That impact 65 million years ago was not a good thing for the dinosaurs. It threw a large amount of dust into the atmosphere, effectively blocking sunlight. The dinosaurs were cold-blooded, meaning they could not regulate their body temperature. Faced with a sudden drop in temperature, the dinosaurs were in some trouble.

"But, having said that, I don't think that impact was the main cause of the dinosaur extinction. Consider that birds, with their migratory abilities, were not affected. Sea creatures, notably sharks and crocodiles, also came out okay. Also consider that close examination of the fossil evidence suggests that the dinosaurs did not die suddenly, but died over the span of a few million years. Such a gradual extinction does not suggest that a sudden cataclysmic event was the cause.

"Throughout the Earth's history, the continents have moved. When the dinosaurs thrived, the continents were set much closer to the equator than they are now. Continental drift came along and the continents moved away from the equator and toward the polar regions. The land that the dinosaurs inhabited became colder, and the dinosaurs could not react. They were cold-blooded, which meant they would freeze to death pretty easily. And the dinosaurs did not understand the situation and could not figure out that they had to migrate. Finally, remember that ice ages occurred throughout Earth's history, and one bitter ice age after the continents had moved could have spelled the end for the dinosaurs."

"Well, the one question that I've been meaning to get to is this, Missy. Will we see any dinosaurs on this planet?"

"That's a tough question. I would say that there is a very good chance. The planet is similar to Earth in many ways, and evolution of life forms could have followed parallel paths. Of course, if dinosaurs did live here, and a mass extinction killed them off, then we are late to the party, so to speak. But, if there are dinosaurs here, then we aren't looking in the right places. They would not be living on the ice cap or on the frozen tundra. Our best chance of finding them would be the tropics and the warm grassland areas."

"But I read once that dinosaurs occupied every continent on Earth, including Antarctica."

"Yes, but you have to remember that during those times, Antarctica occupied a different spot on the Earth, and had a much warmer climate. In fact, all the continents were crunched together in the tropics or semi-tropic areas."

"I see," said Josh, seemingly lost in thought. "Well, I think we should save the tropics until the end. In the mean time, we have a lot of other parts of this world to explore."

"Yes," said Missy. "So where to next?"

Josh picked up his globe and studied it. "If we stay in this latitude, we can circumnavigate the planet. It looks like we will run into more tundra, the edge of a large ocean, and maybe some boreal forest. So shall we head west?"

"Okay," said Missy. The plane banked to the west, stayed at a low altitude, and headed over the tundra.

8

They flew over tundra for several hours, picking out occasional herds of animals. Josh's routine each time was to climb out of the rover on the rope ladder, take some pictures, and do some casual observing. Josh was going through these usual motions one day when he found a group of large animals that looked a little like musk oxen. As he was taking pictures, he noticed something moving in the distance. It was just a quick flash, and then it was gone. Josh was curious, and crept in the direction where he saw the movement. This was tundra, it was flat, barren grass. There were no trees or hills to hide behind. What the devil did he see?

Josh wandered around the area, staring at the ground for footprints. After about a half hour, he saw something. It was a depression in the soft tundra grass. It was shaped like the bottom of a boot. It was fairly big, and Josh thought that it looked like a human being's footprint. He stepped inside the footprint, and found that his foot was about the same size as the footprint in the grass. He looked around for more footprints, and, sure enough, he found a line of them. They appeared to be moving away from the animals.

Josh sent a message to Missy. "Missy, I found some strange footprints here. They belong to a creature that walks upright on two legs, and probably wears some kind of boot. The footprints are very similar to those of a human. I'm going to follow the tracks and see where it takes me. I may be gone for a while."

"No problem, Josh. I'm waiting patiently for you."

Josh found the tracks and slowly started to follow them. He was wondering if the creature was running, because it was gone from sight. Josh realized that he may never be able to catch this thing, whatever it was. But he kept on, nonetheless. At least the trail was clear and very easy to follow.

After walking about a mile, Josh came to a stream, with trees surrounding it. He paused to drink out of the stream. The water was very cold, but tasted good. Then he proceeded downstream. At this point, there were no footprints to follow. The foliage became thicker as Josh moved on.

Then he heard the unmistakable sound of ocean surf in the distance. It was coming from straight ahead. He kept walking through the forest, following the meandering stream. Finally, he could see the coastline, and a beautiful blue ocean.

He called Missy. "Missy, I've been following the tracks. They led to a creek surrounded by trees. I started following the creek, and now I see the ocean. I still haven't found the creature I've been tracking."

"Sounds interesting," said Missy.

As Josh approached the ocean, there was a great beach full of sand and a few black rocks. On the beach sat a group of about ten creatures. The creatures looked human.

Josh approached them, holding his hands up high to demonstrate that he was not carrying weapons. The creatures were sitting cross-legged in a circle, and Josh could make out that they had a small fire burning in the middle of the circle. They were eating something tough and stringy; Josh could tell by the way the food tugged at their teeth. They were wearing clothes and boots, obviously made from animal skins. They kept eating, not acknowledging Josh's presence.

When they finally noticed Josh, they started talking amongst themselves. They did not appear frightened by Josh. As Josh grew closer, he could tell that these beings were ruddy-skinned and something very close to human. They had human body parts, human hair, eyes, nose, teeth, everything that a human being has. They had primitive weapons alongside them, mostly spears and knives. Alongside the ocean were a few small wooden boats.

"Hello," Josh said, keeping his hands in the air, and hoping he did not sound scared.

"Yadufar," one of the men said, looking over at Josh. He did not appear angry or frightened.

Josh was trying to think of a way to communicate with these beings when they did not have a common language.

He stepped closer, and drew two circles in the sand with his finger. He pointed to the first circle. "Here," he said, pointing down to the ground. "This is us." Then he pointed to the second circle. "This is the sun," he said, pointing to the sky at their sun. Then Josh stood up and held his hand above his head. "I am from here," he said. He moved his hand down to the first circle. "I came from out there to here. I am from another world."

The beings just stared, looking confused.

Then Josh drew a picture of a shark in the sand. "Have you seen this?" Josh said, and pointed to the ocean. No response.

Then Josh drew a picture of a seal. He asked the same questions. The creatures started murmuring amongst themselves, then one of them nodded in the affirmative.

"Dax," he said. "Shrapu noxi dax."Josh wondered if dax was the word for seal, and that they had seen seals.

Josh drew a picture of a crocodile, then of a large prehistoric bird. He got no response to either. This was very slow, methodical work, but Josh had initialized communication with the beings.

After a while, Josh called up Missy at the ship.

"Hello, Missy. I am communicating with some primitive human beings down where the creek runs into the ocean. If you can find me, I would like you to come and bring a little bit of food as a peace offering."

"That sounds amazing, Josh. Sure, I can come. What kind of food?"

"Fish, and maybe some soft meat like chicken. And a few servings of vegetables. I'm taking a few chances here. I'm not sure what they like."

"I think I can find you, but stay connected and I can home in on the signal."

"Okay, thanks so much, Missy. Hope to see you soon."

In a few minutes, the rover appeared, hovered overhead a bit, then slowly descended into the sand. The natives were watching this spectacle in awe. Josh walked into the rover, and noticed that plates of food were already arranged. He took the plates, two at a time, out to the natives. He didn't bother with silverware. When all the food was out by the circle of natives, Josh came and sat with them. Everyone ate heartily. Josh was relieved that they were enjoying the food. Then Josh walked back to the rover.

"Thank you so much, Missy. Everyone is enjoying their food. Your cooking has been an obvious success."

"You're welcome, Josh. Meeting fellow humans on a strange planet is certainly something worth celebrating."

"I'm going to borrow the globe for a little bit," Josh said, as he picked up the globe and carefully walked out of the rover with it.

"You are doing great, Josh. This is exciting. I'll talk to you a little later."

Josh sat down in the midst of the group, holding the globe. Everyone was looking at him, expecting some explanation of what the globe was. In haltingly poor communications, Josh eventually explained that the globe was their world. They didn't understand. Their world was flat, of course. And, what is he talking about, "our world", like there are other worlds out there? Josh was patient, extraordinarily so. He was able to locate a point on the globe that corresponded to their location. And here was the river running into the ocean. And here was the ocean. Josh showed them how enormous the ocean was. And there is much more. Josh showed them the other land masses, the other oceans, and the different kinds of vegetation. He explained to them the jungle, the desert, the forest, the ice caps, and where they lived, the tundra. He told them that he would explore their entire planet in his rover.

Josh pointed at the sun, and tried to explain that the universe had many thousands of such suns. Josh came from a different world that had a different sun. He tried to explain that the stars were really just other suns, far, far away.

He looked at the faces of the people in his audience. There was a mix of expressions. Some were bored, some were confused, some were probably saying to themselves, "Who cares?" But a few of the people, particularly the older men, seemed very interested. One of them asked if he could see Josh's ship. Josh agreed, and the two of them walked over to the rover, and stepped inside.

"What is your name?" Josh asked the man.

"Gronk," the man said.

"Missy, please introduce yourself to Gronk."

"Hello, Gronk. I am the ship's computer. You may call me 'Missy'."

Gronk was completely confused. Josh could see that he had a lot of explaining to do.

It would be simple to explain to a modern-day human that Missy was the voice of a computer, and that the computer ran the ship. But this was almost hopeless. Gronk had no idea what a computer was, or even what a machine was. Josh decided to take the easy way out.

"The ship talks," Josh said. "The ship's name is 'Missy'. " Amazingly, Gronk seemingly understood these simple English sentences. "Would you like to fly with us a little?"

Gronk thought about it, and then nodded yes.

"Let's take Gronk for a short ride, Missy. Maybe over the ocean and along the coast."

"Okay," said Missy. "Hang on, Gronk. Here you go."

As the rover lifted off the ground, Gronk nervously gripped his armrests.

"It's okay, Gronk," Josh said, knowing that his words were not understood, but that Gronk could understand Josh's calm voice.

As the rover gained altitude, Gronk peered out the window at the ground below, where he saw his friends staring up at the rover in fascination. Gronk waved, but they would never see him waving through such a small window.

The rover headed out over the ocean. Josh pointed out the ocean, and some of the animals, like seals and dolphins, or whatever their relatives would be on this planet. Gronk stayed with his face glued to the window. Josh picked up the globe, and showed Gronk where he lived, and the ocean next door, and how large the ocean was.

The rover banked left and headed along the coastline.

"You need to change seats and sit on the left side of the plane so you can see the coast," I said to Gronk, making elaborate hand gestures to explain.

Gronk understood. He moved over and looked at the coast. Most of it was barren and rocky, as it reached up to touch the endless tundra.

Finally, the rover headed back up the coast to Gronk's home. It hovered a bit, then slowly eased downward to the ground. Gronk's friends were all staring in amazement at the descending hunk of metal. When the rover touched the ground, Gronk headed out the door, and began talking with his friends. He was very excited, waving his arms about wildly, while the others listened closely.

While Gronk was talking to his friends, Josh asked Missy what she thought of the humans here.

"Quite intelligent," Missy said. They have some language skills. They also can make tools and clothing. They can make fire. Obviously, they are good hunters because their food and their clothes come from animals that they hunt. It appears most of their clothes is from the skins of seals, or some similar marine mammal. That implies that they are fairly good at maneuvering a boat through the ocean waves. Their boats are made out of wood. They obviously got the wood from the trees that surround the river bed. Somehow, they figured out how to make a tool for cutting. They can make boats that stay afloat on the ocean, which in itself is quite impressive. And they have made spears to use in the hunt. Their technology, by our standards, is still primitive, but they are certainly an intelligent bunch."

"Here's what I don't get, Missy. This planet is a hundred or more million years younger than Earth. Human beings were not around on the Earth that long ago. Why are they living on this planet in a semi-advanced state?"

"We don't know exactly when the first humans lived on the Earth. The fossil evidence suggests that it was about a million years ago, but that may not be the final answer. Humans may have lived much earlier than that, and the evidence has not yet been found, or cannot be found. But, for the sake of argument, let's say that humans appeared on this planet far earlier in its history than did humans appear on the Earth. Why might that be?

"If we accept the theory of evolution, then we know that organisms evolve because of random mutations in their DNA. Most of the random mutations are worthless, but a few leads to beneficial results. The path that life forms take in the evolutionary process is random, and, basically, the luck of the draw.

"But the interesting thing about this planet is that it is not just humans that are ahead of schedule, but all mammals that we have seen so far. I don't have a quick explanation for this, only some guesses. One guess is what I just talked about, the great dice roll of evolution happened, and this planet got lucky rolls. Favorable mutations happened at a faster rate than on the Earth.

"A second guess is that this planet did not experience the large number of mass extinctions that the Earth did. Those things set the Earth way back. It's like, life was evolving normally on the Earth, then all of a sudden a mass extinction comes along, and you're starting all over. Without the mass extinctions, the life forms advance at a faster rate than on Earth.

"A third guess is the configuration of the continents is different. At the similar point in the Earth's history, the landmasses were clustered around the equator. The predators of the tropics were fierce, and many life forms were wiped out because they could not survive against those predators, including the dinosaurs. The interesting counterpoint is Australia, which broke off from the rest of the continents early on. Unique life forms survived on Australia. They may have existed on the other continents, but quickly went extinct on those other continents. Koala bears, platypuses, and emus were simply no match for dinosaurs.

"But on this planet, landmasses do not hug the equator. They are spread out. The higher latitudes provide a refuge for the mammals to escape the fierce predators of the tropics."

"So, of these three ideas, Missy, which one do you favor?"

"I don't have a favorite. In fact, it may be a combination of all three, or even some fourth one that I haven't thought of. Maybe when the guys back on Earth analyze all the data that we send them, they will have a better idea."

Josh happened to glance toward the rover's door, and noticed Gronk standing there, holding his spear.

"Oh geez, Gronk, how long have you been standing there?"

Gronk made no reply, probably because he did not understand my words. I opened the door and invited him in.

Gronk started communicating. "I am an elder person in our little group. I am valued for my wisdom, not for my ability to hunt wild beasts. I want to go with you when you explore the world. I want to see what the world is like. Then I want to return, and tell my friends everything that I learned. I have talked this over with the others and they all agree that it is a good thing and an exciting opportunity."

"Wow, Missy, what do you think?"

"I have no objections. Interactions with the culture of this world is a main objective of your research. I don't believe Gronk poses a threat to us. We can bring him along. But he may be separated from his group for a month or more."

I explained to Gronk, as best I could, that he would have to be gone for thirty days or more. He said that was fine. With that agreement, we welcomed him aboard as part of the crew.

Gronk came aboard, set his spear against the wall, and had a seat.

"Well, we might as well go, Missy. I say we head out over the ocean, capture some video data, then explore the ocean depths."

"Sounds good," said Missy.

The rover ascended vertically into the blue sky, while Gronk looked out the window and waved to his friends.

9

The rover headed out over the ocean. The ocean was a sparkling blue, with gentle swells visible on its surface. Gronk stayed by the window, transfixed by what he was seeing. A few animals that looked like seals were swimming around and playing.

"We'll be heading underwater soon," announced Missy, and the rover began a gradual descent. Gronk gripped his armrests tightly, not understanding why the rover was about to crash in the water.

"It's okay, Gronk," Josh said reassuringly. Gronk got the message that things were fine, and seemed to relax a little.

The rover flattened out its descent just as it was about to touch the water. It landed on the surface smoothly, and gradually slowed to a stop. Waves rippled against the rover's windows. The rover remained still for a minute or so, then began a slow descent into the depths. Gronk did not appear frightened, but was fascinated by what he saw. The ocean was alive with life. There were small fish in abundance, some with bright colors. There were big, fast-moving fish, something like sharks. And there was everywhere the deep, eerie quiet of the ocean. Soon, they were too deep for sunlight to penetrate, and Missy turned on the lights. There was a large floodlight at the front of the rover, which illuminated the undersea world very brightly. There were also lights inside the rover. As Josh could recall, they had never been turned on before.

"Are you collecting data here, Missy?" asked Josh.

"Yes, Josh. Water temperature, chemical composition, pressure, sonar soundings to chart ocean depths, and videos of all the marine life."

"Great, Missy. You're the best."

"Thank you, Josh."

Suddenly Gronk pointed excitedly out of the side window, and uttered a confused grunt, as if to say, "What the hell is that?"

Josh looked in the direction that Gronk indicated. It was an enormous set of green tentacles, maybe thirty or more feet long, and a large number of them. The creature wasn't threatening the rover, but it was a frightening sight, nonetheless.

"It looks like a giant squid," Josh said. "What do you think, Missy?"

"Yes, it certainly does. Squids on Earth have the ability to change color quickly. I suspect it is the same here. Maybe the squid is used to hiding in tall grass on the floor of a shallower part of the ocean."

"Let's hang around and watch it for a while. It doesn't seem bothered by us."

"It doesn't recognize us as some kind of fish, so it thinks we are part of the natural underwater landscape."

Suddenly, the squid turned and came toward the rover.

"Missy, let's get out of here," Josh said, with obvious concern.

"That's not a good idea, Josh. We can't outrun the squid."

"Well, what can we do then? That thing can destroy us if it wants.

"I think I got this," said Missy. "Hang loose."

Tentacles started encircling the rover. Josh could make out the suckers along the tentacles, as they closed around the rover. What possible interest would the squid have in the rover? Josh couldn't begin to guess, but such questions now were hugely irrelevant.

The rover creaked under the pressure of the tentacles, as the squid's grip on the rover tightened. The rover was lifted up, then twisted around. Josh and Gronk both fell over as the rover was turned sideways. Suddenly, the squid's grip on the rover loosened. Was the squid backing off? Unfortunately, no. The squid's tentacles attached themselves again, and shook the rover. Josh's head banged against the rover's wall, and he felt dazed. But the squid soon gave up, and this time it looked like the squid had had enough. Everything got quiet. Josh stood up slightly, feeling the bruise on the side of his head.

"Missy, what did you do?"

"I electrocuted it," Missy said. "The only thing was, the first shock was not strong enough. The doggone squid was tough."

Then it occurred to Josh to check on Gronk. He waved Josh off, signaling that he was unhurt.

"Is the rover damaged at all?"

"It's fine," said Missy. "The walls creaked a little, but there was no damage."

"You need to take care of that bruise on your head," Missy said. There is a first aid kit in the storage cabinet. You can use some medicine and a bandage, then an ice pack. Josh followed Missy's suggestions. Luckily, Gronk was unhurt. Josh didn't imagine how. Gronk was thrown around the same way that Josh was.

The rover held its course, staying at a depth of one thousand feet. The ocean here was completely black. Josh and Gronk looked out the windows into the blackness, illuminated by the rover's floodlight. Josh and Gronk each had some lunch, while looking outside at the strange fish that inhabited these depths. Suddenly, Gronk pointed out the window. Josh looked out and saw another giant squid, this one red.

"My God," said Josh. "This planet seems to be full of these monsters."

Missy angled the rover away from the squid. Fortunately, the squid was diverted by something else, something that looked like a large shark, maybe twenty feet in length. The squid swam toward the shark. The shark didn't know what to do. For an instant, the shark thought about attacking the squid, then it backed off. The squid's tentacles started encircling the shark. The shark tried to escape, but the suckers on the squid's tentacles were holding the shark fast. The tentacles squeezed the shark, almost like a boa constrictor squeezing some small animal.

"Let's get out of here," said Josh. "Missy, I'm sure by now you've got most of this on video."

"It's all on video. I'm steering away now, Josh."

"Excellent. I hate to piss that thing off."

The rover made a hard turn and headed away, maintaining its depth at one thousand feet. Now that they were past the squid, there wasn't much to get excited about. The rover made its way through the blackness of the deep ocean, going past schools of small fish, and the occasional deep-water shark.

Gronk looked out his window the whole time, stunned by his experiences in the underwater world.

After a few hours, Josh thought he noticed something. It was a whitish gray shape on the side of a large rock.

"I see something, Missy," he said. "Maybe it's nothing, but it seems out of place here. Maybe it's a dead carcass. It's a little below us, and slightly to the left. Do you see it, Missy?"

"Yes, Josh. It's strange looking. I don't think it's a dead animal. It's way too big. It almost looks like the wreck of a boat."

The rover crept up on the strange object. Josh thought it might be a sunken boat, similar to the boats by Gronk's home. But that didn't seem right. This thing looked metallic, not wooden. Could it be that some groups of humans here had become advanced enough to use metals? If so, that would be impressive.

They came closer to the object. Josh could see some detail. It didn't look like a boat. It was the wrong shape. What the heck was this thing?

"Oh my God!" Josh said. "It's a spaceship."

10

Missy pulled the rover up to the side of the spaceship. The rover hovered there in the open water, while Missy and Josh studied the ruins. The craft had struck the underwater mountain head-on, at a shallow angle, and a slow speed. Josh reasoned that the craft had hit the water at a low angle several miles away, then slowly descended, its speed being slowed by the water. As a result, the craft sustained minimal damage, only being scrunched like an accordion on impact, but the accordion effect was not intense. As Josh looked around, he could see no other wreckage apart from the main body. There was a sort of cockpit with a clear window, probably made out of some plastic-like material. A creature was in the cockpit. Josh assumed that this creature was the pilot. The creature was not human. It was an ugly reptilian form, with the head of a crocodile, and the body of a human being. It appeared to have two arms and two legs, ten fingers, and opposable thumbs. Its teeth were sharp and frightening. Josh reasoned that the body was preserved so well because of being kept very cold. The water temperature here was thirty-six degrees Fahrenheit, according to Missy's data. The rest of the craft was somewhat similar to a fighter plane on the Earth. It had two pairs of wings, going straight out from the sides. Its fuselage was oval and metallic. Josh could not tell what kind of metal went into the craft's construction. There was also no way to determine how long ago the crash occurred.

"Missy, is there any way to move the plane out of the ocean and onto some land, so we can study it more?"

"Maybe, Josh. I have a couple of things we can try. But it depends on how heavy the plane is. My first idea is to use a magnetic field. Of course, this assumes that the plane contains some metals that can be affected by a magnetic field. These include iron, nickel, and cobalt. Normally, all of these metals should be affected by magnetic fields at the low temperature where we are at. So it all depends on what the plane is made out of."

"You said there were a few ideas, Missy. What other ideas are worth trying?"

"We do have a set of belts on the rover. The belts can be used to grab onto the craft, hold onto it, and allow the rover to fly off, carrying it."

"Which idea do you recommend, Missy?"

"I recommend trying out the magnetic field approach first. If the craft is too heavy, the magnetic field will not be strong enough to carry the craft. Then we have to use the belts. The problem with the belts are that I have to physically guide the belts from here, so they encircle the craft, and fasten themselves. This is a tricky procedure that I am not looking forward to."

"Okay, Missy. Let's go with the magnetic field, and see where that takes us."

"Sure, Josh. Okay, here we go."

The rover came over the top of the alien space craft, then settled down to rest on top of it. Josh heard the hum of the electro-mechanical motor, and then the rover lifted slowly up through the water.

"Where is the alien ship?" Josh asked, as he could not see under the rover.

"It's with us, Josh," said Missy cheerfully. "We got it. If it breaks loose from us, you'll hear a loud crash as it falls into the rocks below."

The rover continued ascending at an agonizingly slow pace. Josh calculated that, at maybe one foot per second or a little more, say one hundred feet per minute, give or take, it would take ten minutes to ascend one thousand feet to the ocean's surface.

That estimate turned out to be reasonably accurate. After several minutes, the inky blackness of the ocean started to brighten somewhat to a dark gray, then to a light gray, and finally to a clear white. Then the rover broke the surface, and emerged from the depths.

"Now," Missy said, "I suggest we find the nearest piece of land, probably a small island, and put this thing down, remove the alien ship, and examine it."

"I have a suggestion," said Josh. "I might be able to go underwater, and fasten the cables from the rover to the alien ship. That way, we would have the magnetic field plus the cables holding it. We would never lose the thing."

"The water's cold, Josh. And you don't have a wet suit or scuba gear to deal with it."

"What is the water temperature, Missy?"

"It's fifty-one degrees Fahrenheit. You could die of hypothermia in minutes."

"I'd like to give it a try. I've swum in water nearly that cold before. The trick is to get in very slowly, so don't rush me, Missy."

"Okay, Josh. I have the three pairs of cables hanging down from the rover along either side of the alien ship."

"Okay, Missy. But before I go, I want to know how Gronk is doing. He hasn't spoken in a while"

"I am okay," Gronk said, then added, "I am lost."

It was the first coherent communication in English from Gronk, without resorting to any arm movements. He must have learned a lot of words by listening to us, Josh reasoned.

"You're doing great, Gronk. We are very happy to have you as part of the crew." That was probably too difficult a sentence for Gronk to understand, but Josh knew that Gronk could pick up on the tone of voice, and he would take it as a compliment.

"Okay, Missy. No more procrastinating."

Josh put his feet into the ocean water, and immediately pulled them out. My God, that water was cold. He tried again, and kept his feet in the water for a few seconds. From his experience in cold water swimming, Josh knew that the feet were more sensitive to cold than any other body part. So the old maxim among cold water swimmers was "get your feet in the water and the rest is easy." Well, nothing is easy in water that is this cold, but that is the idea.

It took Josh a few minutes before he could get his feet in the water and keep them there for a while. Then, he slowly lowered his body into the water. When the water was up to his neck, he pushed off the side of the boat, and swam with his head out of the water, and keeping his feet kicking. The idea was to burn calories quickly. After a few seconds, he lowered his face into the water. In second place after the feet were the ears. Once Josh seemed adjusted to the cold, he swam back to the side of the boat. He could see the three pairs of cables hanging from the rover along the sides of the alien ship.

"Okay," Josh said to himself. "Just take your time and do this in three easy steps."

He dove underwater, found the first pair of cables, pulled them together, and fastened them with their strap. He pulled the strap through the metal hinge, and tightened it as best he could. Then he came to the surface to get some air. He wanted to rest, but knew that every second that he spent resting would mean more time for his body to get cold. So down he went for the second time, found the cables, brought them together through the metal hinge, and pulled it tight. Then back up for air, and the same thing one last time, and he was done.

It had started to rain while Josh was doing his work, but Josh hadn't even noticed. Josh climbed back into the rover, and took a hot shower, then had something to eat with Gronk.

"Nice job, Josh," Missy said.

"Thanks, Missy. That water was too hot, I need to cool off."

Missy chuckled. Wow, a computer that could understand humor.

"Well, Josh, I think the next step is to cart our alien ship to the nearest spot of land we can find. I don't believe there are any continents nearby, so we're probably talking about a small remote island. I can do a radar sweep, and see what is out there. But the bad news is I don't think we can fly and tow that thing along. The best we can do is tow it through the water."

"Okay, Missy, we're all okay with that." By now, a hard driving rain was pounding against the ships, and the waves had grown considerably larger.

"What do you think about this storm, Missy? Anything to worry about?"

"Only seasickness, Josh. If you're worried about typhoons or tornadoes, forget it. The water is too cold to support that kind of activity. It'll just be a rough ride, that's all. Oh, and by the way, my radar scan picked up a mountain fifty miles away. It must be on top of a small island. So I guess that's our spot to land. Fasten your seat belts and take your motion sickness pills."

"How are you doing, Gronk?" Josh asked, but he already knew the answer. Nothing bothers Gronk. The only time he ever saw Gronk get nervous was when the rover was taking off from his home base.

Gronk shrugged, and made a small gesture with his hands, basically saying that this was nothing. Josh wondered if Gronk had a lot of experience boating in rough seas hunting seals or just fishing.

Meanwhile, the rover made a hard left turn, and headed through the turbulent seas toward some unknown tiny spit of land.

11

Shark attack! The rover creaked as the body of the enormous shark slammed into it. Then the shark banged the rover again.

"My God, the damn thing wants to tip us over and throw us all into the water."

Josh grabbed his laser gun, and aimed it at the shark. But there was a basic problem in physics here. The laser beam, a form of light, travels faster in air than in water, and is thus diffracted or bent, once it hits the water. It is a very poor weapon to use at a shark that is swimming underwater.

Gronk understood our confusion. "Here," he said, as he picked up his spear.

Josh noticed only now that it was more than a spear. It had a rope hanging from its end. It was a type of primitive harpoon.

Gronk stood outside on the deck of the rover, holding his harpoon, and watching the shark. When the time seemed right, he threw the harpoon forcefully, and hit the shark in the back. The shark now could sense danger, and quickly swam away, leaving behind a trail of blood.

"Wow, Gronk, that was amazing."

Even Missy got into the act. "Very well done, Gronk. You quite possibly saved our lives. You definitely saved the rover and the alien ship that we are towing along."

Gronk seemed to partially understand. "Thank you," he said, simply.

"How big was that shark, Missy?"

"Gigantic. It looked to be about twenty-three feet long. As big as anything on Earth."

"Am I wrong to call it a shark? Maybe it was some pre-historic monster like a mosasaur or something."

"I don't know exactly what it was," said Missy. "But, for lack of a better word, let's call it a shark."

With the shark gone, Josh looked ahead. The island was there, with a large mountain in its center. Besides the mountain, Josh could make out green rolling hills, heavily forested. The shoreline ahead of them was rocky, and Josh could see waves crashing into the rocks.

"We can't drive the rover into those rocks on the coast, Missy. I think we have to circle the island and find a natural harbor where we can land."

"Yes," said Missy, and the boat turned to parallel the shoreline.

"What about coral reefs, Missy? Are we in any danger of striking a coral reef, and damaging the rover?"

"No," said Missy. "The rover is made out of reinforced steel, and coral reefs will not damage it. Furthermore, the coral reefs, if there are any, would be more likely to rub against the bottom of the alien ship, not the rover. The alien ship is sitting on the bottom of the rover, so the alien ship will have to absorb most of the impact with the coral reefs. Nonetheless, Josh, that is something that I will think about, and we will proceed extremely slowly once we enter the shallow water. "

"Sounds good, Missy."

The rover was making progress, following the shoreline of the island in a clockwise manner. So far, there was no place to land the rover.

"What about flying to some spot on the island, Missy? Then we wouldn't have to worry about coral reefs or rocky cliffs along the coast."

"To do that, we would have to abandon the alien ship. Our combined weight makes it much too heavy for us to fly."

"Well, unfortunately, Missy, I can't abandon the alien ship. It is the first evidence we have of an alien life form capable of interplanetary travel. The scientific value of that ship is enormous. In fact, when we finally land on the island, I want to note our latitude and longitude, then pick up the thing with the main ship, and haul it back to Earth."

"That sounds good, Josh. I think you have plenty of room in the cargo hold of the ship, where you can store the alien spacecraft. But I don't think you can bring along any dead aliens. They would be hanging around for close to four hundred years, and their bodies would become skeletons and eventually dust."

"Just a minor detail, Missy, but why are you speaking of aliens in the plural? All we saw was one alien."

"Well, you never know, Josh. There may be more aliens on board, somewhere. I hope the alien ship keeps some kind of record or log of its travels. Then we can figure out where the ship came from."

"Yes," said Josh, "and good thinking. Look, Missy. I think we might have a good harbor coming up a little ahead of us."

Indeed, there was a large bay coming up that provided a wide protected harbor. Missy saw it, and steered the rover toward the center of the bay. When the rover entered the bay, Missy cut power, so the rover would only go at one mile per hour through the shallow water. Waves, some of them large, were striking the rover from the rear. But the rover held to its direction and speed. Josh and Gronk were impatiently waiting for the rover to reach the shore, which was probably a half mile from the mouth of the bay. At the rover's slow speed, this seemed to take forever. Finally, however, there was the sound of pebbles and then a sandy bottom as the rover pulled up on the beach. The rover and alien ship were now half on the beach and half in the water.

"Josh, can you unstrap the alien ship for us?" said Missy.

"I guess so," said Josh. "I'm hoping I will be able to reach all the clips so I can unhook everything."

Josh climbed off the rover and jumped into the shallow water, which came up to his knees. It was cold, but not nearly as cold as Josh's last experience. Unfortunately, the operation was trickier than what Josh had hoped for. All the clips were on the bottom of the alien ship and rubbing against the dusty bottom of the ocean. Josh went into the rover, found its tool shed, and took out a shovel. Then he crawled next to the alien ship, and dug a depression below and to the side of the alien ship. Now he could reach underneath the cables, and pull them out to the side, where he could unlatch them.

When he was done, Missy de-activated the electro-magnet holding on to the rover, and the rover flew a couple of feet away and landed on the nearby sandy beach. The alien ship stayed where it was. Enough of it seemed to be on dry land, so it wasn't in danger of floating back into sea. "But what about high tide?" Josh thought, and then quickly realized that the planet had no moon to influence tides.

"Well, Missy, there is a lot to do. I suggest we start with opening up the cockpit, and removing the captain from his spot, and learning what we can about his biology."

"I agree, Josh. But you have to be careful with your pronouns. You never know, the captain of the ship may be a female."

"Yes, you are right. Unfortunately, the English language doesn't have a gender neutral pronoun in the third person singular, and I don't want to always have to say 'he or she' whenever I'm talking about someone. So how about if I just say 'he' when I don't know something's gender, and we both understand what I mean?"

"Okay," said Missy. "I was really just joking with you anyway."

With that, Josh waved to Gronk, asking him to help out with the task of removing the captain. Gronk came over, and Josh explained what they needed to do. But before they could get to the captain, they had to remove the plastic cockpit.

"How do I get this thing off, Missy? I'm sure it has an air-tight seal."

"Maybe there is another way to get onto this ship," Missy said. "And then, the best of all worlds is if we can find an eject button that still operates."

"I don't know, Missy. I have a feeling that any other way into the ship is also air-tight, and is controlled by the panel in the cockpit. But we'll look around."

Josh and Gronk inspected the ship's exterior, looking for any way to get in. They couldn't see the ship's bottom, which sat in the ocean mud, but they did see something like an exhaust pipe sticking out the back. It was much too small to climb through, and, besides, it was under water and flooded.

"We're not finding anything, Missy. I suggest we focus on the window to the cockpit. If we can't pry it off, we can just break it. What do you think?"

"Yes, I agree, Josh. Come and grab a crowbar from the toolbox, and whatever else you might need."

Josh came aboard to the rover, grabbed a crowbar and a hammer, then went back to the alien ship. He tried to pry open the cockpit window, then tried to hammer the crowbar into the edge of the window. Nothing worked. He looked around the perimeter of the window, thinking there might be a release button somewhere. But he saw nothing.

"We're going to have to break this window," he said to Gronk. Gronk seemed to understand. Josh took the hammer and whacked the window hard. The window did not break, but a fracture pattern appeared. He tried once more, and this time the entire window broke and fell into the cockpit. Then he motioned to Gronk to help him remove the pilot's body from the cockpit. Standing on the plane just to the back of the cockpit, they each reached down and tugged at the pilot's body. It wouldn't budge, no matter how hard they tried.

"Missy, can you be of any help here? We just can't get this thing's body out of the cockpit. In fact, it won't move at all."

"Maybe, Josh. I can give it a try." Missy maneuvered the rover to just in front of the alien ship.

"Josh, can you take these cables that are lying on the ground, and wrap them around the alien's body?"

"I think so, Missy. The problem is, we can't move the body at all, but let's give it a try."

The first cable was easy. It went around the alien, slightly below the neck. Josh was able to wrap it completely around the beast.

The other two were tough or impossible. To get the cable around the beast's stomach, they would have to move him slightly, nudge him a little off his seat.

"Missy, I've only got one cable attached, but can you lift the body a few inches so I can strap in the next two?"

"Probably, Josh. But I can't lift him completely out of there with only one cable around his upper body. The cable will just slip off if I try."

Josh heard the whir of machinery as the alien's body was lifted up an inch or so. Josh hoped that Missy could hold things there, as he put a second cable around the alien's stomach, and snapped it into place. Then he was actually able to put the third cable around the alien's hips, and snapped shut.

"We may have it, Missy. Can you try to lift him out of there?"

More whirs and hums as the cables tugged at the alien's body. The alien was lifted out of the cockpit, and then rested on the sandy beach in front of his ship.

"Wow, success, Missy! Great job."

"Is anyone interested in how much that thing weighs? I can tell it pretty accurately from the tension placed on the cables."

"Sure, I'd like to know. And so would Gronk, right Gronk?"

Gronk nodded his head.

"Two thousand seven hundred pounds, give or take."

"My God, Missy, are you sure?"

"Yes, the method I used is pretty accurate."

"Wow. Well, let's measure its length."

"I've already done that, Josh. I measured it with the viewer that I use. It is 25 feet long, including its tail, which is five feet long. I believe the thing walks upright, which means he is twenty feet tall, roughly the same as a two-story building. He has the head of a crocodile, but the hands and feet similar to a human being. He has five fingers on each hand, including an opposable thumb. He has five toes on each foot. He has protective hard bony scales along his back, so it is very hard to hurt him, unless you go for his stomach, which also has some bony protection, but not so much as his back. I suppose that is so his stomach can expand and contract while he eats and breathes.

He has a very tough set of teeth that lie in sockets, so if one tooth breaks, another will grow to replace it. When he runs erect, he can probably go very fast, like maybe twenty-five miles per hour, much faster than a human. He has the ability to taste, feel, smell, hear, and, of course, see."

"How are you able to deduce so much, Missy?"

"I am extremely observant, and can draw good conclusions quickly. I am also quite modest," Missy added with a bit of a chuckle.

"I've heard that crocodiles on Earth have something in their blood that can kill any infection. Is that true, Missy"

"Yes, Josh, that has been demonstrated in lab experiments. I suppose you are wondering if this alien creature has that same ability."

"Yes, Missy. That is exactly what I was wondering."

"There is no way to test that, Josh, unfortunately. The creature is dead, and the chemistry of his blood has changed. Even if his blood could be tested, we don't have any toxic germs that we could throw into some dish and mix it with the creature's blood. But, if I had to make a guess, I would say that this creature is biologically so similar to the crocodile of Earth that I would expect the same properties of immunity."

"I guess it's very hard to kill a crocodile without modern technology."

"You are exactly right, Josh. In fact, if it were not for human beings and their advanced technologies, there would be no way to kill a crocodile. You would just have to wait for it to die of old age, and the lifespan of a crocodile on Earth is about fifty years. Some live much longer.

"Crocodiles on Earth have no natural enemies, only man. If human beings were not around, crocodiles would come close to ruling the world. The only shortcoming for them on Earth is that they are pretty much confined to the water – rivers, lakes, and, in the case of salt water crocodiles, the oceans. Crocodiles can move around on the land, of course, but they are vulnerable there, and prefer the water, where they are undisputed kings.

"The crocodiles that we see here have evolved to the point where they can live comfortably on the land. In fact, the land might be their preferred environment. With this thing that we just dug out of the cockpit; it seems nature has created the perfect monster."

12

"I guess our next chore is to try and learn whatever we can from what's inside the ship."

"Yes, Josh. I can't begin to guess what we might find there, but we just have to start looking."

Josh motioned to Gronk, and the two of them climbed into the cockpit. They had to move carefully, because everything was covered with shards of plastic from the broken window. The first thing they looked for were buttons or computer screens. There were none. There was a cabinet off to the side. Josh opened it, and a bunch of papers and assorted junk fell out onto the floor. There were many pieces of paper with strange writings. There were some papers with mysterious drawings. Then there were some bits of junk, that Josh thought maybe were some kinds of good-luck symbols.

"Missy, I think we need your help with this junk. It might be something important, I have no clue. Can you take a crack at it? Maybe you can make some sense out of it."

"Sure, Josh. Bring the stuff over, and I'll do my best with it."

Josh motioned to Gronk, and the two of them loaded up their arms with the junk, and walked over to the rover. Once in the rover, and unceremoniously laid everything on the floor, making sure that Missy could see everything.

"It looks like a lot of secret scribbling," Missy said.

"Well, if Missy is confused, then this stuff must be undecipherable. Let's let her continue to think about it, and you and I get back to the alien ship."

Josh and Gronk crawled back into the cockpit and looked around some more. Josh couldn't see anything more there. But there was a stairway leading down from the cockpit into the depths of the ship. The stairway was large, with stairs spaced very far apart, and a ceiling that was massively high. Josh and Gronk had to both be careful not to fall, because the stairs were so widely spaced and there was no handrail. At the bottom of the stairs, they were in a basement. The whole thing was flooded with at least three feet of water. Other than that, everything was dark, and Josh decided to get a flashlight so he could see. So he went back to the rover, got a flashlight, then went back to the ship. He was surprised to see Gronk wading through the water in the basement. Apparently, his eyes were not bothered by the dark. Gronk was pointing at something excitedly. Josh followed him into the water, and gasped in surprise and disgust. There was a large group of crocodiles partially submerged in the water and chained together. Josh guessed that they were prisoners being exiled to this planet. In any case, it was time to get back to Missy and report.

When he reported to Missy, Missy suggested a plan of action. They could use a pump to get the water out of the basement. Then they could use a flamethrower combined with a fire extinguisher to burn the bodies. Normally Josh would be sickened by such an idea, but these creatures did not generate any emotions in him. So he agreed with Missy. But first, he decided to take some photographs of the gruesome scene in the basement. Then he went back to the rover and retrieved the pump. Fortunately, the pump had a long pipe attached that could be stretched to the outside of the cockpit, so the water could be dumped onto the sand outside the ship. It was not that heavy. Josh managed it, but had to let Gronk carry the flashlight. Then he and Gronk began the long process of draining the water from the basement.

It took several hours to complete this job. When they were finally done, they counted eleven of the crocodiles chained together on the floor, their bodies starting to stink.

"I guess we're ready for the flame thrower and the fire extinguisher," Josh said to Missy, noticing now that night had fallen.

"Try and be careful, Josh. You don't want to burn up the ship. It might still provide some useful information. But now I understand why the alien ship was so heavy. It had the captain and eleven other crocodiles, each weighing something like two thousand seven hundred pounds."

"Yes, Missy, we will be as careful as we can."

With that, Josh and Gronk carried this new equipment, along with the flashlight up through the cockpit and down the stairway to the basement. Josh explained to Gronk what needed to be done. He handed the flame thrower to Gronk, and explained how to use it, then kept the fire extinguisher for himself. Josh pointed at the first one of the bodies, and motioned to Gronk to shoot the flame thrower at it. Josh pointed the flame thrower, and pressed the trigger. The beast started to burn up. Josh squashed the stray flames, then waited while the crocodile burned up. When the body was completely incinerated, Josh doused the fire. Then they moved on to the second crocodile. This was slow work, and they had to be very careful. Finally they finished the gruesome job. All the crocodiles had been incinerated. There were burn marks on the floor but no real damage to the ship. It was time to head back to the rover.

When they were back in the rover, Josh explained that they still had some investigation to do around the ship, but they would like to do that in the light of day. With that, Josh and Gronk sat together, had a large delicious meal, and drifted off to sleep.

When Josh woke up, there was bright sunshine pouring through the windows. Gronk was moving around in the rover, doing some kind of stretching or yoga.

"How did you sleep, Josh?"

"Wow, really good, I guess. Boy, I was exhausted after all that work yesterday. I think we need your help again, Missy. Can you somehow move the alien ship so it is resting completely on dry land? That way we don't have to worry about anything getting flooded."

"Sure, Josh. I can do that right now. I'm going to sit the rover on top of the alien ship, turn on the electro-magnet, and move it."

With that, the rover hovered in the air, gently moved over to the alien ship, and sat on top of it. Josh could hear the hum of the electro-magnets as they turned on. Then the rover lifted up, carrying the alien ship along, and eased it down smoothly on the sandy beach. Then the rover disconnected the electro-magnet, and touched down some feet away.

"Thank you, Missy."

"You're always welcome, Josh. Have fun over there." Josh chuckled at that.

Josh motioned to Gronk, and the two of them left the rover and climbed into the cockpit of the alien ship. Gronk immediately saw something.

"What is this?" Gronk muttered. He was holding up a large transparent bag with a lot of junk in it.

"Where did you find this?"

"In here," Gronk said, pointing to a metal box. Josh looked in the box but couldn't see much of any interest. Then Josh noticed some tubes coming out of the bag with the junk in it. On the ends of the tubes were small connector pieces, looking almost like electrodes.

"You know what I think this is?" said Josh, facing Gronk, but talking mainly to himself. "I think these guys set up a system to feed themselves intravenously on their trip. If we knew how much they consumed each day, and we know how much is left in the food bag, we could estimate how far they came to get here." Then, as an afterthought, Josh added, "That big metal box over there. I bet that's a portable refrigerator to keep their food from spoiling.

"I wonder if the prisoners in the basement had the same setup. Unfortunately, it was dark when we burned them all up, and we may have burned their life support up along with them without even thinking about it."

Josh and Gronk crawled down the stairway to the basement, and looked around. Indeed, Josh found the charred remains of several refrigerators, some "food" lying around on the floor, and a few remaining strands of tube. The rest of it was all burned up. Of course, the focus had been to burn up the stinking corpses, paying little or no attention to anything else. But, in any case, their investigation did answer one important question, how the aliens ate on their trip.

"I think we need Missy to help us figure out some things," Josh remarked, and they headed back to the rover.

"Well, Missy, we've determined that the aliens were fed intravenously through tubes. The tubes came out of large bags of junk that sat in a type of refrigerator. As for the guys downstairs, the prisoners, almost all their stuff is burned up. But we do have an intact refrigerator, bag of junk, and tube for the pilot.

"Now, Missy, if you're still with me, here's the thing. If we knew how much gunk the aliens consumed, and at what rate they consumed it, we might be able to take a stab at how far away their home planet is."

"Interesting," said Missy. "We don't know how fast their ship was going through space, but we can take a wild guess, say fifteen thousand miles per hour. Our best guess as far as food consumption is how much is left in the big refrigerated bag. We can assume that whatever is there is enough to get them back home, plus a margin of safety.

"The big unknown is how much they consume each day. We could cut open the pilot's stomach and liver, and see how much stuff is sitting there. Of course, I am guessing that the biology of these beings is similar to their counterparts on Earth. But we have to remember that some or most of this stuff is expelled as bodily waste. We don't know how much. Did the pilot have any kind of catheter or other similar device on him?"

"I don't know. His body is lying in the sand. But I have to be honest, Missy, I am not looking forward to cutting that thing open to look at his insides."

"Here is another thought, Josh. If you can find the fuel tank, measure its volume. I assume that they ran out of fuel and that is why they crashed, but there still might be some small amount of fuel in the fuel tank. If there is, we can chemically analyze it. Then, if we know how much fuel can be carried in the tank, we can make a pretty good guess at the potential range of the space craft."

"That sounds a lot better, Missy. Gronk and I will get right on it."

Josh and Gronk entered the alien ship and walked to the basement. There was nothing there except some storage cabinets and a lot of empty space where the prisoners were chained together. So it was back to the rover and Missy.

"Missy, I suspect the fuel tank is on the underside of the ship. Are you able to flip the ship over for us?"

"I think so, Josh. I have to maneuver the rover to the side of the ship and then use the rover's arms to flip the ship over."

The rover did exactly that, and in a few minutes, the underside of the ship was facing up.

Most of the underside was taken up by a very large tank, which Josh assumed was the fuel tank. It was made out of metal, and Josh didn't know how to get inside of it. He needed to burn a hole somehow. So it was back to Missy, who was able to find an acetylene torch for him to use.

Josh knew that acetylene was not effective on all metals, so it would be a little bit of a gamble to see if it would work on the ship's fuel tank. He powered on the acetylene torch, which threw out a small pinpoint flame. Then he aimed it at the center of the fuel tank and went to work. After five minutes, the torch had managed to produce a small dent in the tank. He didn't know how thick the tank was, but this could really be a big job. The problem was, he needed something bigger than a small peephole, so he enlarged the area cut by the torch. He had to take a break after fifteen minutes. A larger dent was taking shape, but he didn't know how much thickness he still had to penetrate.

"Welcome to shop class," he laughingly told himself as he struggled clumsily with the torch. Finally, after about an hour divided between drilling and resting, the torch broke through and he heard it penetrate empty air. Now all he had to do was widen the hole. Actually, he needed to widen it quite a bit. Another hour and he had a hole that was large enough so he could stick his hand and a flashlight through. He looked around through the hole that he made. The tank was about four feet thick, so he could just barely reach the other side of it with his outstretched arm. There were a few damp spots but he couldn't find what he really needed, which was a puddle large enough to bring back to Missy. The way to proceed, Josh reasoned, was to lower a robotic vacuum through the hole that he made, let it roam around and capture whatever it could, then run the junk through a sieve to separate the solids from the liquids. Finally, with a little bit of luck, he could have a liquid specimen to take to Missy for analysis.

So, he proceeded with this plan. He got a robotic vacuum from Missy's tool shed, replaced its garbage bag with a brand new one, and went to the basement. He was just able to fit the contraption through the hole that he made, then he turned the power switch on, set it down, and let it roam around. This was going to take some time, so he went back to the rover, where he and Gronk had a nice lunch and a nap.

13

Josh woke up a few hours later, and headed back to the alien ship's basement to check on the robotic vacuum. He brought along his laser gun, which he could use to measure dimensions. When he reached the alien ship, lying upside down, he looked through the hole he created, and, indeed, found the robotic vacuum. It had returned to its starting position. He picked it up and looked inside its garbage bag. There was a mixture of solid and liquid, but a fair amount of liquid, probably enough to fill a small cup for Missy to analyze. Then he used his laser gun to measure the dimensions of the fuel tank. He got measurements of 40 feet by 40 feet , and 3 feet deep. That gave him 4800 cubic feet of total volume. He converted that to gallons, knowing that there were about seven and one half gallons in one cubic foot. That meant that the fuel tank, when full, could hold about 36,000 gallons.

What did that tell him? Well, it would depend on the kind of fuel that was used. But, as a first order approximation, if the space craft could get 1000 miles per gallon flying through the near vacuum of deep space, then it had a range of about 36 million miles with a full tank. If that estimate was accurate, then the aliens must have come from a nearby planet in the same star system. But it was time to check all this out with Missy.

After Josh explained his reasoning, Missy agreed that the ship must have come from a nearby planet. One issue, however, was that there was no fuel remaining for a return flight. So did they ever plan to return? Or did they have a secret stash of fuel hidden someplace on this planet? Or did they just badly miscalculate?

But now it was time to analyze what the robot vacuum had collected. Missy instructed Josh on throwing the stuff into a sieve to separate the solids from the liquids, then using the rover's highly advanced mass spectrometer to analyze the liquids. Missy explained that the fuel had to be liquid, and the solid matter that the vacuum had picked up was not fuel, just garbage. After a few minutes, the mass spectrometer had some results. Missy pointed out a group of about six elements, and identified them as kerosene. After that, what was left was small amounts of liquid hydrogen and liquid oxygen.

"There might be more liquid hydrogen and liquid oxygen than we have seen," explained Missy. "Some of it probably evaporated. In fact, I'm surprised that we have any of it to see at all."

"So do you have any conclusions or theories so far, Missy?"

"First of all, these creatures are obviously quite intelligent. They have proven themselves capable of space travel. But they have not perfected it yet, and I'm still confused about why they ran out of gas before they could return to their home planet. Unless we are missing something, this was extraordinarily poor planning on their part.

"Beyond that, I agree with you, Josh. The range of the alien space craft on one full tank of fuel means that they had to be coming from a nearby planet orbiting the same star. There is nothing on their ship like a solar sail or a hydrogen scoop, so their only means of propulsion was the liquid fuel, for as long as it could be burned.

"Of course, our real goal is to locate the home planet of the crocodile creatures. We don't know a whole lot, but let me try to get us started. First, we can safely assume that the crocodile planet appears as a very bright object in the night sky. It is quite close to our planet, and, if it has a normal albedo, that is, it reflects light as most planets do, then it will be one of the brightest objects in the sky, analogous to Venus, Mars, or Jupiter from the Earth. Granted, Mars is not nearly as bright as Venus or Jupiter, except when it is closest to the Earth, but at all times it is a brighter than average object.

"Now that we are looking for bright objects in the sky, we have two possibilities. First, the crocodile planet is closer to the sun than our planet. In that case, we should see it close to the sun as either an evening star or a morning star, similar to Venus from the Earth. The second possibility is that the crocodile planet is farther away from the sun than our planet. In that case, we don't have a lot to go on, except that it is a bright object in the night sky. Keep in mind that most of the constellations in the night sky here will be different from what we are used to on Earth, and that makes it tough to identify a planet."

"Maybe a stupid question, Missy, but possibly Gronk can help us, especially if we are stuck in the difficult second case. If he has been watching the stars, he might know something."

"Good idea, Josh, and I would encourage getting what we can from Gronk, but I wouldn't put a lot of hope into it. Gronk and his colony impress me as simple hunters and fishermen. I don't think they travel the oceans like the ancient Vikings. They wouldn't have much practical use for stargazing."

"You're probably right, Missy, but I do want to try."

It was getting late in the afternoon, and soon the sun would set, and they could view the night sky. The rover carried along two telescopes, an eight-inch reflector for general observing, and a four-inch refractor for viewing planets at high magnification. Josh took them both outside and set them up on the beach. Soon the sun set, and stars began popping into view. Josh found Gronk, and explained to him what was going on. This was a real challenge, because Josh had to explain that these little dots in the sky were real objects, most were stars, but some were planets, and one of those planets was the crocodile planet. Gronk seemed to understand things with some difficulty. Then Josh explained that the stars did not move through the sky but the planets did. So, if you notice some object changing its position over time, then it was probably a planet. Finally, the big question for Gronk – did he spend much time watching the stars, and did he notice some stars that moved around compared to the other stars? Gronk couldn't say for sure. In fact, he seemed quite confused by what Josh was trying to explain to him.

Josh decided to start with the refractor telescope. Night had fallen. It was quite dark in a world where there were no electric lights. Josh made a quick run to the rover to grab a flashlight, then came back and set up the telescope with an eyepiece to maximize the magnification. It was always trickier to find things under high magnification because the telescope's field would be smaller, and the heavenly bodies would jump around quite a bit with just a small movement of the telescope. But Josh had spotted a very bright evening star that just might turn out to be the crocodile planet. If so, he wanted the largest possible magnification to view it.

Understandably, it took a good few minutes before Josh could line up the telescope to point at the bright evening star just above where the sun had just set. If this object was a planet, it would be closer to the sun from the planet they were on. He looked through the eyepiece lens, and turned the knob to bring it into sharp focus. Was it a star or a planet? A star, when focused, would appear as a bright point of light. A planet, on the other hand, would appear as a disk. Josh looked intently at the object as it came into focus. My God, it was a planet! There was no doubt about it. The image was a circular disk, and, as Josh looked closely, he could make out a few surface features. He could see some mountain ranges, and some flat, sunken areas that might be oceans. He could see some thin lines, which might be rivers. And he could see ice caps that were prominent, but not as large as the ones on this planet. Could this be the crocodile planet? Josh thought it was very possible, but he had more investigating to do.

He set up the reflecting telescope, which was good for searching bigger areas of the sky. Planets that were farther from the sun than this planet could lie anywhere in the sky, and possibly could not be seen at night if they were on the daytime side of the planet right now. But Josh made a reasonable assumption that the planets in this system followed a path known as the ecliptic, so their declinations, or effective latitudes, would be somewhere between -23 and +23 degrees. That could narrow the search a bit. Josh picked out a group of the brightest stars, and, one by one, looked at them through the reflector telescope. Out of six stars that he viewed, one of them was a planet, but its disk was so small that Josh couldn't make out any features on its surface. Josh stayed outside the entire night, thinking that during this period he should see almost every star and candidate planet in the sky. It was a long night. Josh saw many objects rise, traverse the sky, and then set. He trained the telescope on most of them, hoping that a few of them would be planets. But as the sun came up in the east to mark a new day, all Josh had found were two candidate planets. The most interesting one was the one closest to the setting sun, the evening star. The image of it was very clear, a fact that indicated that it was close by. The other planet was farther from the sun, fainter, and probably a long distance away.

Now Josh wrapped up his all-night observing, grabbed the two telescopes, and headed back to the rover. He told Missy about the two candidate planets. Missy suddenly sounded excited, something very unusual for a computer.

"Josh, I think I know where the crocodile planet is. I managed to decode the scribbling that you found in the cockpit of the alien ship. I admit it was hard work, after all it was an incoherent language and incoherent drawings. But a few of the drawings started to make sense. One of them was a map and set of instructions for where to land on our planet. Another was a map and set of instructions for the route through space. Anyways, the long and short of it is that the crocodile planet is close to us, and is closer to the sun than we are. It may be the closest planet to the sun in this solar system."

"That sounds like the planet I saw last evening, the evening star. Like I said, it is the strongest candidate for being the crocodile planet."

"So now that we know where the crocodile planet is, Josh, what do we do?"

"We go there, Missy. It will be our first contact with a civilization that is capable of space travel."

"I'm not sure that is a good idea, Josh. After all, these creatures are monstrous, and probably savagely cruel. And they are very smart, and have developed an advanced technology. Going to visit them will be extremely dangerous. Not only that, but they are far different from humans, and there may be no way to communicate with them."

"I realize all of that," said Josh. "Maybe all we can hope for is observing them, and learning what we can about their society."

"You are the boss, Josh. You can always just fulfill your obligations on this planet, and then go home. But, if you want to visit the crocodile planet, then I am at your service to do that."

"I have one question, Missy. The guys on Earth have been monitoring this area of the galaxy for any kind of signals, like radio waves. They got nothing from this planet, but they also got nothing from the crocodile planet. Why not?"

"Well, Josh, you have to keep in mind the time frame. It takes 500 years for a signal to travel at the speed of light from the crocodile planet to Earth. And you have been traveling through space for 625 years, as measured on Earth. So, that means that the crocodile planet would have had to send a signal 1125 years ago for it to be received on Earth before your departure. The conclusion is that the technology on the crocodile planet is younger than 1125 years."

"Makes sense, Missy. I should have thought that."

"Now, Josh, if you really want to go to the crocodile planet now, then we will still have to come back and finish our exploration of this planet."

"Yes, Missy. As long as you approve of that plan, that is what I want to do."

"Okay, Josh. I approve, for what that is worth. But you are the boss. Whether I approve or not makes no difference."

"Gronk, what do you want to do? Do you want to come with us to the crocodile planet, or go home to your friends?"

Gronk excitedly signaled that he wanted to fly with us through outer space to see the crocodile planet.

"So, Missy, I assume we need the main ship to take us to the crocodile planet, right? Or can we do it in the rover?"

"I recommend the main ship, Josh. The rover might be able to make it, but has not been sufficiently tested for space travel. And, it would take way too long. Traveling thirty million miles at a maximum speed of 3000 miles per hour would take over one Earth-year."

"Okay, Missy. So, let's pack up our things and head over to the main ship."

Josh took a minute to check his notes. "As I recall, Missy, the main ship is at a latitude of 36 degrees south and a longitude of zero. Where are we now, Missy?"

"We are at 49 degrees south latitude and 20 degrees west longitude. Applying the law of cosines in spherical trigonometry, I calculate that we are thirteen hundred and sixty-five miles from the main ship. That means a flight time in the rover of two hours."

"Missy, I haven't slept all night. I'll try to get some sleep now, and then we can head for the main ship for our flight to the crocodile planet."

"Sounds good, Josh. We can leave when you're ready."

Josh lay down and fell asleep instantly. He dreamt that he had finally returned to Earth and was enjoying a pleasant walk in the park with Laura.

14

Josh woke up around noon. The rover was still parked on the beach.

"I'm awake, Missy. We can leave whenever you and Gronk are ready."

"Gronk has been ready for hours. After all, this will be his first experience in outer space."

"Okay, so I guess we might as well go, Missy."

The rover took off vertically, with Gronk staring out the window with his usual fascination. Almost directly below, Josh could see the alien space craft tipped upside down, and then the monstrous body of the crocodile captain. The rover banked left and headed out over the ocean. The island, which they nicknamed "crocodile ship island", was behind them but still somewhat visible. Josh could make out lush green forests, and a mountain peak in the island's middle. As the rover sped away, the island got smaller and smaller until it finally disappeared from sight. Now there was just endless ocean as far as they could see. Ocean swells moved through the water, but soon even these could not be seen as the rover continued to gain altitude.

Josh realized that he was very hungry, and guessed that Gronk was too. Missy helped them to prepare a wonderful dinner of steak, potatoes, and vegetables with blueberry pie for dessert, and orange juice to drink. Josh ate as slowly as possible to savor the taste of the meal. Gronk also enjoyed it, as he shoveled food into his mouth with his hands. By modern standards, it was terrible table manners, but it didn't bother Josh. He considered Gronk a good friend, and he was happy to see Gronk enjoying his food.

As Josh was finally finishing his meal, they saw some land up ahead. There was a ridge of mountains just off the coastline. As they approached the land, Josh could see greenery on the seaside edge of the mountains and brown barren scrub on their tops. The rover, meanwhile, had begun a long, gradual descent. They passed over the ridge of mountains, and Josh noticed the sharp contrast. Lush greenery gave way very suddenly to barren desert on the other side. Josh watched as they flew over the top of the mountain ridge. The ride became bumpy as they flew over the ridge. Gronk gripped his armrests tightly in response to the turbulence.

"It's okay, Gronk," Josh said reassuringly. "A little turbulence is normal on a flight like this. See the mountains below us?" Gronk looked out the window and nodded his head.

"Mountains create bumpy air," Josh explained. He motioned with his hands that air had to rise to pass over the mountains, then fall away on the other side, and that made for a bumpy ride through the air.

The landscape became drier and soon was a desert, with only sand and scrubby bushes to dot the ground. Then, ahead of them, they could make out the protective dome of the ship that transported them through outer space. The rover slowed down, and continued to descend until they were very close to the ship. Then the rover descended vertically and rested on the sandy ground next to the ship. Josh and Gronk came out of the rover. Gronk looked at the huge structure housing the space ship, and appeared confused. Josh tried to explain to Gronk what was going on, and why they needed another ship to travel through space. Gronk seemed only partially to understand it all.

Gronk started walking aimlessly around, then suddenly appeared excited. He pointed down at the ground. Josh came over to have a look.

"My God," Josh said aloud. "Footprints. In the middle of the desert, no less."

Josh bent over to study the footprints. They were larger than what a human being would make. They were also spread quite far apart, which suggested a large animal that took big steps. The forward portions of the footsteps stuck out, so it looked to Josh that the creature walked on two legs and had feet with five large toes.

"What do you think of these footprints, Missy?" Josh said.

Missy, who had been studying the footprints along with Josh, gave a frightening interpretation. "I think it is a creature similar to the crocodiles that we saw on the alien space craft. In fact, it might even be the same species of animal. The length of the stride and the size of the feet suggest that the creature might be twenty or more feet tall, stands upright on two legs, and probably is somewhat intelligent, considering its curiosity about our ship."

"Is this thing dangerous?"

"Yes, I would say so," said Missy. "If it behaves anything like the crocodiles on Earth, then it could be very vicious and violent, and would probably try to harm us and our ship. Not only that, it is a very large and powerful animal."

At this point, Gronk pointed to a trail of footsteps leading away from the ship and into the desert.

"I wonder how recent are these footsteps," said Josh. "If they are fairly new, then maybe the animal is still nearby. We should try to hunt it down."

"That would be very dangerous," said Missy, without elaborating.

"The problem is, we can't allow this thing to destroy or vandalize the ship. For starters, it is my only way back to Earth."

"Well, Josh, like I keep saying, you're the boss, so if you want to go after that thing, you can. All I can do is advise against it, and warn you that you are chasing a very dangerous monster."

"Good, so that settles it. Do you want to come along, Gronk? We can chase after that monster."

Gronk seemed to understand, and nodded yes. Gronk never tired of adventure, Josh thought.

With that, Josh and Gronk waved goodbye to Missy, and then headed out on foot, following the path of the footsteps. It was an easy path to follow, but it turned into a long hike.

Then Josh remembered that he had two rocket belts in his backpack. Using them, they could catch up to the creature. Josh put his on, then helped Gronk to get into his. A few minutes of demonstration and Gronk was ready to go. They took off vertically until they were about one hundred feet off the ground. At this altitude, the horizon was about ten miles off, using the extremely rough approximation that the square root of the height in feet was equal to the horizon distance in miles. Of course, Josh also assumed that the planet was close to the same size as Earth.

When they reached about one hundred feet of altitude, they spotted the beast almost immediately, walking at a brisk pace and heading away from them. There was a kind of oasis or watering hole in the distance where the beast was probably headed.

For several minutes they followed the lumbering monster, slowly gaining on him. Josh and Gronk both got out their ray guns, preparing for a fight. When the beast could hear the gentle hum of the motors in the rocket packs, he turned to face them. He looked just as the monster that was piloting the alien space craft. He was probably twenty feet tall with the head of a crocodile, and the body, partly human and partly crocodilian. It walked on its hind legs, but its front legs doubled as arms. Its eyes were reddish green, a very unusual color, reflecting anger and hatred. Its stomach was lined with scales, some of them bony.

Josh motioned to Gronk, and they descended together to about twenty feet so they were staring the crocodile in the face. Environmentalists would not approve of what Josh was thinking. He wanted to murder a life form that was recently discovered. Josh rationalized this easily. The monster was not indigenous to this planet. It came from another world, and probably meant to do harm to the local life forms.

Josh and Gronk both drew their weapons. The monster was now about fifty feet away, and Josh felt that he could shoot it from that distance. But he was surprised. Instead of calmly waiting to be shot, the creature leaped into the air, its mouth gaping wide, as it stared at Josh and Josh's weapon. It seemed to know that Josh held a weapon. Its enormous teeth clamped down on Josh's right forearm, forcing him to drop his weapon. Gronk fired at the beast, hitting him somewhere in the face, but the beast was not deterred. Suddenly, something like a lightning bolt flashed out of the sky, striking the beast, which then fell to the ground in a mottled heap. Josh looked up and saw the rover descending toward them. It was the most beautiful sight in the world to Josh, who was about to be killed by this alien monster. But the monster was not dead yet. As the rover continued to descend, the monster leapt to its feet, and jumped into the air, grabbing the rover angrily in its mouth. Josh and Gronk both emptied their weapons into the monster's throat, chest, and face, until it collapsed to the ground. The monster was dead. Josh could be quite sure of that. But so was the rover, which lay in a tangled heap on the ground, its body a mass of twisted metal garbage. Josh couldn't believe it.

"Missy," he cried out, but there was no response. "Missy, Missy, Missy, please come back. You just saved our lives, and I love you. Please, Missy, come back, you can't die now." Josh was bent over the side of the rover, crying like he never cried before. Missy was gone.

Josh finally gathered himself together. He and Gronk strapped on their rocket belts and began the return trip to the ship. The sun was going down, shadows were lengthening, and Josh realized there was not too much daylight left. The trip back seemed long, but it was only about ten miles. Eventually, they saw the ship in the distance, encased in its protective shield. Josh was afraid of what the ship's computer would say, after he confessed that the rover was destroyed.

Minutes later, he entered the ship with Gronk. He explained to the ship's computer what had happened, while he fought back bouts of uncontrolled crying.

The ship's computer listened patiently and calmly, as computers normally do. Then the computer said simply, "Let's go retrieve the rover and see what can be done." Hearing these words, a faint glimmer of hope flashed through Josh's mind. Could the rover actually be repaired?

"But first," continued the computer, "we have to get you stitched up. Your arm looks like a hunk of hamburger. I'll call one of the robots to fix you up."

The computer called the resident robot medic, who showed up promptly, and began working on Josh's arm. The robot disinfected the wound, then began the process of stitching it up. In the mean time, the computer removed the ship's protective bubble. "We need to find the rover and retrieve it," the computer explained matter-of-factly.

Josh explained that he did not know the latitude and longitude of the rover's remains, but it was close by, and he could point the ship in the general direction. The ship took off vertically to a height of a few hundred feet. The sun was just setting, and Josh hoped that they would be able to find the rover in the twilight gloom. With a pair of binoculars, Josh could see the rover fairly quickly, and pointed to it. The ship obediently moved to where Josh was pointing. In a while, they reached the twisted mass of rubble that had once been the rover, and the enormous body of the monster lying next to it.

"Twenty-six stitches," the robot medic said, as it finished stitching up Josh's arm. "You are going to be fine, but you may have a scar for the rest of your life. The important thing is to be extra careful with that arm for several days, so the wound can heal. That was quite a bite that the creature gave you."

"I know," said Josh. "I hope I will be okay, and I am praying for Missy and the rover."

"Who is Missy?"

"Oh, sorry," said Josh. "That is the name that I gave to the rover's computer."

"I see. Well, we will both pray for her, then."

Meanwhile, the ship was hovering a few feet above the rover's wreckage. Josh heard a loud noise of mechanical parts moving. "What you hear is the door to the ship's basement opening up from below," the computer explained. Then gigantic mechanical arms descended, encircled the rover, and brought it back up and into the basement.

"We're going to need the robots," the computer said, issuing a stream of commands to the robot force. Josh wasn't sure if it was his place, but he rushed down to the ship's basement to observe what he could of the salvage effort.

The ship gained altitude and began flying, while the robots continued to examine the wreckage, oblivious to the ship's motions. "We need to find a more secure place," the computer explained. "Somewhere where the monster's friends won't come looking." Sure enough, the ship steered away from the dead body of the monster, and also avoided its original landing spot. In a couple minutes, it touched down in another part of the same desert region. The computer directed the return of the protective bubble, and things were back to normal.

In the mean time, the team of robots had hoisted the rover up onto a hydraulic platform, which raised the rover about ten feet above the floor. Then the robots, some of them on ladders, started examining the various large dents. Josh watched with interest as they used hot water and suction cups to pull some of the dents into place. Josh thought this was an old-fashioned method, but it seemed to work with the tools that they had available. But Josh guessed this would be a very long and arduous job. After a while longer, Josh retired to the main cabin, where he enjoyed a nice supper with Gronk.

Once Josh had eaten, he realized how exhausted he was. He lay down and fell asleep at once, assuming Gronk was doing the same.

He woke up, with the sun shining in on him. He felt very groggy. He had slept through all of the night and probably most of this morning. He climbed out of bed, cleaned up a little, had a small breakfast of toast and some fruit, then anxiously headed downstairs to observe the salvage operation on the rover. As he walked down the stairs, holding the hand railing, shots of pain shot through his right arm. Wow, the robot medic was right. This injury was serious, and he did have to be extra careful.

He arrived at the basement, where there was a lot of activity going on with the rover. The rover's appearance had improved dramatically. It was no longer a heap of twisted rubble, but was starting to assume its old shape. There was still work to be done, but Josh found this encouraging. Then he noticed two of the robots, each with their own workbenches, working with large magnifiers and holding soldering irons, as they worked on Missy's circuit boards. Josh felt good about what he saw, but clearly there was still work to be done.

"Any guess as to how long it will take to fix the rover?" Josh asked the computer.

"Well, first of all," said the computer, "we aren't sure that the rover can be fixed, at least not to its fully functional form. But the robots are very good at what they do. If all goes well, and there are no complications, then I'm guessing another one or two days. If the damage turns out to be more serious than we thought, then it's anybody's guess. I know the next thing for us to do is to fly to the crocodile planet, and have a look at it. I think, before we do that, we have to finish up with the rover – either get it fully functional, or determine that it cannot be fixed."

"Yes," said Josh. "I agree completely. The rover is a marvelous machine, and we all hope that it can be fixed."

"Absolutely," said the computer.

"I have to hand it to you and the team of robots," Josh said. "After the encounter with the monster, I did not have any hope that the rover could be repaired. Now I have some hope."

"I know how much you like the rover, Josh. In fact, you have made excellent use of it in your data collection. And I know how attached you are to Missy. So, the robots are trying their very best to bring Missy and the rover back to life."

"How did you know about Missy?"

"Everything that Missy experiences, including her interactions with you, gets automatically downloaded to me. I know everything, Josh."

"Well, it looks like I have a long wait with nothing to do," Josh said. "I think I'm going to go outside with the rocket belt and explore some."

"Okay, Josh. But be very careful with your arm. Another violent encounter and you could wind up losing it."

"Yes, I realize that," said Josh. "I will be extra careful."

Josh strapped on his rocket belt and asked Gronk if he wanted to come along. Gronk quickly agreed, strapped on his belt, and the two of them stepped outside. They took off, Josh moving about randomly, and Gronk following. Josh didn't know exactly what he was looking for, maybe some forms of animal life, or some unusual plant life that he hadn't noticed before. He wasn't sure if he would find anything at all interesting, but flying around was something he could do as he waited to hear about the rover. So he and Gronk spent a couple of hours flying about aimlessly, until something caught Gronk's eye. He made grunting sounds, tapped Josh on the shoulder, and pointed. It was some kind of bird in the distance. Josh fetched his camera from his pocket and started recording a video of what they were seeing.

Josh and Gronk cautiously moved closer to the thing. After a while, it started to take shape. It was a huge bird, and it was moving very quickly. It seemed to notice Josh and Gronk because it maneuvered in their direction for a while. Then it lost interest, and continued along its path at an oblique angle from them. Then Josh noticed that there were more than one of these things.

Josh was videotaping the leader of a group of four birds. They had enormous wingspans, Josh guessed twenty feet or so. Their mouths were full of frighteningly sharp teeth. Josh was thankful that the birds were not interested in him. But naturally, he wanted to follow them.

The maximum speed afforded by the rocket belt was about thirty miles per hour. Right now, they were at the maximum, but they could not keep up with the birds. It wasn't even close. Those things must have been going fifty or sixty miles per hour. Josh admired them for flying so swiftly, and appearing to do it effortlessly. He wondered where they were going. Was this some kind of migration season or what?

Then, to answer his question, the group descended on the lifeless carcass of the dead crocodile. The four birds landed on top of the carcass, and started feasting on it. It was a disgusting scene, but interesting scientifically. The birds were very alert scavengers. Apparently, they had exceptional senses to pinpoint the carcass from several miles off. Josh and Gronk cautiously advanced nearer to the scene, with Josh running his video machine. Thankfully, the birds ignored Josh and Gronk. Supposedly, they looked at the two human beings as small, insignificant flying creatures who could do them no harm.

As they came closer, Josh noticed the features of the birds. They had feet, just like birds of Earth. They had two eyes, and a mouth filled with sharp teeth, that they used to tear into the carcass. They had bony things sticking out from the backs of their heads. Josh believed they were similar to the prehistoric Pteranodon of Earth. He would discuss this with the ship's computer later. Right now, he was focusing on capturing a good video.

One of the birds paused in its eating, and looked up at Josh and Gronk, who were hovering in the air about thirty feet away from the scene. The bird issued a large, frightening cry of some kind. Josh's instinct was to run away, but he quickly realized that running away was a bad idea. The birds would identify him and Gronk as prey. Then Josh and Gronk could not come close to escaping these fast flyers.

When Josh thought that he had captured enough video data, he motioned to Gronk, and the two of them slowly backed up. The birds all had gone back to eating, and paid no attention to the two human beings. After Josh and Gronk had backed up to a few hundred feet of the birds, they turned around and headed back to the ship. Josh kept nervously looking over his shoulder, but all he saw were the birds silently eating. Probably, they figured that the humans had been trying to sneak in and steal some of their food, but now were scared off. If that was the case, good.

In about half an hour, Josh and Gronk could see the large protective bubble of the ship. They continued toward the ship, descending until they hit the desert floor. Then they turned off their rocket belts, and entered the ship.

16

"I saw those birds," said the computer. "But they were way off in the distance."

"That's okay," said Josh. "I got the whole thing on video."

As he said that, Josh downloaded his video stream to the ship's computer. "I think this ought to get sent to Earth," Josh added, saying the obvious.

"Of course," said the computer, as it started to study Josh's video. "Yes, these creatures resemble the prehistoric Pteranodon of Earth. But there is one big difference. The Pteranodon was toothless. It was not a carnivorous reptile. This thing that you saw has teeth, and I believe it to be carnivorous. It looks like it can fly at 65 to 70 miles per hour when it is chasing something, or it can easily glide along at 50 miles per hour. Obviously, it has very long, powerful wings. There were four of them together. That implies some sort of social behavior and maybe a hierarchy, where an alpha male figure leads the group and makes big decisions like where to go next. The ones that you found had long bony crests sticking out from the backs of their heads. This is similar to the Pteranodons of Earth. It is a subject of debate what the purpose was of those crests. My own opinion is that the crest was a kind of rudder that helped the Pteranodon steer itself, while maintaining stability in flight. The Pteranodons of Earth had no teeth, and hence their diet was mostly fish. In that way, they resembled the sea birds such as albatrosses. But the ones that you saw had very sharp teeth, and could consume meat, as well as scavenge for the meat of dead animals. I don't think the Pteranodons had any interest in you and Gronk, other than curiosity."

"So are these things faster than any birds on Earth?"

"No, Josh, not by a long shot. Peregrine falcons have been clocked at over 200 miles per hour. Golden eagles have been clocked at over 75 miles per hour. But for an animal as large and weighty as the Pteranodon, a speed of 65 miles per hour is quite impressive."

"Do these things migrate?"

"Probably not. It is most likely that they establish permanent homes in comfortably warm climates. But that is just my guess. They certainly have the ability to migrate. They may be comparable to albatrosses, who sometimes migrate, not because of climate, but because their food sources are often seasonal."

"It would be interesting to follow these Pteranodons with the rover, if and when the rover is repaired."

"That's an interesting idea, Josh. The only problem is it will take another day or so before the rover is repaired, if it can be repaired. And, by then, our Pteranodons will be gone. Unfortunately, it is impossible to track them without putting bands on their legs, and good luck with that."

"So can we say that we have seen dinosaurs on this planet?"

"Good question. Most of the scientific community does not consider these Pteranodons, or 'pterosaurs', to be dinosaurs. On Earth, the ancestry between dinosaurs and pterosaurs splits off into separate evolutionary paths long before the pterosaurs came into existence."

"Why are you calling them pterosaurs?"

"That is just a general name for these flying reptiles. Pteranodons are just one of the many pterosaurs."

"I would really like to follow these birds to wherever it is that they call home. I'm just trying to think if there's a way." Josh stared down at the floor, thinking. "How many transmitting beacons do we have? Can we spare any of them?"

"We have lots of them, Josh. But I'm not sure what you're thinking. We can't implant one of them on a bird. The bird wouldn't let us, and has very sharp teeth and claws. We don't want to mess with one of those."

"Here's a thought," said Josh. "We could bury a beacon in a hunk of meat, then try to feed the hunk of meat to the birds. Maybe one of them will wind up with the beacon in its intestines."

"That might work, Josh. The problem is, it is a dangerous thing to do. I assume you would be flying to the birds with your rocket belt. If the birds see that you are carrying food, they may attack you and fight you for it. They would kill you, for sure."

"Well, let's see. I could have the meat wrapped up in some kind of scented paper. Then I could fly above them, at, say, one thousand feet, unwrap the meat, and drop it in their midst."

"That's the craziest thing I've ever heard, Josh. The thing is, it might work, as long as the birds don't notice you. And you have to hope that they are still where you think they are. And you have to hope that they are still hungry enough to go after your slab of meat. A lot of big ifs, Josh."

"Okay, so that settles it. Can you help me get the scented paper and the slab of meat?"

"Yes, I can have that ready in a few minutes, Josh. Are you really sure you want to do this?"

"Yes, I am sure. Thank you so much for your help, Mr. Computer."

"You're welcome, but I have to strongly advise against doing this."

"Your advice is appreciated. Let me know when you have those things ready. In the mean time, I'm going to get inside my rocket belt."

Josh took his time strapping on his rocket belt. By the time he was done, the computer directed him to the 3-D printer. There, Josh found a large slab of fresh meat, and some aluminum foil that smelled of peppermint. Josh assumed that the birds would not be interested in peppermint. Josh embedded a beacon in the slab of meat, and was ready to go.

Then, with rocket belt attached and the slab of meat in hand, Josh stepped out of the ship onto the desert floor, and took off into the blue, windless sky. He had made this journey before, and he knew the way to the dead crocodile, and where he hoped the birds would be. As he was flying, he forced himself to gain altitude. He had mentioned one thousand feet to the computer. That was really high. Josh did not have an altimeter, so he had no idea when he would reach one thousand feet. When his eyes seemed at the same level as the surrounding hills, he guessed he was one thousand feet, or maybe even higher. Then he continued flying in the general direction of the dead crocodile. In only a few minutes, he spotted it, and, yes, the birds were still there feasting on the carcass. At thirty miles per hour, Josh arrived at his chosen overlook point in about twenty minutes.

Now the task was simple. "Just take the slab of meat out of its peppermint-smelling paper, and drop the damn thing, then get the hell out of there." Josh told himself exactly that. He stared directly below him. One of the birds looked up at him. This was a scary moment. If the bird viewed Josh either as prey or as a threat, he could soar the one thousand feet and attack Josh. Josh wouldn't have a chance against the faster carnivore. Then again, they were busy eating. If Josh was something to eat, Josh was no competition for the huge dead carcass that they already had. "Come on, Josh, stop dawdling, and just drop the damn thing."

Josh reviewed his basic physics of a falling body. Start with the formula that distance equals one half the acceleration multiplied by the time squared. He knew the distance was 1000 feet. He thought the acceleration due to gravity would be about the same as that of Earth, or 32 feet per second per second. So the time falling would be the square root of 1000/16. So the thing would take about 8 seconds to hit the ground. If there was no significant air resistance, it would accelerate at 32 feet per second per second for 8 seconds, which means it would hit the ground going something like 250 feet per second or approximately 160 miles per hour. He had to hope that it wouldn't hit one of the birds. He moved a little to the side of them, thinking it would not hit the ground in the midst of them. He took a last look at the birds. The bird that was watching him had gone back to eating. All seemed well. Bombs away! He let the slab of meat go. He didn't wait to see where it landed. What would be the point? He just wanted to get the hell out of there. He sped away at thirty miles per hour, and, 8 seconds later, he heard a distinctive plop as the slab of meat hit the ground. He was glad of one thing. The sound was the sound of an object hitting the ground, not an object hitting the body of a bird. That was good. He didn't look back at the birds. That would just slow him down. He just kept flying straight for the ship.

After a few seconds, he descended from one thousand feet to fifty feet. That would make it harder for the birds to see him if they were looking for him. But fortunately, it didn't seem that the birds were interested in him. So he just kept going until he saw the large protective bubble of the ship. He slowed down, planted his feet on the ground, and entered the ship through the door in its bubble.

"I'm back," he announced somewhat proudly to the computer.

"Yes," said the computer. "I am homing on the tracking device now. It seems to be sitting idly there. That may mean nothing. Maybe one of the creatures ate it, and maybe not. We don't know. But at least it was delivered as planned. You did your job, Josh."

"What is our maximum range on tracking a beacon?"

"An awfully long way, Josh. It's basically a short-wave radio signal, that can go thousands of miles if it needs to."

"So I guess now we sit and wait, and, if we're lucky, we see some movement in the beacon."

"Exactly right, Josh. And, by the way, I have some fairly good news from our team of robots. They say that the rover should be fully functional sometime tomorrow."

"How about Missy, the rover's computer?"

"Missy will be fine. There was some damage to a few chips on her mother board, but the robots are able to manufacture and program replacements. They have access to all the specs."

"That is really great," said Josh. "Among other things, if the birds take the bait, we will be able to follow them in the rover."

"That's right," said the computer. "Let's hope that the robots are correct in their prognosis. But I have a lot of confidence in those guys."

With that, Josh and Gronk ate a nice supper. Josh explained what he had just done, and Gronk seemed to understand. After dinner, they went to sleep. As usual these days, Josh fell asleep almost at once and slept soundly.

17

When Josh woke up, he asked the computer for status on the beacon and the rover.

"Good news, Josh. First, the beacon's location has changed. It has been moving at about 50 miles per hour. That is consistent with the assumption that it is sitting in the intestines of one of the birds. The other good news is that the rover is now operational. The robots, who have been working 24 hours a day, have just reported this to me."

"That's great, Mr. Computer. I think what I'd like to do before anything else is take the rover for a low-stress test run. Just get comfortable with it again, see if there are any new glitches."

"Sounds good, Josh. The rover is waiting for you just outside."

"You seemed to know what I wanted before I said anything. Thank you very much, Mr. Computer."

"You're welcome, Josh. I assume next you will want to chase down the Pteranodons. First, I need to hear from you after your test ride with the rover. I want to know if there are any performance issues."

"Sure," said Josh, as he walked through the door of the bubble and stepped into the rover.

"Hi, Josh." Josh immediately recognized Missy's voice.

"Hello, Missy. I sure am happy to hear your voice again. For a while, I was afraid that you were gone for good. That horrible monster attacked you while you were saving our lives."

"Well, Josh, I am happy that I saved your life and Gronk's life. But it looks like you got a nasty gash on your arm."

"Yes, Missy. The monster did that. The robots on the ship washed the wound and stitched me up. I have to concede, your advice was right-on. We probably shouldn't have chased down that monster."

"But, in the end, it was a good thing for science, Josh."

"I suppose so. Are you up to speed with what has happened since then?"

"I think so, Josh. The crocodile monster was killed, some reptilian birds came to feast on its carcass, and now you want to track down those birds, and see where they live."

"Exactly, Missy."

"And what do you hope to find out once you track those birds?"

"I don't know, Missy. Maybe nothing, maybe something big. I just don't know. I am just really curious about those things. They seemed to show up out of nowhere. I wonder how far they had to fly to reach the carcass."

"So I guess I can home in on the beacon, and we can follow that and see where it leads us."

"Yes, Missy. Do you have the frequency to tune in on?"

"Yes, Josh. In fact, I'm tuned right now to the beacon."

"Well, I guess we are on the same page on that one. But before we chase down the birds, I promised the ship that I would take you for a test ride, just to make sure you are working okay, and to sort out any bugs."

"Okay, Josh. Where are we going?"

"Well, we might as well head out to the monster's carcass, and see what is left of it."

Josh pointed in the general direction. The rover took off vertically, then headed in the direction that Josh indicated.

They reached the dead crocodile's carcass in a minute or so, and Josh was impressed at how much faster was the rover compared to the rocket belt. The carcass was completely consumed. All that remained was a pile of bones. Even the eyes and the tongue were gone. The Pteranodons certainly did a thorough job of cleaning things up.

"Where to now, Josh?" Missy asked.

Josh couldn't think of another place to go. He simply said, "Back to the ship to report that our test flight was successful. Then we pick up Gronk, assuming he wants to come along. Then we home in on the beacon, and follow it."

"Sounds good Josh," Missy said, as the rover made its way back to the ship. Josh entered the ship, told the computer that their test was successful, then asked Gronk to come along after the birds. Gronk enthusiastically agreed, and they both walked out and boarded the rover.

"I'm homed in on the beacon's frequency," Missy said. "I can't tell how far away it is, but it will be more than a few miles."

"That's okay, Missy. We can enjoy the scenery during our journey."

The rover banked slightly to the left to get on course and then flew across the desert. The rover had a normal cruising speed of about 600 miles per hour, but Josh sensed they were not going that fast. He could tell by looking down at the ground and watching things move by.

"How fast are we going, Missy?"

"About half-speed, Josh. Three hundred miles per hour, or thereabouts. I'm being extra careful because I don't want to fly a little off course and lose the signal."

"That's a good idea, Missy. I wasn't impatient or anything like that, just curious."

In a few minutes, they passed over a row of bleak mountains, and, once again, Gronk nervously gripped his armrests. As before, Josh explained that everything was fine, and turbulence like this was normal when going over mountains. Gronk understood and seemed to relax a little.

The scenery changed dramatically on the other side of the mountain range. Instead of desert, there were green rolling hills, covered with scattered trees. Some distance ahead, the land appeared to flatten out. That's where the rover was headed.

"I have a couple questions, Missy," Josh said.

"What, Josh?"

"First of all, this is a respectable distance that the birds had to fly. Does that surprise you?"

"I'm not surprised that the birds are capable of covering that distance in a reasonable amount of time. After all, you saw them cruising with very little effort at fifty miles per hour. So they could cover the distance in two to three hours, and maybe not even get tired. What does surprise me is why they would choose to make the trip. They must have ascended to a very high altitude to be able to see something that far away with a mountain range in the middle."

"And either their eyesight or their sense of smell must be incredible, so they could make out a twenty-five-foot carcass from so far away."

"Absolutely right, Josh. Either that, or they were on some routine patrolling mission that took them to the other side of the mountains, and then they saw the carcass."

"Maybe they heard the sounds of the fight, and decided to come over and investigate."

"Another possibility, Josh. One thing for sure, these birds have impressive physical traits, and they are quite intelligent."

Josh turned his attention to the land ahead of him. It was becoming flatter. There were broken clumps of trees, and a very large lake in the background. Gronk was the first to notice something, and he started gesticulating wildly as he pointed.

"My God," Josh said, almost in a whisper. "Those are dinosaurs."

18

Below them was a small herd of plant-eating dinosaurs, that looked lot Brontosauruses. Josh stared in amazement. They were beautiful animals in a way, but massive beyond belief. Their bodies must have been sixty feet long, and their necks rose up to the tallest of trees. They were wandering gracefully along, paying no attention to the rover.

"Fifty-six feet long, in case you were wondering," said Missy. "And thirty-eight feet tall. I estimate their weight at sixty thousand pounds."

It looked like a closely knit family, with large males, slightly smaller females, and adolescent teenagers about half their size. Beyond them was a group of creatures that looked like elephants, with long snouts and tusks. The elephants looked like dwarfs compared with the Brontos. The rover kept flying slowly, and suddenly Gronk pointed. "Birds," he said. Indeed, there were, quite possibly the same group that Josh had come to know and to track. They were overhead, making lazy circles in the blue sky. Josh guessed that they were waiting for something to die so they could do their scavenging.

The trees were full of things that looked like orangutans, some sitting around calmly, others making raucous noises, and still others practicing acrobatic tricks as they swung around on the branches. Like orangutans of Earth, they had extremely long arms, human-like heads, and reddish-brown skin.

"I'm a little confused, Missy," Josh said. "We have mammals and dinosaurs living here at the same time. On Earth, the mammals weren't around until the dinosaurs became extinct."

"Earth is the weird case here, Josh. There is no reason for the mammals to hold up their development until the dinosaurs died off. The two kinds of beasts can certainly live at the same time. As long as the dinosaurs do not exterminate the mammals, the mammals can multiply and evolve normally.

"The real interesting point is why on Earth could not mammals evolve at the same time as the dinosaurs. There are many theories that try to explain this. In my opinion, it was the drifting continents that simultaneously led to the demise of the dinosaurs and the rise of the mammals. Dinosaurs thrived in tropical climates, while mammals thrived in temperate, cooler climates. At the time of the dinosaurs, continents were scrunched together near the equator, so basically the entire Earth was tropical. Then the continents drifted toward the polar regions. The cold-blooded dinosaurs could not adapt, while the mammals not only adapted but thrived. Mammals, unlike dinosaurs, are warm-blooded, which means that they could regulate their body temperature regardless of the surroundings. Mammals also had skin that was covered by fur, which kept them warm in cold conditions. So, as the continents drifted apart, mammals loved it, and dinosaurs did not."

"Interesting, Missy," said Josh, as he continued to scan ahead in the direction of the large lake. Along the edges of the lake were hundreds of animals of various kinds. Some were like horses or wildebeests, some were like the pre-historic duck-billed dinosaurs of Earth, some were like great bisons of the old American west.

Then, surrounding the lake, were the huge crocodilian monsters. Josh felt immediately afraid when he saw them. One of them ran after a horse-like creature. The horse-like creature had no chance. The crocodile outran him, and started tearing him to pieces. Josh couldn't watch it. Then another crocodile leapt out of the water and attacked another animal, some kind of duckbill.

Josh was sickened as he saw this bloodshed. He saw the crocodiles as monsters, that had very nearly killed Missy. They were aliens from another world. They did not belong here. They had invaded a peaceful group of living things, and turned it into a horror show. Josh regrettably watched more, as a dozen or so of the innocent animals were mercilessly slaughtered by the crocodiles, leaving bloody stains everywhere.

"Missy, I think we should declare war on these crocodiles. We should kill as many of them as we can. It is for the survival of the native wildlife on this planet."

"That is a tough call, Josh. Who is to decide if this is alien invasion or natural predation?"

"These crocodiles are from another planet, Missy. I cannot agree that it is natural predation. I say we kill as many of them as we can for the survival of the living beings native to this planet."

"You are the boss, Josh, and I will obey your instructions, as always."

"Let's kill them, Missy. Start with the ones on the ground, and then proceed to the ones swimming in the lake."

"Okay, Josh. I understand," said Missy, as she steered the rover to the perimeter of the lake and began to sweep along its shore in a counterclockwise fashion. The first crocodile was easy to kill. He did not expect it. The others, now sensing the danger, began to scatter. But the rover was faster. Missy quickly gunned down two more along the shore, who were trying to run away. Some of the crocodiles had seemed to escape into the nearby forest, but they were too big, and couldn't hide from Missy, who shot several of them as they tried to run away. God, there were a lot of these monsters, Josh thought, as more and more of them were gunned down by Missy. When Missy had completed the counterclockwise encirclement of the lake, Josh counted twenty-seven crocodiles killed. Now it was time to go after the ones swimming in the lake. Josh could see what a lot of them were up to. They would sit motionless, pretending to be a piece of wood, until some unsuspecting animal came nearby. Then they would spring onto the poor beast, immediately killing it. But these crocodiles were too big to go unnoticed in the water. Missy spotted them easily, and picked them off, one by one. A few of them sensed the danger, but where could they go? There was no escape, and Missy kept on with the slaughter.

When it was all over, there were sixty-five crocodiles killed. The water in the lake was stained with their blood. The sand along the shore of the lake was similarly stained in their blood. Josh felt no sense of guilt for what was just done. He and Missy had saved this world from a group of horrible monsters, that had invaded from another planet.

The remaining animals seemed to sense that a great danger to them has been eliminated. They started joyfully splashing around in the water, and playing with each other. And the animals along the shore appeared definitely more relaxed, now that the crocodiles were gone.

"I think we should make one more sweep of the area," said Josh. "Let's make sure that we got them all."

"Okay," said Missy, as she began a second encirclement of the area. They did find three more of the crocodiles, running away, trying to hide in the forest. Missy quickly shot them down. Then one last sweep over the lake itself, but there was nothing.

"I wonder if there are more large groups of these things running around all over the planet," commented Josh.

"I don't know," said Missy. "But it would be a fantastic piece of luck if we happened to run into all of them on this little venture."

"Well, I guess we might as well head back, Missy."

"Yes, Josh. In one sense, this little mission was a success, because we saw dinosaurs."

"Right, Missy. And we got them on video." Josh took a last look around, and saw the giant birds swooping down and feasting on the many dead carcasses. There were quite a few birds this time, a group of over ten of them.

It was a quick flight back to the main ship. Missy downloaded the video files to the ship's main computer, which transmitted them to Earth.

"I'd like for Gronk and I to have a good sleep, and then we can head off to the planet of the crocodiles. Everyone seemed to be in agreement.

Josh and Gronk enjoyed a nice supper. The rover was docked onto the main ship, and both were protected by the bubble. They were ready to head off into outer space tomorrow. Josh explained this to Gronk, who was excited about the prospect.

Before drifting off to sleep, Josh reflected on the day's events. It was a truly momentous day. They had seen dinosaurs on the planet. They had also seen a wide variety of life, such as orangutans, horses, duckbills, bison, and wildebeest. By killing off the crocodile invaders, Josh had preserved one corner of native life on the planet. He thought about how happy the animals seemed to be once the crocodiles were gone, and he realized that he and Missy had done a very good thing.

Josh woke up some time later. The sun was already up. Gronk was doing his yoga. Josh asked Gronk if he was ready for his first flight through outer space. Gronk seemed to understand, and quickly nodded yes. Josh explained to the ship's computer that everyone was ready for the journey. The computer ordered the removal of the protective bubble, and in a few minutes, everything was ready for the trip.

Josh and Gronk took their seats, and fastened their seat belts. The computer's voice came over the intercom.

"We will soon begin our journey to what we call the "Crocodile Planet." That is the home planet of the monstrous beasts we have encountered several times so far. I don't know if we will actually land on the planet or not. That decision is up to Josh. But we all need to be very cautious because these creatures are dangerous and have an advanced technology.

"As for our trip, we will be traveling 30 million miles through outer space. At our normal interstellar speed of 80% of the speed of light, this would take us three minutes. But this is not an interstellar trip, it is an interplanetary trip, and everything is different. For one, our solar sails will be almost useless because we will be traveling toward the sun on most of the trip. It is analogous to a sailboat going against the wind. To make any progress, we would have to tack back and forth against the solar radiation. We will use our hydrogen scoop and our nuclear power capabilities to reach a respectable speed of one million miles per hour.

"The bad news is that we will accelerate at a rate of a little more than 4g's for about two hours to reach that speed. This is well within your biological tolerance, but will be uncomfortable. I suggest taking motion sickness pills if it gets too bad for you. Once we have reached our target speed, we will spend the rest of the trip either accelerating at 1g or decelerating at 1g. This is the same as the gravity on Earth, so you can safely and comfortably move about the cabin, and feel a normal gravity.

"All told, the trip should take us about 27 hours, or slightly more than one Earth Day. At the end of that time, we will be in orbit around the Crocodile Planet. Okay, here we go."

The ship ascended vertically, quite slowly for several minutes, while the view of the planet receded. Gronk looked out the window in fascination, even though he had seen similar scenes before. Gradually, the blue sky began to turn light purple, then dark purple, then black.

"Welcome to outer space, Gronk," Josh commented. Gronk looked confused.

Then the ship banked to adjust its course, and the acceleration began. Josh and Gronk were pushed back into their padded seats, where they would be for the next couple of hours. They were headed for the Crocodile Planet. Josh fell into a deep slumber.

19

He had bad dreams of monsters coming after him, trying to kill him, and he knew why. They wanted to exact revenge because he had killed a bunch of their buddies the other day by the lake. Josh tried to fly away with his rocket belt, but the monsters chased him. The monsters could run fast, even faster than Josh could fly with the rocket belt. So Josh took off into the sky to get away from them. But he couldn't get away. They were coming at him in fighter planes, coming down and strafing him with bullets. Josh felt the bullets go through his body, but he somehow stayed alive, and kept trying to dodge the fighter planes. It was hopeless. Josh knew that. The rocket belt could not match the speed of the fighter planes. It wasn't even close.

One of the fighter planes flew close by to Josh, and Josh felt an irresistible strong tug as a tractor beam latched onto him. Then he was aboard the alien ship, flying off through outer space to some other planet. They reached the other planet, and Josh was ushered out of the plane into a room that looked like the waiting room of a doctor's office. A voice boomed over a loudspeaker.

"You have been found guilty of a serious crime, and must now face punishment."

He was taken to another room that was much like the one he was just in, except other people were there. There was one door that led outside to a dusty street. He started talking to the other people in the room, who all spoke English.

"Do you people speak English?" Josh said. They all nodded.

Just then, Josh heard screams coming from the dusty street outside. A man fell over hard, then was lifted to his feet and helped back into the room. The man did not appear to have any broken bones, but he was very bloody, and he was gasping for air and obviously in a lot of pain. The others in the room felt sympathy for him but could do nothing.

"What is this place?" Josh asked. "I haven't been here before and I've never seen anything like it."

"Some people call this place 'the waiting room'. It is better known as 'hell'. It's where people who die get punished."

"Do we ever get out of here?"

"Never. We are stuck here for eternity. Each one of us suffers a horrible death, and we go through that horrible death over and over again for all eternity."

"My God," said Josh.

One other man went out to the dusty street. Everyone heard his cries of agony as he was mangled to death. Then, he was released, and came back into the room to await his next turn.

A uniformed man came into the room from the street, and pointed at Josh. "You're up," he said. "Good luck to you."

Why the heck was he wishing me good luck, thought Josh. Anyways, Josh followed the man into the street. He was sweating profusely. He had no idea what was to come. The man strapped Josh's ankles together with leg irons, and then handcuffed his hands. Whatever was going to happen, Josh could do nothing to stop it. He was led into the middle of the street. At the other end of the street was one of the crocodile people. The thing was enormous, standing on its hind legs, just as Josh remembered. Twenty feet tall, and weighing close to three thousand pounds. The thing headed toward Josh, slowly at first, then picked up speed until it was charging. Josh couldn't do anything but stand there and watch. The thing came close to Josh. Josh could smell its stinking breath, and see its yellow eyes and razor-sharp teeth. It slashed Josh with one of its claws, opening up a huge cut along Josh's chest. Then its jaws came down to bite Josh in the head, and probably decapitate him.

"No!," Josh yelled. "No! No!"

Josh felt a gentle tug on his shoulder. He opened his eyes. It was Gronk.

"You scared," Gronk said. "Maybe bad dream."

"Yes," said Josh, surprised to see the darkness of outer space. "it was a terrible dream, a nightmare." He patted Gronk on the head, thanking him for waking him up.

It was the worst nightmare Josh could ever remember. He wasn't sure about the inner meanings of dreams, but he knew there was a lot of studying about them. What did this dream mean? Was it trying to make him feel guilty for killing those crocodiles by the lake? If so, it didn't work. Josh hated those monsters, whom he regarded as the enemy. If anything, the dream made Josh more aware of the horror some of the creatures felt who were attacked and killed by the crocodiles. They had no defense to the crocodile's lunge and bite. The crocodile could run faster than any of them, and could kill them easily. The creatures could do nothing to stop it. That was what Josh had felt like a minute ago. Guilt for killing the crocodiles? Not a chance.

20

The flight went smoothly. The only uncomfortable part was when the ship had to change from accelerating at 1g to decelerating at 1g. To prevent Josh and Gronk from hitting the ceiling with their heads, the ship had to tip itself over. So Josh and Gronk strapped themselves to their seats, the ship flipped over, and the seats flipped over along with the rest of the ship, so now Josh and Gronk were experiencing Earth-like gravity from the other direction.

This maneuver took place shortly before the halfway mark of the flight. The computer announced that they had about fifteen hours until they reached an orbit about the Crocodile Planet. Josh and Gronk enjoyed a good meal, then sat back and rested.

It seemed like a very long time until the computer announced that they were approaching the Crocodile Planet. They could now see it out the ship's windows, but could not make out any details. After a while, as they got closer, they could make out mountain ranges and bodies of water, and lights. The trouble was that they were approaching the planet on the side opposite its sun, so they were looking at the dark side of the Crocodile Planet.

Soon they settled into an orbit. They were now pretty close to the planet, and could make out the shapes of landmasses. Even though it was dark, there were enough artificial lights so that features could be seen.

"It looks like we have some trouble," said the computer.

Just as the computer was speaking, Josh noticed a huge blue cloudlike shape heading straight for the ship. It was round, and large, and growing, and moving quite rapidly. The computer sent the ship into a dive to evade the object, which flashed by at high speed. It didn't look like a solid object, it looked more gaseous.

"What was that?" Josh asked, as he fought back his feelings of nausea.

"I'm honestly not sure," said the computer. "It was not a missile, certainly. It looked like some form of plasma energy, the kind of stuff you see in stellar nebulas."

"Where was it coming from? Who shot that thing?"

"I see a space station," said the computer. "It's in orbit, just like we are, but ahead of us. They must have seen us, and decided not to take any chances, and fired on us."

"Look," said Josh. "It's firing another one of those things at us." Indeed, another huge blue cloud was heading their way. "Damn," Josh said. "Those things move fast."

The ship veered sharply right, avoiding the mass, but not by much.

"Thank God our ship is fast," said the computer. "Right now our speed is about 700,000 miles per hour. Those things are coming at us at maybe 5000 miles per hour. So the ship is able to move out of the way in time. The challenge is to spot those things in time. The damn things are invisible to our ship's radar. When we ping them, the signal does not echo back, it just goes right through the gaseous cloud."

"What would happen if one of those things hit the ship?"

"It could completely disable the ship, Josh. I assume that it contains electrically charged material that would damage our circuitry and possibly render the ship useless."

"I suggest that we attack that space station, and take away its capability to destroy us," Josh said.

"I have to agree, Josh. In fact, we have no other option. If we do nothing, the space station will use us as target practice, and eventually score a devastating hit."

With that, the ship rolled so that the space station was directly ahead. Six laser beams shot out from the ship. All of them struck the space station less than a second later. For a while, nothing happened. Josh wondered if the space station was made out of some super-strong metal alloy that could resist laser beams. Suddenly there was a huge silent explosion, and the space station blew apart, sending debris in all directions. The computer took the ship into an evasive maneuver to avoid getting hit with debris, but it was probably unnecessary. The ship was too far away from the space station. Josh was surprised to see such a large explosion without hearing any noise, but in outer space, sound waves are not propagated, so there was nothing unusual about it.

"Ooh geez," Josh said. "That was something, but now I'm worried about what else our crocodile people have in store for us."

The ship continued in its orbit. It was still moving at 600,000 miles per hour, which meant that it completed one orbit in about five minutes. The alien ships, leaving from the planet's surface, could not match that speed. The acceleration required on take-off would be impossible. If there was another space ship in orbit that could launch warships, then the warships could benefit from the momentum of the space station, and it might be possible. The other danger might come from surface-to-air missiles, but it would require very expert shooting to hit a target moving 600,000 miles per hour.

Now they were on the daytime side of the planet, and at a low enough altitude where they could make out some detail.

"I have a question, Mr. Computer," said Josh.

"What is it, Josh?"

"Why were they exiling bunches of them to another planet? And why did we find those guys tied up in chains in the basement of their ship?"

"I don't know, Josh, but my best guess is that they were some kind of political prisoners or prisoners of war that were being exiled."

Just as the computer was talking, Josh spotted a land-based missile heading for them.

"Watch out," he instinctively yelled, and the computer dodged the incoming missile, turning sharply to the right. But there were more of those things coming. Unfortunately, in the last few minutes, they had drifted to a lower altitude, and that put them within range of the missiles. The ship turned sharply up, and Josh watched a missile zoom by. A second missile was approaching, and the ship went into a dive to avoid it. Then two more missiles came. The ship bobbed and swerved, barely avoiding the missiles, as they zoomed by.

"I think I see where they are coming from," the computer said. "I'm going to try to take out their missile battery." The ship adjusted its position, and then a barrage of lasers shot out from its front. Seconds later, there was an explosion on the ground, and a huge ball of flames rose into the sky. Apparently the missile battery was destroyed.

"What do you want to do now, Josh?" asked the computer.

"I want to continue to explore this planet, and, if it's safe, land on it, and look around.

"Are you sure, Josh? This place is nothing but trouble."

"Yes, I am sure."

The ship continued its gradual descent through the partially cloudy sky. Josh looked out the window and saw much the same things that he would see on Earth -- large oceans, lakes, rivers, mountains, forests, deserts.

Then it happened. A large thud, a blinding flash, and Josh instinctively knew that a missile had hit. *My God, where did that come from?*

"I didn't see that coming," Josh said.

"Neither did I," said the computer. Josh looked around the ship. Fortunately, nothing was on fire, but there was damage from the impact.

"We have some engine damage," said the computer. "Our hydraulics are still good, and we have only minor structural damage. As we stand now, we don't have enough power to get out of here. But, with some skill, we can glide the ship down and land on the planet. Then, if left alone, the robots can work on repairing the damaged engine. Lucky for us, the crocodiles can see that we've been hit, and they've decided to leave us alone and let us crash land.

"Have you ever flown glider, Josh?"

"No, Mr. Computer, I can't say that I have."

"That's what the ship is now. With no engine to power it, it is a gigantic glider. The nice thing is that we don't have a specific runway to land on. We put her down wherever we can. That should make things easy."

The ship lost air speed and altitude fairly quickly, but the computer manipulated the controls to avoid a catastrophic dive. It pointed the ship into the wind, and lifted the nose up, in preparation for landing. The computer was aiming for a large grassy area between two clusters of forests. The scenery was quite beautiful, but Josh didn't spend any time enjoying it. He was too nervous about coming out of this thing alive. Then, of course, was the real worry. Josh was in imminent danger of being marooned on an alien planet, inhabited by monsters, with no escape possible.

21

Josh looked out the window onto a grassy field. A group of crocodiles were walking upright, methodically making their way toward the ship, which lay helplessly on the grass.

"Here's what we'll do," said Josh. "I'll go outside and surrender myself to the crocodiles. Gronk can stay here. The robots can attempt to repair the ship. "I'll take my laser gun, and my pocket phone, so I can communicate with you guys."

"They will probably kill you, Josh," said the computer.

"Better me than Gronk, and better me than the whole ship. After all, this whole thing was my idea, and I should bear the responsibility of failure. So, if this is the last that I see of you guys, I love all of you and hope that somehow, we all make it back to Earth together."

With that, Josh grabbed his portable phone and his laser gun, and stuffed them in his pockets. Then he took a deep breath and went out to meet the crocodiles. He noticed first that the air was breathable, and the gravity was about the same as the Earth's. The air temperature was comfortable.

He held his hands in the air, hoping that the crocodiles would understand that he was surrendering, and not looking for a fight. He slowly walked forward toward the group of crocodiles. These beings were truly monsters. Josh couldn't believe that he was surrendering to these beings, but it seemed like the most logical thing to do.

When the crocodiles had reached him, one of them reached out with its claw, and whacked John hard on his arm, twisting him around. John heard the clinking of chains, and the monsters tied Josh up in the heavy chain. It reminded him of the crocodiles that they found tied together on the crashed space ship a while back. He wondered if that would be his fate. It might be the better option, getting sent back to the other planet, where maybe he could meet up with his friends.

The crocodiles walked back through the meadow toward a group of trees, pulling Josh along. The crocodiles were walking incredibly swiftly, and Josh could not keep up. He kept falling over onto his face into the dirt. The crocodiles kept bending over and pulling Josh back up to his feet. Josh didn't understand why the crocodiles didn't just kill him. Where were they taking him?

Eventually they came to something that looked like railroad train tracks. Off to the side was a tall building that may have been some kind of depot. One of the crocodiles walked over to the building, and did something, Josh couldn't figure out what. After a few minutes the crocodile came back out, and started talking to the other crocodiles, explaining something. Their communication was completely foreign to Josh. It wasn't even words, it was a series of grunts with different tones, like a type of musical chant, except not harmonious. In fact, it was discordant and ugly. But the crocodiles understood each other and kept talking. In a few minutes, something that looked like a train came along the tracks. The crocodiles pushed Josh roughly into the train, then got in themselves. The train was obviously much bigger than a train on Earth, because it had to carry such enormous creatures. There were no seats on this train. Everyone was expected either to stand or sit on the floor. Josh sat on the floor. As the doors closed, Josh noticed the putrid smell of the crocodiles in a room with no ventilation. He had to fight himself to avoid throwing up.

The train noisily gathered speed until it was going maybe fifteen or twenty miles per hour. As the train moved along, Josh noticed an unusual group of trees alongside the track. They had trunks like redwood trees, and multi-colored leaves like deciduous trees on Earth in the fall. The other trees looked a little like oak or elm trees, or the African baobab.

The train continued on its course, going through forests alternating with grassy plains. Josh didn't see any more train stations. The train ride took maybe one hour, and then Josh could see that they were entering some kind of city. There was a large number of quite tall buildings, and an occasional crocodile roaming the filthy streets, filled with garbage and feces.

In the distance was an enormous coliseum that reminded Josh of the ancient Romans and their brutal gladiator games. The train continued to approach the coliseum. Josh deduced that the coliseum was their travel destination, and he was right. The train began to slow down as it pulled up next to the coliseum. When it stopped, the crocodiles grabbed Josh and led him to a dark, filthy room, which appeared to be a part of the coliseum complex. The crocodiles undid his chain, and threw him roughly to the floor of the stinking place. Everything about this planet was a stinking mess, Josh thought.

Josh sat on the cold floor, wondering what was to come next. The room that he was in had one open-air window that was straight ahead of him, with iron bars on the window. Josh looked through the window and could see an area of stony desert, mostly barren sand with occasional clumps of rocks. Circling this area were rows of seats. The seats were massive and were spread out by huge distances. They were obviously meant for crocodiles.

Josh finally figured it out. He was in a huge arena, like the ancient Roman coliseums. Spectators were starting to gather to view whatever spectacle would take place. Josh felt in his pocket to make sure he still had his laser gun. It wasn't a powerful laser like the one on the rover or on the main ship, and he was sure he could not kill a crocodile with the thing in his pocket. But the cold steel comforted him when he realized it was there for him. The crocodiles failed to take it away.

As time went by, the seats in the stadium filled up, as bloodthirsty crocodiles came in anticipation of bloodshed and gore. Was ancient Rome really this bad? He couldn't help comparing himself to a gladiator. Maybe that's what he was.

After some time of nervous waiting, Josh heard some doors open. Two crocodiles, one from each end of the arena, came onto the sandy floor. The crowd of spectators started making loud noises. The two crocodiles cautiously circled each other, making occasional lunges, then quickly backing off. The crowd obviously didn't like this kind of strategic maneuvering. They were after blood and gore. One of the crocodiles swung a claw at his enemy, but the blow was easily deflected.

It took several minutes of this maneuvering before one of the crocodiles lost patience, and lunged wildly at his opponent. He managed to bite his opponent in the ribs, and out poured a gush of deep red blood. The other crocodile beat and clawed at his attacker, trying to force him to loosen his grip. But the attacking crocodile was not deterred, and maintained his bite on his opponent. Eventually, the defender fell over, hitting the ground with a gigantic thud. The attacking crocodile launched his teeth in a deadly bite on the other's neck, and soon it was all over.

The crocodile that was still alive was quickly surrounded by ten or so crocodiles that were armed with some sort of guns. They grabbed the victorious crocodile, and wrapped a steel chain around him, then led him into a side chamber. Josh saw that the crocodile was in the chamber with several other crocodiles, all of them in chains. Josh remembered the crocodiles on the crashed space ship from the other planet, who were also tied up in chains. He wondered if their fate was to be flown off to the other planet and dumped off, to survive by whatever means they could. Meanwhile, the body of the dead crocodile lay in the sand, covered with blood and feces. Nobody was bothering to clean up this mess.

Then some crocodiles came into Josh's room, opened the bars on the window, and roughly threw Josh out into the sandy arena. Then they closed the window behind Josh. Josh stood there alone, in terrified confusion. The crowd of crocodiles in the spectator area were reacting to Josh, with what Josh loosely interpreted as laughter. Finally, a door at the other end of the arena opened up and a crocodile came out. As all the crocodiles on this planet, this was a huge monster, every bit of twenty-five feet tall, with bony skin, large piercing eyes, and huge feet. The crocodile looked around the arena, perhaps a little confused, unable to find his opponent. Finally, the monster spotted Josh. Josh remembered the horrible nightmare he had, and it seemed like this was that nightmare coming to life. But there was nobody to wake Josh up from the nightmare. He understood that this was a fight to the death. If he wanted to live, he would have to kill the crocodile.

22

Josh reached into his pocket for his laser gun. His gun was just a pocket-sized thing without much power. It was nothing like the weaponry that the rover had or the main ship had. But, right now, it seemed like Josh's only hope. He also had his phone. It wouldn't be much help because there was no one who could save Josh. But he turned the video feature on, and shoved it back in his pocket. The phone could videotape whatever was about to happen. It could operate through Josh's clothes

He aimed his laser gun at the advancing monster, and pulled the trigger. He saw the beam impact the beast's chest. He kept the trigger pressed down. The monster moved out of the way of the beam. On the monster's chest was a pink burn mark. The laser gun had found its mark and the monster had felt some pain. But Josh needed more than that. The monster's skin was hard and thick, and Josh's gun was a virtual toy compared to what he needed.

The monster's eyes. That's what Josh needed to concentrate on. His eyes were not well protected, and were thus somewhat vulnerable. If he could seriously damage the monster's ability to see, then he might be able to gain some advantage. At least, he could have some time to come up with a plan.

Meanwhile, the monster was advancing toward him, and growling angrily. The monster could move at twenty-five miles per hour. Josh could not outrun the monster. Josh aimed his laser gun at the monster's right eye and shot. He didn't know if he hit the eye or not, because the monster lashed Josh with its claw, cutting Josh badly in his side and across his chest. But now the monster had backed off a step. Josh aimed at the other eye and shot. A miss. His hand was shaking. Josh concentrated on keeping a steady hand, then fired at the monster's other eye. He thought he got it. The monster growled in pain and swiped at Josh, cutting his skin badly again. Josh's laser gun was in a tangled heap on the sand. The monster had destroyed it. Josh ran away along the edge of the arena. The monster tried to chase him, but it was obvious that it couldn't see very well. At one point it bumped into the wall running along the edge of the arena.

Josh had to kill the monster but without his weapon. It seemed like an impossible task. Maybe the monster couldn't see very well, but he could feel his way around and eventually find Josh and murder him.

Take a step back and think, Josh told himself, as the monster was still far away. What tools did Josh have? Josh made a mental list of everything, whether it was useful or not. There were some rocks of various sizes in the arena. There was a rotten old log, about ten feet long, lying around in the sand. There was the dead crocodile, which got killed in the last fight. And Josh had the clothes he was wearing, including his belt. And, oh yeah, there was blood on Josh's body and on the body of the dead crocodile. And there was feces around the dead crocodile. Josh wasn't sure how any of this was useful but that's what he had, and that's what he would have to use to kill the monster.

Josh looked over at the monster. The monster was advancing slowly toward Josh. How did the monster know where Josh was? Either it could still see pretty well, or it was using its other senses. Josh ran around to another part of the arena. The monster stopped, looking confused. It moved around some, mostly turning its head side to side. Then it seemed to finally zero in on Josh and it started slowly toward him again. Josh picked up a grapefruit-sized rock that was lying in the sand. He threw it hard just to the monster's left side. It hit the sand, making a loud kind of splashing sound. The monster stopped and turned its head to the left toward the sound. It seemed to stare for a while, then turned back and aimed again at Josh and started again walking toward Josh.

What the heck was going on? Well, the monster could not see well, if at all. It bumped into the wall earlier because it couldn't see it. When Josh threw the rock, the monster pointed its head in the direction of the sound. Therefore, the monster could hear things, but it wasn't using its hearing to find Josh. So how did the monster know where Josh was? He could smell Josh. Of course! It was a process of elimination.

So now what could Josh do? He had some valuable information. The monster was guided by smell, and could hear but not see. Josh had to find a way to take advantage of that. He could try to lure the crocodile into some sort of trap. But then he would need a way to kill the crocodile. His laser gun was gone. What else could he use as a weapon? Rocks. The log that was sitting on the ground. But the log was too heavy. Josh wouldn't be able to lift it up. So he was left with rocks. He needed to find a rock that was big enough to do serious damage to the crocodile. But the rock also couldn't be too big or Josh wouldn't be able to pick it up and throw it. Meanwhile, the monster continued inexorably to march toward Josh. As long as the monster couldn't see, it moved slow enough that Josh could out-maneuver it. Josh ran to the opposite side of the arena. The monster stood still for a few seconds, then moved its head around, trying to figure out where Josh was.

An idea began to form in Josh's mind. It seemed like a long shot, but it just might work. Josh found a large rock, sitting along the edge of the arena. He walked over to it and picked it up. It was very heavy. Josh guessed it probably weighed about sixty pounds. But Josh could lift it. He hauled the rock up in his hands and lifted it over his head. Yes, he could do that. He lowered the rock back down so he was carrying it underhanded. Then he walked over to the big log and laid the rock next to the log. Now for the hard part. He walked over to the body of the dead crocodile. The dead crocodile's feces were scattered about on the sand near the carcass. Josh stripped off his clothes. He wiped his clothes on his own blood, where the monster had swiped him. Then he covered his body with feces from the dead crocodile. While he was doing this, he kept looking at the monster. It was some distance away, moving its head around. It seemed to be confused by Josh's sudden movements.

Covering his body in feces was the most sickening thing Josh had ever done in his life. At one point, he had to stop and throw up. He didn't know if he could go through with this, but he had to. It was a matter of life and death. With his body covered in crocodile feces, Josh picked up his bloody clothes and walked to the log. He set his bloody clothes on the log, and waited. The crocodile would smell his bloody clothes. The crocodile could also smell his feces-covered body, but that would just seem normal to the crocodile. Josh's own scent would be hidden by the feces.

The crocodile was walking slowly toward the log, driven by the scent of Josh's bloody clothes. Josh picked up the rock that was lying next to the log. The crocodile continued to slowly march toward Josh. Josh waited. The crocodile continued to approach Josh's bloody clothes. It was starting to move more quickly now, as it seemed to sense that it was about to finish Josh off. Josh raised the rock over his head. The crocodile bent over and lunged at the log, digging its teeth deep into the wood. Josh's clothes were totally destroyed. With the crocodile's mouth full of wood, Josh slammed the rock on top of the monster's head. There was the sound of cracked bones. The monster's blood splattered everywhere. The crocodile's huge body lifted up in the air in some sort of death spasm, then crashed down to the floor of the arena. The sound was deafening. Josh backed up in fear, not knowing if the crocodile was still alive or not. Josh waited. The crocodile did not move. The crocodile's body was not moving, as it would if it were still breathing.

Josh stood for several seconds, just waiting, still not believing that the crocodile was dead. But everything remained still. Then the spectators in the arena stood up and lifted their arms into the air. They started making noises. Josh thought they might be cheering. Yes, the crocodile was dead. Josh had killed it. Josh's body was stark naked, covered in blood and stinky crocodile feces. He looked and smelled disgusting, and he knew it. But he stood for a moment in triumph, enjoying this glory. He felt like a conquering hero.

A crocodile approached Josh from one of the coliseum doors. He walked slowly to Josh. Josh was not afraid. He knew the crocodile did not mean to hurt him. The crocodile held out a claw, and Josh saw that the beast was handing Josh some kind of award. It was a large, round, gold coin. Josh took it, and bowed his head in thanks. The spectators in the arena were roaring their approval.

 Josh could not believe this. The crocodiles were barbaric, bloodthirsty creatures. But, if it was possible, there was a tiny spark of good in them. Josh wondered if the monster he had killed was some kind of evil criminal. Then Josh wondered if the crocodiles he saw on the other planet were also evil criminals that had been sent there in exile.

The crocodile that had given the gold coin to Josh now showed him the way to the exit. He opened the door for Josh and let Josh out into the land of freedom. It may have been his imagination, but Josh thought he saw the crocodile waving goodbye to him.

Josh walked out the exit door into the streets of the city. He did not have his laser gun. It was destroyed in the battle. He did not have his clothes. He remained stark naked and covered in feces. He wanted to wash off the feces but there was no water around, and he had nothing that he could use to wipe the feces off. And, he realized that he was better off being covered in feces as he walked through the sprawling city of the crocodiles.

Josh pulled out his phone and tried to call Missy. It didn't work. His phone was unable to make calls here. Josh was going to have to find his way to the ship by himself. He thought he knew the way. First, he had to find the railroad tracks. He would follow the railroad tracks to the depot, then make a left turn and walk through the forest to the ship.

23

Josh could see the ship in the distance. After a brutally long walk in his weakened condition, he wanted to jump for joy. Soon after he left the coliseum, he was lucky to hear a train going by. He followed the noise, found the train tracks, then followed them through the night. Luckily, none of the city dwellers bothered him on his walk. Maybe staying covered in feces was a good idea after all. When he reached the distinctive grove of trees, a strange mixture of redwoods and baobabs, he began looking for the depot. When he saw the depot, he turned left and began hiking through the woods. By now, it was early morning. He could see his way around but didn't know how to find the ship. So he just walked straight ahead. He got lucky. Very lucky. He did manage to see the ship ahead and a little to the left, as he hiked through a flat meadow.

When he reached the ship, the ship's computer welcomed him home. Josh was overjoyed. He wanted to tell his story to everybody, but first he needed a shower, and then he needed to eat a good meal. He asked how the ship was doing. The computer told him that the robots had fixed the engine, and the ship was back in good shape. They were ready to leave at any time, whenever Josh wanted. Josh explained that he needed a shower, some food, and some time to sleep.

After taking a hot shower, and eating a delicious meal, a robot came to administer to Josh's injuries. He had several places on his body that needed stitches. The crocodile had cut him up badly. After that, Josh lay down and instantly fell asleep. When he next opened his eyes, it was dark outside, and Josh was surprised that he had slept through the entire day.

"What do you want to do, Josh?" asked the computer.

"Let's get out of here, please," said Josh. "I've seen enough of the crocodile planet."

"Sounds like a good idea," said the computer. "Fasten your seat belts, and we're ready to leave."

Josh and Gronk fastened their belts, and the ship took off vertically into the night. Josh looked out the window at the crocodile planet. He was glad to leave this place behind.

Josh privately admitted to some second thoughts about leaving the crocodile planet. He felt that there was some work that was left undone. He would have liked to find the space port, which trafficked unfortunate crocodiles from here to the other planet. He would have liked to destroy that, to save the other planet from an invasion. But there were many problems with doing that. First, Josh didn't know how to find that space port. A long shot lead might be the crocodile that won his fight before Josh. That crocodile was wrapped in chains. Josh wondered if he would be exiled to the other planet. Following that crocodile to wherever it was being sent might take them to the space port. Of course, this was a difficult and dangerous undertaking. At some point, their ship or rover would come under fire from the crocodile planet. And, even if they could find the space port, there were likely several of them. They would have to scour the whole planet, looking for these things. No, leaving this place behind was the right decision.

The computer announced that their travel time would be much shorter in this direction. This was because they were traveling away from the sun, and the solar sails could catch some of the radiation pressure. Instead of twenty-eight hours, they could make this return trip in about fifteen.

The ship leveled off and began accelerating at 4g's. Josh was used to this acceleration by now and he hardly felt it. He started relating his exploits on the crocodile planet to Gronk and the computer. Gronk could not understand, of course, and the story was too long and complicated to translate for Gronk. But the computer understood and seemed impressed with what Josh had accomplished.

"I think me and Missy are very impressed, Josh. You managed to kill a crocodile in the arena with no weapons. The thing was, what, twenty-five foot tall, and several thousand pounds."

Josh showed them the award that he was given for winning the fight.

"Put it here, Josh, by the mass spectrometer. Let's see what this thing is made of."

"Well, I can't right now, Mr. Computer. We are still accelerating at 4g's, and, if I try to stand up, I'll get blown out the back of the ship. Once we reach our cruising speed, I will put it there."

As it turned out, the ship finished its 4g acceleration in a few minutes, and Josh took his award and placed it in the mass spectrometer. A minute later, they had some results.

"98 percent gold, Josh. Basically, it's pure gold. It's like an Olympic medal. Take good care of that thing."

"Wow," was all Josh could say. He walked over to retrieve his gold medal, treating it with a new kind of reverence.

He settled back in his seat, ignoring the pain from his injuries, and went back to sleep.

Josh slept on and off during the entire ride back. He woke up as the ship was decelerating and preparing to land. They were approaching the sunny side of the planet. Josh could make out desert and semi-desert areas.

"We're headed back to our old home, before we left for the crocodile planet," the computer announced matter-of-factly. Soon they touched down. It was early morning. Josh wanted to round up Missy and the rover to take a trip to the tropics, the only part of the planet that they hadn't seen yet.

24

The rover was freed up and ready to go. Josh and Gronk got in the rover, and Josh instructed Missy to take a course toward the equator, then zigzag around a little through the tropics.

"Okay," said Missy. "It will be a few hours of flying time to get near the equator. I hope you and Gronk can stay busy, or, at least, not get too bored."

"We'll be fine, Missy," Josh said, laying his head back in the seat and relaxing. Gronk kept looking out the window. Josh looked out occasionally. He saw desert, and then grassland, then some scattered trees. As the hours passed, the vegetation got more lush. Clouds were popping up everywhere now, and Missy took a detour to dodge around a bad thunderstorm.

"I would say we are in the tropics now," Missy finally announced. "What would you like to do?"

"Cruise around at low altitude and low speed for a while, and let's just look around," Josh said. "And take the usual measurements of air pressure, humidity, and temperature."

"Sure, Josh. Just to let you know, we seem to be approaching a herd of elephant-like creatures up ahead a few miles away."

Josh looked out the view screen and didn't see anything. "You have good eyes, Missy."

"You will see them in a couple minutes, Josh.

Finally, Josh saw them. There was a large herd of about fifty animals, that looked exactly like elephants. They were drinking out of a river, and eating shrubbery. Some of them had tusks and some did not. Josh guessed, as elephants on Earth did, that the ones with tusks were the males. As the rover passed overhead of them at a low altitude, some of the elephants looked up at the rover, not out of fear but out of curiosity. Most of them ignored the rover.

"This is beautiful animal life, Missy. Let's make sure we have enough of a video to send to Earth."

"No problem, Josh. It certainly is a spectacular scene."

Meanwhile, Gronk was looking out the window in amazement. "Big animals," he said, keeping his sentences simple and to the point. It occurred to Josh that Gronk had never seen an elephant or anything like it. He had seen huge animals during his travels with Josh, but, before that, maybe some big fish, maybe even a whale, but no huge land animals.

After a while, the rover moved on across dense jungle interrupted by occasional rivers and lakes. Josh pointed to one of the lakes, and said, "Let's have a look there, Missy."

The rover cruised over the inland lake. Josh looked around for whatever life forms he could see. There were lots of birds, some of them in brilliant colors like parrots on the Earth. He saw a few birds diving down from the trees, trying to catch fish in the water. At the far end of the lake, Josh saw a few dinosaurs. There weren't many of them. They were plant-eaters, and they were lounging around, some of them sitting by the lake, some of them lying down and sleeping. They were huge beasts, similar to the old Brontosaurus of ancient Earth.

"Let's get some video of those dinosaurs," Missy. Missy knew what he meant and she cruised over the heads of the small group of Brontosauruses and got some good video to send back to Earth.

"Can you get any data on the water in the lake, Missy, or do we need to go underwater for that?"

"Yes, Josh, we need to go underwater to get that data. What do you think?"

"If you don't mind getting wet, let's do it," said Josh.

"Okay, Josh, here we go." The rover eased itself down to the water's surface, and then gently submerged. There were lots of strange-looking fish, lots of different colors, and some strange shapes. Some of them looked like lionfish, except bigger. Most were small and very brightly colored.

"The chemistry of the water is very similar to that on Earth," said Missy. "Water temperature is 79 degrees Fahrenheit, water pressure is normal."

They came again to the surface. There was a group of birds with long necks that looked like geese, floating on the surface of the water, and examining the rover.

"Let's not disturb this beautiful group of birds," Josh said. "When they go on their way, then we can take off."

"Sounds good, Josh," as the rover sat in one place on the lake's surface. Josh looked around. There were lush green forests, with birds in the trees, and, of course, the dinosaurs lounging around at one end of the lake. There were some kind of monkeys or chimpanzees hanging from some of the tree branches, and Josh did manage to spot an orange animal that looked like an orangutan. He had seen one of those before some days ago, so he guessed that they were indigenous to this planet.

The birds dispersed, and the rover was able to take off vertically from the surface of the lake. It was a beautiful sight from above.

"There's an ocean some place nearby, right, Missy? I see if on the globe."

"Yes, Josh, we are a few hundred miles from the ocean. Do you want to go there?"

"Yes, of course," said Josh. "I want to take some measurements of the water chemistry, and observe the aquatic life. We haven't yet seen marine life in the tropics."

"Okay, Josh. We should be there in twenty minutes."

The rover banked to adjust its course, and then rapidly accelerated. Josh looked out the window and saw nothing but dense jungle. Gronk, as always, was fascinated by the scenery. In a few minutes, they could see the blue water of the ocean ahead. The rover continued to make its way through some salty air. As they approached the ocean, the vegetation started to change from lush jungle to scraggly bushes. They were over a large sandy beach, and the rover paused in the air so they could study the scene. They saw a large group of shorebirds. There was also a group of five large mammals, that looked like sea lions, lying on the beach next to each other, probably sleeping. Some of the birds landed on the backs of the sea lions, and were picking off insects. Waves were gentle and rolling as they approached the shore.

After a while, the rover flew out over the ocean. When they were about thirty miles out, Missy asked if this was a good spot to submerge. Josh said yes, and the rover descended until it landed on the water. Then it gently submerged. Immediately, they saw hundreds of small, brightly colored fish darting around. It reminded Josh of a fancy aquarium, where you see so many exotic fish in one place.

The rover cruised along underwater, while Missy gathered data on water temperature and chemistry. They did see one large fish placidly swimming by. It looked to Josh like a manta ray. The fish completely ignored the rover, and just swam by, minding its own business.

"Pretty much identical to ocean water on Earth," Missy announced, "but with zero pollution."

The rover continued on its course through the undersea depths. The water gradually became darker as the rover continued to descend. Eventually, everything was black, and Missy turned on the rover's headlights so that they could see out the windows. There weren't many fish at all at these depths. The few fish that they did see had gigantic eyes that could gather the small amount of light coming to them. Missy took another set of measurements. Again, they were very similar to what we could expect on Earth. After a while, the rover slowly began to surface. As it came to the surface, there was a large group of fish that looked like dolphins, swimming underwater, then popping out of the water to breathe, then going underwater again. Josh would have liked to see a whale, but he was not so lucky.

"What now, Josh," Missy asked, as they cruised along the surface.

"I say we fly along for a while. I'd like to see an island or island chain."

"Okay," said Missy. "Believe it or not, I think I know just the place. We flew over it a while back when we were looking for places to park the ship." The rover rose vertically into the air, then banked, and accelerated in a new direction. Soon they saw a chain of three islands lying in a row, just ahead of them. They were all pretty small, maybe a few miles across each.

"Let's pick one and land on a beach someplace. I don't care which one and I don't care which beach."

Missy guided the rover to a beautiful white sandy beach on one of the islands. Josh and Gronk made themselves some nice dinners, then they got off the rover, and walked a little on the beach, and sat down, and ate. The place was magnificent. On one side were gentle ocean waves slowly rolling their way into the shore. Across the water were more islands, their mountaintops shimmering in the distance. As Josh and Gronk looked inland, they saw lush green forests, and then some hills, leading eventually to a volcano. Josh knew that Gronk would never understand deep concepts expressed in English, but he felt the need to give Gronk some sort of closing speech. He turned his tape recorder on, and began.

"Gronk, you live on a beautiful planet. Yes, there are some dangers. There are giant squids that live underwater. There are dangerous sharks and ichthyosaurs roaming the seas. But the worst of all are the crocodile men. They came from another planet. We have killed a lot of them, but I don't know if we got them all. But, overall, your planet is beautiful and unspoiled. I hope you and the other inhabitants here can appreciate that fact, and maintain the planet's unspoiled ecosystem. It's possible that there may come other humans like myself to live on this planet. If that happens, it will be thousands of years in the future, and I assure you they will come in peace. I will explain to them what a beautiful world you have here, and what a peaceful group of human beings you are."

Josh then rewound the tape, and handed the recorder with its tape to Gronk. He showed Gronk how to play the tape whenever he wanted, so he could play it for his friends. It was a huge hope that Gronk and his friends would be able to make sense of the tape, but Josh felt that it was worth the effort.

"Well, Gronk, I guess we might as well call it a day. We can get some sleep, and then head back to your friends on the tundra."

Gronk slowly nodded. Josh got the feeling that Gronk would miss spending time with Josh and Missy.

127

They went back to the rover. "Missy, do you think you can find Gronk's old home where his friends live?"

"No problem, Josh. I know what the coordinates are, so I can definitely get us there. It is about a ten hour flight. If we leave now, we'll get there in the middle of the night. Maybe we can wait until later in the evening. Can you find something to do for a few hours?"

"Sure, Missy. We have a beautiful beach and some ocean. I don't think Gronk would mind hanging out here a while."

Gronk nodded his approval, and they spent the next few hours relaxing on the beach and swimming in the warm, salty water. Then, as the sun was setting, they dried off and headed back to the rover.

"It's a little early," said Missy, "but I guess we can take off now and arrive around sunrise. Keep in mind that Gronk's people are nomadic, and we may have to spend some time searching for them."

"Yes, I figured that," said Josh. "Gronk, say goodbye to the tropics, at least for now. I mean, who knows, maybe you and your friends can figure out a way to come down here someday."

Gronk, as usual, was glued to the window. He finally signaled that he was okay to start the trip. The rover rose vertically from the beach, arriving eventually at its cruising altitude. Then it banked to set its initial heading, and began accelerating.

25

The long flight through the night was going to be boring. Josh felt sorry for Gronk, who always loved to look out at the scenery. But now there was nothing to see. The whole long flight would be during the night. Josh glanced over at Gronk. He was getting up from his seat, and walking over to his bed. Josh was happy to see him getting some sleep.

"Missy," he said. "I know we need to keep our voices down so Gronk can sleep, but I have one question that is nagging me."

"And what's that, Josh?"

"All the time we spent on the planet, we never saw any land-based carnivores, except for the crocodile monsters that came from another planet. We saw sharks and giant squids under water, but we never saw land-based carnivores. Why do you think that is, Missy?"

"Well, Josh, the first possibility is that they live on the planet, but they don't live in places that we have visited. The carnivores, and I assume you are thinking of carnivorous dinosaurs, will almost certainly live in the tropics. We have not explored the tropics extensively, but have really only taken a sampling of the tropics.

"A second possibility is that they once lived here but are now extinct, for whatever reason. Maybe they got into a war with another group of carnivores, were wiped out, and then the other carnivores were wiped out with them."

"Interesting," said Josh. "Probably a way-out idea, but maybe they got in a war with the crocodile people. The crocodile people are warlike and aggressive. They are also very intelligent, and can communicate with each other. A primitive species of carnivores would have no chance of defeating them in a war."

"Yes, exactly, Josh. The only thing is, we haven't seen many of the crocodile people, and it would require a lot of them to win a war."

"Yes, but there are some unanswered questions about the crocodile people. We only saw them in one little area. We didn't see them any place else. Why couldn't we find more of them? Then they had to be transported here from the Crocodile Planet. It would take many hundreds of missions in a space ship to build up a significant population."

"Yes, Josh, but with a superior technology, a small number of them could wage a war against primitive dinosaurs. So I think the war theory is a possibility. The crocodile people simply went to war against other species competing for the same food sources."

"I have one idea," said Josh. "Could it just be due to the vagaries of evolution? Evolution happens because of random haphazard mutations in an animal's DNA. Over 99% of the mutations never go anywhere, because they are not beneficial to the species. But, very rarely, the random mutations hit on something that sticks, and there you have an improved species. Maybe all the random mutations that were happening never hit on the possibility of carnivorous dinosaurs."

"Yes," said Missy. "In fact, your idea is the most likely explanation. The random process of evolution on this planet never led to the birth of carnivorous dinosaurs."

"But over billions of years, the evolution on the Earth certainly created these beings. Is anything systematically different here?"

"Well, yes, things are different here. One big difference is this planet doesn't have a moon. With no moon, there are no tides. With no tides, there are no tide pools. Tide pools, those shadowy areas along a coast that are alternately dry or submerged in water, are breeding grounds for many different kinds of life forms, including the amphibians. Dinosaurs on Earth ultimately came from the amphibians. Just an educated guess here, Josh, but, without the tide pools, the richness of amphibian life would be diminished."

"But this planet does have plant-eating dinosaurs. We saw them. Can the plant-eating dinosaurs evolve without these tide pools that you are talking about?"

"Good question, Josh. Dinosaurs can certainly evolve without tide pools, but their evolutionary pathway comes from amphibians. At least, that is the history on Earth. But without tide pools, the amphibian life would not have much diversity. Then the dinosaurs that evolve from those amphibians would also lack some diversity. So, in theory, I suppose it's conceivable that, without the tide pools, not all dinosaurs could evolve. And from that we can theorize that maybe plant-eaters evolved but not carnivores. But, as you can see, this is all very hypothetical guesswork."

"Well, yes, Missy, but your hypothetical guesswork, as you call it, is about the best we can do. We certainly don't have the resources or the time to do massive digging of fossils and so forth. I think your theory about the tide pools is the most logical."

"Thank you, Josh. It is an interesting question that you pose."

"How much flying time do we have left, Missy?"

"A few hours yet. Try to get some sleep, Josh."

"Good idea, Missy." Josh closed his eyes, and, in a few minutes, was gone. He woke up later with the morning sun shining through the rover's windows.

"Good morning, Josh," Missy said. "We can start looking for Gronk's family. We are over the tundra now, and pretty close to the region where Gronk is from."

Josh nudged Gronk gently to wake him up. Then he pointed out the window and explained to Gronk that they were close to his home. Gronk looked around, then excitedly pointed at a spot along a coastline to the arctic sea. Josh looked where Gronk was pointing. It looked familiar. It was probably exactly the spot where they had met Gronk. But Josh didn't see any people, at least not yet.

"Do you see anything, Missy?" Josh asked.

"As a matter of fact, I do," said Missy. "I see a small colony of human-like figures on the beach. It looks like they're building something."

After another couple of minutes, Josh began to make out some detail. He saw the humans that Missy was talking about. He also saw what they were building. It looked like a very large boat. It reminded Josh of his mental images of what the Vikings rode in when they did all their groundbreaking exploring.

The rover hovered over the group of humans for a few seconds, then moved off to one side, and slowly descended. Gronk looked out at his friends and started to wave, but it was no use. They were still too far away. But the humans seemed to understand that it was their friend Gronk who had finally returned.

When the rover finally touched down, they let Gronk out, who immediately started talking and gesticulating with his friends. Gronk certainly had a lot of explaining to do. After all, he had traveled across a good portion of the world. He had also taken an interplanetary flight to another planet. He had seen dangerous sea creatures, and numerous land animals, including some dinosaurs. He had also seen enormous prehistoric birds. He had seen horrible crocodile beings from another planet, and their space ship, crashed underwater. He had seen deserts, oceans, islands, and forests, as he traveled all over the planet. As Gronk was explaining all this, his friends stared at him in a mixture of amazement and disbelief.

"Missy, I have a couple of requests," Josh said. "First, I would like a nice meal for every one of the humans, just like we gave them when we first met them. Second, I would like to give Gronk a copy of the globe." He went and fetched the globe. "Can we do that, Missy?"

"Of course, Josh. Just put the globe down here by the 3-D copier, and we should have a new one in a half hour or less. In the mean time, I can have food ready in just a few minutes."

"That's great, Missy." Josh walked out of the rover, and sat with Gronk and his friends. Gronk was continuing his talk about his exploits. As Josh approached the group, they all looked to him, possibly expecting some confirmation of Gronk's stories. Josh nodded his head, pointed to Gronk, and said simply, "Everything he says is true."

Nobody spoke English, but, thanks to Josh's facial expressions and hand gestures, they all seemed to understand. Everyone was impressed. Gronk went on talking for a few more minutes, and then Missy called to say that the food was ready. Josh went to the rover, collected the food, and passed it out. They all had a wonderful meal together, as they talked about Gronk's exploits.

Then Missy announced that the globe was completed and Josh went back, picked it up, said that this was a present to Gronk, and explained, as best he could, what the globe represented. With his fingers, he traced the route that Gronk took in exploring the planet. He would stop at many points along the way, and give an explanation, like "This is where we saw the giant birds," or "This is where we saw the crocodile monsters."

He drew a sketch in the sand of their sun, and a few planets circling the sun. Then he showed them where the Crocodile Planet was, and how Gronk had flown through space to visit that planet.

Then he explained how Gronk had saved their lives by using his harpoon to kill the monster shark that had attacked their boat. Everyone clearly viewed Gronk with an extra amount of respect and reverence for what he had been through, and what he had done.

When it seemed like they were done talking about Gronk's exploits, Josh asked Gronk to hold up his new tape recorder. Josh took a new, unused tape, put it in the tape recorder, did some talking, then played the recording back, so everyone could see how this marvelous machine worked. He left Gronk with the tape recorder and a dozen unused new tapes that he could use as he wished. Then he announced that it was time for him to return to his world. He tried to make some sort of emotion-filled speech about how much he enjoyed seeing this planet and meeting the people, but he just couldn't. The abstract ideas could not be expressed very easily to people who did not speak the language. But he did his best and tried, and tears soon filled his eyes and his cheeks. He grasped Gronk's hands and gave a final handshake to the strange human from another world who had become his friend.

Then he went back into the rover, and waved goodbye to everyone. The rover vertically ascended for several minutes to reach its cruising altitude, then banked and started its flight back to the main ship. Josh was overcome with emotion. It was a beautiful time that he had with Gronk and his friends. In science fiction movies, it seemed the aliens were always wicked people, but they can be good, too. For every crocodile monster, there is a Gronk. Josh would always remember that.

He was still lost in reverie when they reached the main ship. It was late in the afternoon with the sun getting ready to set. Josh got out of the rover, the ship removed its protective bubble, and the rover docked with the main ship.

"There is one last thing to do," Josh said. "I would like to return to Crocodile Island, retrieve the alien ship, and take it to Earth with us. It has a lot of scientific value. Do you think we can do that?"

"I believe so, Josh," said the ship's computer. "I know where the Crocodile Island is. It's a good flight to get there, but we can manage. Strap yourself in, and we can head out there."

The ship rose vertically from the ground, banked slightly, and headed off. The flight to the Crocodile Island was uneventful. Josh was lost in reflective thought for most of the way.

It was mid afternoon when they reached Crocodile Island, and Josh could see the alien ship stranded on the beach. Josh's ship placed itself a few feet above the alien ship. Then Josh heard a grinding kind of noise as the door to the ship's basement opened from below.

"What now?" Josh asked.

"No sweat," said the computer. "I got this."

The ship lowered itself so that it was almost touching the alien craft. Then Josh heard the hum of a large motor. The alien ship was lifted off the ground and into the basement of the ship. Then the door closed back shut.

"How did you do that," Josh asked.

"Electromagnets", the computer answered back.

"I should have guessed," said Josh. He took one last look around the planet that he had come to love, in his own way.

"Well, I guess we might as well head back to Earth," Josh said, as he reached into the refrigerator to grab a five quart jug of goop.

"Okay, Josh," said the ship's computer. "Take your time and drink your goop, then we'll freeze you and take off.

Josh started drinking the goop. He felt serenely happy with his trip here. He had pretty much explored the entire planet, and had seen and videotaped a good deal of wildlife. He had taken an interplanetary trip and seen the Crocodile Planet. True, that was not a happy scene at all, but it was something to chalk up as an experience. He had several scary adventures, particularly his battle with the crocodile in the coliseum.

Josh finished his five quarts, and lay down on the freezer bed. The straps rolled around his body and fastened him in place. The glass door closed above him. Nitrogen gas started to fill the air, and Josh felt chilly again. He knew this routine. He had been through it before. Finally, the ship ascended into the sky, and when they were surrounded by blackness, set a course for Earth, some 500 light years away.

26

Josh woke up to the sound of soft music. He didn't know why he was being woke up. Everything around him was the inky blackness of deep space. He was not anywhere near the Earth.

"I need your help," the computer said. "We are lost. I was using the star Betelgeuse as a sign post. But I don't see Betelgeuse. I was mixed up and locked onto Aldebaran. I knew, like Betelgeuse, that it was a red giant star. But now I see that it is not Betelgeuse. I have been going in the wrong direction and I don't know how to correct this mistake."

"Wow," said Josh. He couldn't believe that such an intelligent computer would goof up on celestial navigation. Sure, it was a tough subject, but jeez. "Well, we need to home in on a few familiar objects in the sky, and use them to plot a path to the Earth. I will need a pad of paper and a pencil, and a place to sit."

"No problem, Josh. There is a desk and a chair by the view screen. They are both fastened to the floor. In the desk drawer is a pad of paper, a clipboard, and some pens and pencils. Careful, because that stuff can float away if you don't hold them. Make sure to strap yourself in at the desk. The view screen in front of the desk can be manipulated by the controls in front of you to show the view in any direction. You can also zoom in or out as you wish."

Josh unstrapped himself, got out of his bed, and floated over to the chair and the desk. It was a tricky and delicate maneuver to get his weightless body to the chair. As he was about to fly by, he reached out and grabbed an arm of the chair, feeling a strain in his arm muscles to keep himself in place. Then he swiveled around, got himself seated, and strapped himself in. He opened the drawer to find paper and pencils and clipboard, then quickly closed the drawer before anything could float away. Next, he looked at the view screen, and familiarized himself with the controls. As Josh struggled for a very long time with all the knobs, he was grateful that the ships's computer was not a human being, and could not relate to things like impatience.

First, he tried to find Betelgeuse. He knew it was a giant red star in the constellation Orion. So he scanned the sky until he found Orion, then looked for the stars at the corners of that constellation. My God, Betelgeuse was not there. Betelgeuse would not have wandered away in one thousand years or so. It must have blown itself up in a supernova explosion. Josh knew that it was an unstable red giant star that would soon go supernova, but he thought "soon" meant in the next half million years or so. Apparently, Betelgeuse thought differently, and went supernova in one thousand years or less, since Josh left the Earth.

Okay, well that explains the computer's goof. But now comes the tough part. Josh had to sight on some objects in the sky, and plot a course to the Earth.

Josh told himself to stay calm. This was not an easy problem, but Josh could do it. The first step was to pick some objects to sight. In theory, two objects would be enough.

Well, first Josh needed to find two suitable candidate objects to home in on. What kind of objects did Josh need? First, Josh needed to be able to find them. Second, they shouldn't be too far away, because the sighting on them would be the same as the sighting from Earth, and it would tell him nothing. Third, they shouldn't be too close to Earth, because Josh wouldn't be able to find them from so far away from Earth, as their apparent locations would be shifted significantly.

Josh was good at mathematics and physics, but he only had a rudimentary knowledge of the night sky. The Andromeda Galaxy, the Large Magellanic Cloud, and the Small Magellanic Cloud were too far away, and would not provide Josh with any meaningful information. Too bad, because those were things that he had a chance at finding. The "Dog Star", Sirius, was too close to Earth, only about five light years, as Josh could recall. He would never be able to find it, and from here it would be dim or invisible.

Josh talked it out with the computer, who had an encyclopedic knowledge of the stars. He picked out several stars that he might be able to identify, and asked the computer their distances from Earth. He eventually found two good candidates:

Rigel

Distance from Earth: 870 light years

Right ascension: 5 hours, 14 minutes, or 78.5 degrees.

Declination: -8.20 degrees.

Pleiades star cluster

Distance from Earth: 444 light years

Right ascension: 3 hours, 47 minutes, or 56.75 degrees.

Declination: 24.12 degrees.

Josh didn't know that what he had in mind was elegant at all, but he was confident he could figure this thing out with some tough work.

First, for each of the two objects, treat declination as latitude and right ascension as longitude, and thus assign spherical coordinates to them. In spherical coordinates, each object had three coordinates: a radius, a latitude, and a longitude. The radius would be the distance from the Earth in light-years. Now he would have to convert the spherical coordinates of the objects to Cartesian coordinates, as seen from Earth. So now he would have coordinates X, Y, Z instead of the spherical equivalents r, θ and ϕ. Here, θ is latitude and ϕ is longitude. The conversion formulas are:

$$X = r \cos \theta \cos \phi$$

$$Y = r \cos \theta \sin \phi$$

$$Z = r \sin \theta$$

He performed the conversions, and got the Cartesian coordinates of Rigel and Pleiades, as seen from the Earth, with the Earth as the center of the coordinate system. That was the first step in finding the coordinates of the ship. And, once Josh could get the Earth-based coordinates of the ship, it would be a simple matter to plot a course to the Earth.

Next, Josh wanted to take sightings from the ship to Rigel and the Pleiades cluster, but he needed to do something very important first. He needed to rotate the ship appropriately so that the coordinate axes, as perceived from the ship, would be parallel to the coordinate axes as seen from

Earth. Otherwise, his sightings from the ship would be of no use in finding the ship's coordinates relative to Earth.

He needed an object in the sky that was so far away that it would appear in the same position as viewed from either Earth or the ship. The perfect candidate was the Andromeda Galaxy. It was two and a half million light years from Earth.

While he was at it, he would also need to find the First Point of Aries. The First Point of Aries defines the astronomical location of the sun when seen from the Earth at the vernal equinox. The First Point of Aries, to astronomers, was zero degrees declination as well as zero degrees right ascension. It was the astronomical equivalent of where the prime meridian of longitude intersected the equator on Earth. Josh reasoned that, if he could point the ship to the first point of Aries, and sight Andromeda at the same place that he would from Earth, and then he would guarantee that his ship was properly oriented.

He asked the computer how to find the Andromeda Galaxy. The computer told him it was between Cassiopeia and Pegasus, two constellations that may not be recognizable from here. He asked the computer for the coordinates of Andromeda, and the computer gave him this:

Andromeda right ascension: 0 hours, 43 minutes; or 10.75 degrees.

Andromeda declination: 41.26 degrees.

Sadly, this wasn't much help. Josh didn't have enough information to find a celestial body given its coordinates. But he did think of a way to find the pole, the point in the Earth's sky about which all the stars rotate. That would be huge. From there, Josh believed he could find the First Point of Aries, and pretty much anything.

He knew the declinations of Rigel and Pleiades. He only hoped that these two objects, when viewed from here, would be close to where they were when viewed from Earth. Rigel had a declination of -8.2 degrees. Since the declination of the pole was 90 degrees, and was directly above Rigel, Josh deduced that the pole was 98.2 degrees distant from Rigel. He didn't know in which direction, but he had the distance in degrees. He had the computer draw a circle on his viewer that was centered at Rigel and had a radius of 98.2 degrees. It turned out to be a huge circle that swallowed up over half of the night sky. But he wasn't concerned about what was inside the circle. He only cared about the edge of the circle.

Next, he knew that Pleiades had a declination of 24.12 degrees. So Josh knew that the Pleiades was 65.88 degrees from the pole, again since the pole was at 90 degrees. So he had the computer construct a second circle, this one centered at the Pleiades with a radius of 65.88 degrees.

When the computer finished the construction, there were two circles. They intersected each other at two points. One of those points would be the pole. Josh just had to figure out which one.

Josh picked one of the two points at random. The Pleiades had a right ascension of 56.75 degrees. This meant that, if you took a point at the Pleiades, and rotated it clockwise 56.75 degrees about the pole, then you would be on the so-called prime meridian, the line of zero degrees right ascension, or "longitude". So, with the help of the computer and the viewer, Josh performed this rotation. If he had the correct pole, then he was 65.88 degrees below it and along the prime meridian.

Now came the interesting part. To find Andromeda from here, you first had to move up the prime meridian 17.14 degrees to match the declination of Andromeda at 41.26 degrees, then do a counter-clockwise rotation of 10.75 degrees, which was the right ascension of Andromeda. Josh used the computer to perform these operations. Then, much to his amazement, there was the distinctive spiral of Andromeda Galaxy. He had gotten lucky and chosen the right pole, and his methods had worked. Josh felt terrific, but there was much more work to do.

Josh did his rotation in reverse to get back to the prime meridian, then went down the prime meridian 41.26 degrees, where he believed corresponded to zero degrees declination and zero degrees right ascension.

He cautiously made an announcement to the computer. "I believe this is the First Point of Aries. To align our coordinates with those of Earth, first we need to point our ship so it aims at this point."

The computer understood, and the ship began to swing around. It took a few minutes, but eventually the ship was lined up toward the first point of Aries. Josh checked the viewer, and found that it looked good.

"What we just did takes care or right ascension," said Josh. "Now we have to adjust for declination. Let's use Andromeda, and angle the ship up or down until the angle of elevation to Andromeda is 41.26 degrees. That corresponds to its declination as seen from the Earth."

Again, the computer understood and easily performed the maneuver. Josh checked the viewer, and it looked good.

"It looks like it works for Andromeda. Now I'd like to verify it with one other very distant object. I've been studying your data banks, and I think a good candidate is the globular cluster in Hercules. It is 25,000 light years from Earth, which means it should be in the same place whether seen from here or seen from Earth. I have the declination as 36.5 degrees and the right ascension as 251 degrees. Let's make sure we can find it. Do I need to guide you through the procedure, or do you think you have it now?"

"I think I'm okay, Josh," said the computer. The computer aimed the viewer up the prime meridian to match the declination of 36.5 degrees, then swept along the arc for 215 degrees in a counter-clockwise direction. When the maneuver was completed, there, indeed, was the great globular cluster. There was no doubt about it. They had the ship properly aligned with Earth. Now they could take their sightings of Rigel and the Pleiades.

Josh explained that, for both Rigel and Pleiades, they needed two angles. The first angle was how far above or below the horizon it was. Call that angle θ (theta). The second angle was how far counter-clockwise it was from the ship's bow. Call that angle ϕ (phi). The computer was able to measure these angles quickly and accurately. It came up with these numbers:

Rigel: $\theta = -38.04$ degrees $\phi = 80.95$ degrees

Pleiades: $\theta = -0.473$ degrees $\phi = 47.2$ degrees

Now Josh needed to find a vector that was aimed at Rigel, and another one aimed at Pleiades. The vector needed to be expressed in three components – the X direction, the Y direction, and the Z direction. These components would come from the familiar formulas:

$X = \cos \theta \, \cos \phi$

$Y = \cos \theta \sin \phi$

Z = sin θ

Once Josh got these coordinates for the vector to Rigel and the vector to Pleiades, he used a simple but key idea that these two vectors, or lines through space, even though they went to different places, they intersected at the location of the ship.

That gave Josh a system of three simultaneous linear equations in three unknowns. The three unknowns were nuggets of gold. They were the X, Y, and Z coordinates of the ship as seen from the Earth. He solved the system of equations and, indeed, got his coordinates.

X was 111.19 , Y was 464.29, and Z was 176.41.

Now was an important but simple step. Josh had just figured out the coordinates of the ship relative to the Earth. But to plot a course from the ship to the Earth, he needed the mirror image coordinates. He needed the coordinates of the Earth relative to the ship. So he needed to take the negative values of what he just figured out. That gave him:

X = -111.19, Y = -464.29, Z = -176.41

Now his course to the Earth is specified by two angles, θ and φ. θ is the angle of elevation, that is, the angle to point the ship's bow, up or down, so it aims at the Earth.

φ is the longitudinal angle, the angle taken counter-clockwise from the axis of the ship to where the ship would point at the Earth. θ is calculated first, and only after that can φ be calculated. The calculations are:

θ = the inverse tangent of Z divided by the square root of the quantity X squared plus Y squared.

φ = the inverse tangent of y/x .

This gives θ as – 20.28 degrees and φ as 76.53 degrees.

Josh explained this to the computer. The first angle told him to point down by 20.28 degrees. The second angle told him, after he was pointed down, to rotate counter-clockwise 76.53 degrees. And, believe it or not, that was the path to Earth. Josh hoped with all his heart that he did not make a bad mistake someplace.

Finally, how far from Earth were they? This was easily figured out by taking the square root of the quantity X squared plus Y squared plus Z squared. This came to 509 light years.

"We're farther from Earth than when we started," Josh told the computer. "You must have been off-course for a while."

"Sorry, Josh. But thanks so much for helping out. Now let's head back to Earth."

Josh floated back to his bed, strapped himself in, and asked the computer to freeze him. The top of his bed closed shut, and then Josh could see the cold nitrogen gas surrounding him. Soon, he felt very cold and sleepy. He said a silent prayer in his last seconds of wakefulness.

27

Laura woke up. There was a man and a woman standing above her.

"Where am I", she asked.

"Hello Laura. My name is Charles, and this is Sydney. You have been sleeping for thirteen hundred and fifty years, Laura. How do you feel?" said Charles.

It started to come back to her. She and Josh were married. Josh went to outer space, and she agreed to be frozen until he came back.

"What year is it?"

"It's thirty-seven-ninety-six," Charles said, plainly. "You went to sleep in twenty-four-forty-six."

"How is Josh, my husband?"

Charles took a deep breath. "We don't exactly know, Laura. He was supposed to return one hundred years ago. He still hasn't come back. We know that he was on the other planet. He sent back some excellent data and videos of his trip. He did a very good job of exploring the planet and reporting his findings. But he just hasn't come back. We don't know what happened."

Laura covered her face. "Oh my God," she said. "No, Josh, no. Where are you? Please come back and tell me you're all right."

Charles waited a minute, then started to speak again. "There isn't much at all that we can do, Laura, except hope and pray that your husband is okay. We don't know if you will ever see him again. It's very hard for me to say that. I know you and Josh were very much in love. But the unfortunate truth is that he may no longer be alive."

"Oh my God," Laura said, crying uncontrollably. "It can't be true. Josh, come back to me, I need you. Oh God, I can't believe this is happening."

Sydney came to Laura, and gave her a little hug on the shoulders. "I am so sorry, Laura. I really am. We both are. We love what you and Josh sacrificed for humanity. Josh is a hero for doing what he did. He took an enormous personal risk for the potential benefit of humanity and he succeeded marvelously. We all love you and Josh."

Laura sat silently for some time, thinking.

"So what now?" she finally said. "What do I do now?"

"Well, Laura," Charles said. "As you can imagine, the world is a much different place now than in twenty-four-forty-six. You can stay at our facility for as long as you need, maybe one month or more, whatever it takes for you to be comfortable. I am arranging meetings for you with several experts who can help you make your adjustment. First, you will meet with a historian, who is well familiar with life in twenty-four-forty-six. She will explain to you the many differences between then and now, and help with your adjustment. Then you will meet with a financial planner, to help manage your savings. Then you will meet with an occupational therapist to help you get started on your new life. But before any of that, you need to pee out your five quarts of gel. Then, we will escort you to your living quarters, where you will have your own personal robot, who will take care of all your needs, such as preparing food, doing housecleaning, and so forth. So we will leave you to yourself for a while so you can pee out your gel, and be alone with your thoughts."

Charles handed Laura a small locket. "Just press down on this, like so," he said, demonstrating, "when you are ready for us. Then we will take you to your living quarters."

"Okay," said Laura. She got out of bed, and immediately noticed that her clothes stunk horribly. She was grateful to see that there was a set of clean clothes laid out for her, and a nice shower next to the bathroom. She got out of her clothes, went to pee, and then stepped into the shower. She was glad that the toilet and the shower worked in the same way as she was used to. She took a shower, put on her clean clothes, and went back to pee.

She peed on and off for about an hour, until she finally felt like all the pee had gotten out. She pressed the locket as the man had demonstrated, and sat down and waited.

Charles and Sydney soon came. "I'm glad to see you found your new clothes, Laura. Everything fits, okay?"

"Yes, fine," Laura said.

Charles and Sydney led her to the elevator, the same one that she had gone down with Mrs. Kennedy, so many years ago. They stepped inside, Charles pressed a button, and the elevator started upward.

Charles was holding a coat, and asked Laura to put it on. "It's chilly outside," he said.

They stepped outside, and a biting wind hit Laura in the face. There were pockets of snow on the grass and some on the sides of the street.

"What month is this?" Laura asked.

"April eleventh", Charles answered.

Laura couldn't remember April being a cold, snowy month. But freak storms in April did happen.

"We're going right here," Charles said, directing her to a ranch style house on the road. A car sped by silently, not making a sound. How strange that seemed. They walked up the driveway, and into the side door of the house. It looked very much like what Laura was used to. There was a kitchen with a sink and a dishwasher. There was a microwave oven, and a refrigerator-freezer.

"What's this?" Laura asked, pointing to something that looked like a large oven.

"That's what you may have called a 3-D printer in your day," Charles said. "You use it to make and cook food. Your robot knows how to use it. You just tell the robot what you want to eat, and she will prepare it for you."

"And where is this robot?"

"Angela, it's time for you to meet your master, Laura. She is a very nice lady that just arrived from thirteen hundred years ago."

Angela came into the room. She was not at all what Laura expected. She was dressed casually in slacks and a buttoned shirt. She looked very much like a human being, a woman maybe in her late twenties, possibly slightly older than Laura.

"Nice to meet you, Laura. My name is Angela. I'm sure we will have a lot to talk about."

Her voice was relaxed and natural. She did not talk in clipped tones like the robots of Laura's day, that sounded like computers.

"Nice meeting you, Angela. I have a lot to learn, and I hope you will be patient with me."

"It will be my pleasure to help you in any way that I can," said Angela pleasantly.

"Well, Sydney and I will be leaving now. You can press the locket if you need us for any reason. I hope you still have it."

Laura reached into her pocket and held it up.

"Good," said Charles. "Angela will take care of all your needs. I have arranged for the historian to come here to your house for a visit tomorrow morning. The next day will be the financial planner, and then the occupational therapist. I expect you will need several sessions with the occupational therapist. You do have a lot to learn. Do you have any questions for me right now?"

"I don't think so," said Laura. "This is all pretty overwhelming." "That's understandable, but in time you will feel very comfortable here."

"Okay, thank you so much Charles and Sydney. I hope to see you both soon."

Charles gave Laura a hardy handshake, and Sydney hugged her. Then they left.

"So, Angela, I'm pretty hungry. Can you fix me a cheeseburger, medium well on a sourdough roll, with sauerkraut, lettuce, tomato, onion, pickles, and some French fries with no salt? Oh, and a large iced tea with lemon?"

"Sure, Laura. It will take me about ten minutes. And was that sweet or dill pickles?"

"Either one. I guess sweet. Thanks so much, Angela."

Laura relaxed for a few minutes, then her food arrived in ten minutes, just as Angela promised. It was on a plate and came with silverware, just as Laura was used to. Laura gobbled it down very quickly. She didn't realize how hungry she had been. The food was delicious. As she was eating, Laura wondered about television, and if it still existed.

"Angela, is there still television in thirty-seven-ninety-six?"

"Of course, Laura. The television set is right here in the adjacent section of the living room. Did you want to watch something?"

"It might be interesting to see some news, if it's on."

"Well, it's almost twelve noon, and there should be some news then."

"That reminds me, Angela, I need to set my watch. What time do you have?"

"It's eleven-fifty-eight right now, Laura, give or take a few seconds."

"Thanks, Angela." Laura took a few seconds to set her watch, then took her remaining plate of food with her to the other part of the room to watch television.

The news came on. The lead story was about an improvement to a device for capturing carbon out of the atmosphere. Some scientist was working on it, and it looked promising. Next was a story about a team of people attempting to cross the Pacific Ocean in a rowboat. Then there was a story about the growing polar bear population in the Arctic. Then there was a story about some swimmers and runners, and how they were training for the upcoming summer Olympics in Toronto. And the very last story was just a quick footnote: "We have just received word that an astronaut's wife, who has been asleep since twenty-four-forty-six, has been woken up. Her husband is late in returning from his deep space explorations. There is no word on the fate of the husband, but we wish him the best and hope he will return to Earth safely. As for the wife, we are withholding her identity, and we wish her the best in adapting to her new life thirteen hundred years in the future." That was the end of the news program.

Laura was happy that they didn't give her name. It was actually quite nice what they said. And one other thing was noteworthy. There was no talk of wars, rebellions, crime, or the like. There was also no talk about politics. Everything was good, or at least interesting.

"Angela, do we have the use of a car?"

"Yes, Laura. Did you want to go for a ride?"

"Yes, Angela. I would like to see the town. Can you drive me around a little?"

"Sure, Laura. Get your coat on, and then we can go. The car is parked inside the garage."

Laura put her coat on, and they walked together into the garage and got into the car. Angela pressed a button and the garage door opened. She pushed a button to start the car. Laura wasn't sure that it worked because the engine made no sound. The car silently moved in reverse out the garage and down the driveway, and then the garage door closed. Angela gave a voice command to the car, saying that she would control the car manually. Then, with Angela at the controls, the car moved along the suburban road.

After a while, they turned onto something that looked like a freeway. It was a six-lane divided highway with light fixtures on both sides and in the median strip. Laura could see some tall buildings in the distance. The freeway had only light traffic on it. As they approached the downtown area, Angela exited the freeway, and drove around some of the city streets. There were people walking and riding bicycles, even though there was snow on the ground. They came to a monorail station, where people were getting in and off the train, and walking up or down stairs, going to or coming from the platform.

"Can we take a ride on this, Angela?"

"Sure, Laura. I don't see why not." She parked the car in a designated parking zone for monorail travelers. Then they walked up the stairs to the platform.

"Here, Laura. Stick your right thumb in this little slot, like I am doing now."

Laura did what Angela said, and a green light appeared, which Laura assumed meant that they were okay to get on the train.

"What's going on here, Angela? Don't we have to buy a ticket?"

"You did, Laura. With your thumbprint."

"But I don't have any money or any account set up. I don't get this at all."

"The cost of the ride gets subtracted from your net worth. Right now, your net worth is negative two dollars."

"Why did it even let me ride when my net worth was zero or negative?"

"It's okay if your net worth goes negative. You can go down to negative ten thousand, as long as you don't stay there too long."

"Why didn't you have to leave a thumbprint, Angela?"

"I'm a robot. Robots go free."

"What happens if your net worth goes below the limit and stays there for too long?"

"Nothing good, Laura. The system will catch you, give you a warning, and then start taking away privileges."

The monorail started to move, slowly at first, then rapidly sped up. Laura looked out the window. She was somehow expecting to see bright, new, modern, tall buildings, because that was how she pictured the future. But things were largely the same as in twenty-four-forty-six. There were nice neighborhoods with nice houses, and some poorly cared for areas with old run-down buildings. Occasionally you could see sports fields, golf courses, swimming pools, playgrounds, and shopping centers. It was still too cold for people to be enjoying the outdoor sports, so many of the swimming pools and golf courses were empty.

At each stop, people got on and off the monorail. Laura studied them. They were mostly dressed casually, possibly going to work, coming home, or doing some errands. No one paid attention to Laura and Angela. Apparently, they looked just like anybody else. Eventually, Angela suggested they get off the monorail, and transfer to another one. They got off and sat on some benches outside, waiting for their next monorail to come. It was cold, there was a brisk wind, and there were occasional snow flurries in the air being blown about by the wind. In a few minutes, the next monorail came, and Laura and Angela got on.

"This one will take us a little ways through the suburbs and then the countryside," Angela said. The monorail started up, and sped through wealthy neighborhoods with tree-lined streets. As before, Laura spotted occasional swimming pools, golf courses, and athletic fields. People of this era must be pretty active, she thought, as there were a good many facilities devoted to outdoor recreation. Eventually, they left the suburbs, and entered a wooded area. There were evergreen trees and some coniferous trees. The coniferous trees had lost their leaves and were barren, but Laura could see a lot of them, and imagined that the summer and fall months must be beautiful here. In about twenty minutes, they came to a small town, where the monorail stopped, and everyone got off. It was apparently the last stop.

"Shall we get off and have a walk around?" Angela suggested. Laura nodded. They got off the monorail and walked some through the town. It was a quaint-looking place, with mostly old buildings and a church steeple in the center. There were houses and a few shops. Some of the shops were hardware stores, and some were selling toys and games. There were a few people walking around in the streets, but overall, the town was very quiet.

"I guess the children are all in school," Laura commented.

"Yes," said Angela. "We're coming to a school right now. It is just about three o'clock, so the children should be leaving right about now." Sure enough, in a minute or so, Laura saw a group of children leaving the school, carrying lunch boxes, and walking down the street, heading for home. It was almost strange, seeing children in thirty-seven-ninety-six carrying lunch boxes, which seemed a thing of the past.

Angela explained that many children made their lunches at home in the morning, then carried their food to school. The school didn't serve lunch, so the children either brought their food with them or went home for lunch.

Laura looked at the children. They were neatly dressed, and well-behaved, as they walked along toward their homes. Overall, the town was quite idyllic. Again, no one paid any attention to Laura and Angela as they strolled along.

"I guess we can go back," said Laura. Angela nodded, and they headed back to the monorail station. They went back the way that they came, two monorail rides and then Angela's car back to the house.

"Thanks for everything, Angela," Laura said.

"My pleasure, Laura. Remember, tomorrow you meet with the historian."

"Yes, I'm looking forward to that. I guess I'll try to go to sleep now."

Laura noticed her bedding and her bed clothes were exactly what she was used to. She was happy for that. The absence of Josh was weighing heavily on her mind. But Angela, even though she was a robot, had become a good friend to her. A very good friend.

28

The historian reminded Laura of a female super-nerd. She was short, and moved with a nervous stiffness. Laura guessed she was about forty years old. She wore a pant-suit, with a shirt that was scuffed and torn. She wore thick glasses in an age when only a few people wore glasses.

"How do you do?" she said to Laura, offering her hand. "My name is Myrtle. I am a historian. I am well researched in the time period that you came from. I am happy to talk with you about your adjustment here."

Ironically, the woman Myrtle talked like a robot, and the real robot Angela talked like a human being.

"Nice to meet you, Myrtle," Laura said, trying to sound relaxed. "I am anxious to talk to you, so I can understand all the differences between my time and yours. Shall we sit down?"

"Okay," said Myrtle, taking off her coat and sitting at a chair by the large circular table in the center of the living room. Laura sat across from her.

"This is your second day here. How did your first day go?"

"Very nice," said Laura. "My robot, Angela, explained some things to me, and we took a monorail ride into the city and then out to a small country town."

"What did you think of the car ride, and the monorail ride?"

"Well," said Laura. "The cars run silently, which is interesting. The monorail confused me because I could buy a ticket with my thumb, even though I had no money or net worth to buy a ticket. Angela explained that my net worth could temporarily go negative, as long as it didn't stay too negative for too long."

"Yes," said Myrtle. "I guess tomorrow you will meet with a financial advisor, who will help you move some funds into your bank account. Then you should have nothing to worry about. I'm sure you are worth quite a bit of money."

Laura was getting frustrated with this conversation. She shouldn't be the one answering questions. She should be the one asking the questions.

"Myrtle, you know quite a bit about my period of history. What, in your opinion, are the major differences in the average person's life style?"

"Good question, Laura," Myrtle said, and actually seemed to relax a bit as Laura was giving her a chance to talk a lot.

"Well, let's start with things around the house. First of all, just about everyone has a robot. It's probably like in your day everyone having a personal computer or a television set. Robot technology has advanced enormously, and robots are comfortable communicating in colloquial English, and understand a large variety of accents. Robots do everything, like preparing food, doing housework, even grocery shopping."

"How does the robot do grocery shopping?"

"Well, there isn't that much to do. The robot needs to keep the 3-D kitchen robot well stocked."

"I assume the 3-D kitchen robot is this thing over here that looks like a large oven."

"Yes, that is right. So your robot tells the 3-D kitchen robot what to cook. The 3-D kitchen robot only needs to have the right ingredients to prepare what your robot is requesting."

"And how does the 3-D kitchen robot get those ingredients?"

"That is the responsibility of your robot, who will order things that go into the 3-D kitchen robot. They will get delivered to your door, and the robot will take care of it from there. You don't have to do anything."

"And what about utilities, like water, electricity, heating?"

"First, you have to understand that our main source of energy is nuclear fusion. It is the safest, cleanest energy available. Back around the year 2000, people were afraid of nuclear energy, because of some reactor accidents. They were also spooked because there was no obvious way to get rid of the waste products. In your era, people were smarter about using nuclear energy, and they are even smarter today. Nuclear fusion leaves no dangerous waste products. Nuclear reactors have become so safe that accidents are unheard of. They just never happen.

"Nuclear energy is used to drive cars and airplanes, and it is extremely safe and quiet, as you have noticed. Every house and every car is equipped with a small portable nuclear reactor.

"As for water, this resource is distributed much as it was in your time period. Some of it comes from streams, some from lakes and rivers, and some from underground springs. The one enhancement is that now we are getting a lot of our water from the ocean. Desalinization plants remove the salt from ocean water to make it quite drinkable. The only problem is that desalinization is expensive. So the first choice for water remains lakes, rivers, and springs, but ocean water is starting to catch up as the desalinization technology improves. Our sewage treatment technology has improved enormously since your day. All our water and waste products get recycled safely now."

"When we were visiting the small country town at the end of the monorail line, we walked by a school just as children were getting out at the end of the school day. They were all carrying lunch boxes, and they were all walking home."

"Yes, Laura. With 3-D kitchen robots becoming very affordable, school children make their lunches at home and carry them to school. The schools have microwaves available for food that needs to be heated up. But serving lunch at school has become a thing of the past. That option can't provide the variety or the cost-effectiveness to compete with 3-D kitchen robots.

"As for children walking home, this has become the fashion in our time. Several studies many years ago have indicated that children became obese mostly because of a lack of exercise. So, in most schools, school buses were eliminated. That hasn't happened everywhere yet. Many schools are holding out, waiting to see if the lack of school buses really has health benefits. But the data to this point says that the children are much better off walking back and forth to school.

"Of course, in some rural areas, school is several miles away, and then bus transportation is provided. For extreme weather events such as blizzards, then transportation of some sort is provided to the children. But, for the most part, the children take on the responsibility of going back and forth to school on their own."

"I was watching the news yesterday on television," said Laura. "First, I'm amazed that television is still around. It is a vestige of the twentieth century, and I would have expected it to be replaced by something more modern."

"At one time, there arose a competing entity that used holographic imagery from lasers to bring three-dimensional imaging into your living room. It still might become a reality at some point, but it is too expensive to compete with television. For the overwhelming majority of people, paying a huge extra price for the holograms just isn't worth it."

"The other thing I noticed while watching the news was that there was no mention of politics. None. That is far different from my time when there was always a high-profile news item about politics, like some scandal, or an upcoming election, or something."

"Yes, Laura. There are no countries any more. The world is governed by one parliamentary body that oversees everything. There are, of course, local governments that manage schools and public works, and so forth. But national governments have become obsolete. People started to realize the obvious – that moving the world forward could not happen with nation-states competing with each other and fighting highly destructive wars, or even economic wars. So there was a worldwide conference of nations in thirty-two hundred to talk it all over. By the way, the year thirty-two hundred has become very famous for that reason. In the end, national governments were abolished and a world parliament was established."

"Wow," said Laura. "There are an awful lot of people that work in the national governments. What happened to them?"

"They were thrown out of their jobs. No one needed those jobs any more. But they were awarded generous severance packages, and they all came out of it okay."

"I'm sure this didn't go over well with wealthier countries like the United States and Western Europe."

"At first, no. A lot of money started to flow to public works projects in Africa and Asia. But the United States and Western Europe emerged from this much better off, although in the short term that was not so obvious. Money didn't have to be spent on government bureaucracy or on national defense. A health care system was set up to cover every person in the world. And there was a guaranteed income for all retirees."

"That sounds a little Marxist," said Laura.

"Whatever label you put on it, it was a very good thing for the world and for all the people. Yes, there was some upheaval at first. People in the government and in the defense, industry lost their jobs. But the people from the defense industry were quickly put back to work as technological researchers. The biggest casualties were the government bureaucrats who didn't have marketable skills in the new economy. Most of them got by on generous severance packages and eventual retirement."

"Without governments, who provides funding for things like schools, and infrastructure maintenance?"

"Typically, each community is awarded an allowance of so many dollars per year to take care of their public works, such as schools, libraries, roads, bridges, broadband, and so forth. If a community develops a special need that is not covered by the allowance, then they can petition the parliament for more money. These petitions are approved almost automatically."

"In my day, there was the internet. Does it still exist?"

"Yes, the internet is everywhere. Access to it has improved so everyone around the world can access the internet easily. And, yes, we still call it the internet."

"If there aren't any countries any more, does that mean there are no more wars?"

"Almost. Governments don't exist, so there is no government-funded war. But that cannot stop groups of individuals banding together, manufacturing their own weapons, and fighting each other. Of course, these kinds of conflicts never amount to much without the funding of big governments. But they do happen. For example, the battles in the Middle East seem to go on forever. In your day, it was Palestine against Israel fighting for control of the West Bank of the Jordan River or the Gaza Strip. Today, it is the same thing, without Palestine and Israel getting involved. There are warlike people on both sides that just like to fight. I don't know how else to put it."

"Any other conflicts going on besides that one?"

"That is the largest. There are rebellions within China, India, and Africa between minority groups and the ruling class, or, as I prefer to say, between rich people and poor people, because that is really what it is all about. I suppose those kinds of conflicts will always happen."

"What about labor unions?"

"They exist, but at some point, they became so powerful, that laws were put into place to curb their ambitions. If a labor union goes on strike, the company is now allowed to hire substitute workers to replace them. When highly skilled workers go on strike, then it is very hard to replace them, so, in a sense, the highly skilled workers have some protection. But labor unions remain a very powerful force. Typically, their members are paid very good wages and have a lot of job security. The standard joke is that you are better off driving a garbage truck than being a physicist. Obviously, that is not always the case, but it depends on the local governments and how big are their allowances. Sometimes it is true."

"How about crime? Is it a serious problem?"

"Not as bad as in your time. With guaranteed health care, and generous benefits when you are out of work, there are less reasons for committing crimes. The most common crimes now are crimes of passion and crimes of revenge."

"How about religion and wars over religion?"

"There is freedom of religion throughout the world. Anyone can worship in any way that they want. There aren't any wars over religion because there are no governments financing those wars. There is still, unfortunately, random acts of terrorism by individuals. But firearms are illegal now, unless you are a member of the police or the military. So any act of terrorism has to be with homemade weapons or weapons smuggled from the police or the military. It still happens but is very rare."

"What is the life expectancy for humans these days?" Laura had so many questions, she felt like she was just randomly blurting things out.

"Most people live to around one hundred years. Guaranteed health care helps a lot. Healthy eating habits and exercise help even more. People are encouraged to participate in athletics from when they are youngsters in elementary school. Most of them keep it up in one form or another."

"How about air and water pollution?"

"Pretty much everything runs on nuclear power now. There are no fossil fuels being used for energy. Nuclear power is clean. Way back before your time, there was a huge reluctance to accept nuclear power because of a few scary accidents. You may have heard of Chernobyl, Three Mile Island, and Chittagong. But the industry cleaned itself up in terms of safety, and is now able to recycle all the waste products. We have developed technology to remove carbon from the atmosphere. At first, it was very expensive, but, as the human race realized that something had to be done, it was accepted as necessary. There are about three hundred huge facilities scattered around the world that look like overgrown factories. Their job is to remove carbon from the atmosphere. In your time, or maybe a little before, people were worried about the gradual warming of the Earth, climate change, and diminishing habitable areas on the planet. That concern has gone away. We like to say that we have solved that problem, but the cost effectiveness is still a concern. So engineers are working on it."

"I'm glad you mentioned global warming, because that reminds me. This seems awfully cold for the month of April."

"Yes, Laura. In your time scale, this is not April, it is mid-February."

Laura gave her a blank look of confusion.

"Let me explain, Laura. About a thousand years ago, there was an enormous astronomical event on our sun. A solar flare erupted that was thousands of times larger than anything like it ever before. Some people called it a 'once in a century event', some called it a 'once in a millennial event', some called it a 'once per universe event'. To this day, no one knows what caused that massive explosion on the sun's surface. But the shock waves were so severe that they struck the Earth, and disturbed Earth's orbit. Nobody on the Earth felt anything unusual. There was no detectable radiation leaking into the atmosphere, nothing like that. Everyone knew what happened almost at once, because astronomers reported it. But nobody noticed anything on the Earth, except for more widespread Aurora Borealis and Aurora Australis. It just seemed like a benign astronomical curiosity. But then the slowing of the Earth in its orbit became noticeable. Winter started later and lasted longer. The position of the sun in the sky at various parts of the year just wasn't right. It turned out the Earth was taking 367 days to circle the sun instead of 365 and a quarter. After twenty years of this, the Earth was some forty days off schedule. There was a conference about what to do about it, and eventually it was decided to add two extra days to the month of February. That put the Earth back in equilibrium, but it was still off-schedule by 40 days or so. The world leaders decided to just forget about that. Some things are just strange, for example the first day of spring is no longer March twenty-first, it's May the first. But life goes on with the months a little off, and it was no big deal.

"By the way, Laura, I see you are wearing a watch. When did you set your watch, and what time do you have now?"

"I set it yesterday around twelve noon. Right now, I have ten twenty-six."

"And you brought your watch over from your time in twenty-four-forty-six?"

"Yes, of course. Why are you asking?"

"Because the event that caused the Earth to move more slowly around the sun also caused it to rotate more slowly, so the day has become longer. Right now, your watch is five minutes faster than mine. That is not your watch. That is the Earth. The Earth takes an extra five minutes per day to make one revolution. It is also because of the massive explosion in the sun years ago. So as to cause minimal disruption to systems, it was agreed to redefine one second as slightly longer, then one minute is still sixty seconds, one hour is still sixty minutes, and one day is still 24 hours. But this was a huge problem for the watch and clock industry. Everything had to be reprogrammed to fit this new rule. As for your watch, Laura, it will continue to gain five minutes each day. At some point, your watch will say it is nighttime when it is actually mid-afternoon. So either you adjust your watch every day, or you get a new watch.”

“So I guess that affects daylight savings time?” commented Laura.

“Yes. Daylight savings time in the northern hemisphere starts on the first Sunday in May, and ends on the first Sunday after Christmas. But the real tricky problems happened with athletic events, such as track and swimming. World records and so forth were based on clocks in the old era. When the time interval for one second was marginally increased, then all those record books had to be rewritten to reflect the time in the new era. It was a daunting task, to say the least.”

“How about long-distance travel?”

“Airplanes or high-speed trains. Just around your era, trains started to run on a hyperdrive, so they could travel as fast as a plane, like six hundred miles per hour or so. They had to stay under the sound barrier, otherwise they had no limit. So you could take a train from Los Angeles to Boston in about five hours, the same as an airplane, and a little cheaper. But trains need tracks, and planes don’t need anything except air. So planes are more flexible. If you want to go, for example, from Salem, Oregon to Richmond, Virginia, you are better off taking a couple of planes to get there. Trains don’t have that kind of expansive network to go anywhere, at least not yet. And, of course, you have to take a plane to go anywhere over the ocean.”

“And the armed forces?”

“Without the big governments to infuse them with money, they are essentially obsolete. But there is still a need for what we call ‘watchdog services’. These are people and robots who are always on the lookout for violence spurred on by terrorists. Frankly, there is not a lot for them to do.”

“And agriculture?”

“About the same as in your time, but technologically more advanced. Fields for crops are much more productive, and livestock is groomed much more efficiently with more protection from disease. There are still farmers and ranchers who love that life style, and want to keep doing it.”

"What about using the ocean for food?"

"That is a rapidly evolving technology. The ocean, if kept healthy and unpolluted, and with proper fishing techniques, can supply us with as much food as we can possibly ever want. It is a trickier problem than most of us appreciate. We have to maintain clean, unpolluted oceans. We have to try to control fishing so that it is done in select areas in select times, and establish limits on how much fishing can be done. This science is still in its infancy but there is a growing awareness of its importance."

"What about the usefulness of outer space and other worlds?"

"Well, it is questionable that the human race can live indefinitely on the Earth. True, we are doing a lot of good things ecologically to prolong our livable time here, but the time will eventually come when we have to spread out. Your husband is participating in that effort, and I understand that he is regarded as a hero. But it is a tough slog, mostly because of the huge distances and times involved in exploring faraway worlds. Right now, we have a small colony of pilgrims on Mars, and another small colony of Ganymede, the largest moon of Jupiter. But those places are problematical. You can't get by without a space suit and oxygen, for one. Right now, we are terraforming Mars by growing plants that throw oxygen into the atmosphere. But that process will take tens of thousands of years before the atmosphere of Mars is breathable. The same problems exist with Ganymede, except they are made worse because the gravity is so much less than Earth's. Planets which are already Earth-friendly, where a human being can walk around and breathe the air, and not freeze to death – those things are very rare. Your husband has traveled five hundred light years to explore one of them."

Laura had to hold back a few tears with the mention of her husband, and how he is regarded as a hero. "My husband is a brilliant man," she finally said. "I am very proud of him."

"As you should be," said Myrtle.

There was a period of silence. "I am a little tired," said Laura. "This has been a great discussion, and I thank you very much. I am most impressed with you."

"Thank you," said Myrtle, smiling. "If we are done, I'm leaving you a text message so you know how to contact me with any more questions."

"Okay, thanks again so much," said Laura. "I'll probably be calling you again."

Myrtle nodded goodbye and headed for the door.

29

Frank Parsons was a smiling, happy man in his fifties, in good shape, with straight black hair that hung over his ears. Laura had a mistrust of finance guys that smiled too much, but Frank seemed like a nice enough guy, at least on first impression.

"How do you do, Laura. My name is Frank Parsons. I'm the finance guy."

"Nice to meet you, Frank."

"I guess you're the lady I heard about on the news. You just woke up from twenty-four-forty-six?"

"Yes," said Laura. "But I don't like to spread that around."

"I understand," said Frank. "So we may as well get down to business. The people at the space agency gave me access to your husband's bank account data. My access is 'read-only', so I cannot change anything or move things around. All I can do is look. Well, from what I have seen, you are an extremely wealthy woman, Laura. In terms of twenty-four-forty-six dollars, your husband's net worth is approximately two hundred and forty trillion dollars. That's 'trillion' with a 'T'."

"Wow!" said Laura. "I expected that he would have a good amount of money, but I did not expect trillions."

"Well, Laura, there are a few things that we need to do fairly quickly. First, we need to give you access to at least some of that money. Then we need to shelter you from taxes, or you will get slaughtered paying taxes. Not that I have anything against taxes. Taxes are good things because they allow things to work. But, unless we do something, you will have to pay about 70% of your money to taxes."

"Okay," Laura said. "I'm listening."

"Now, Laura, you are the wife and sole beneficiary of Josh's money. The legality here is a little tricky and frustrating. As his wife, you have a legitimate claim to half of the money, but only when he provides written permission for you to access your half. The exceptions are divorce or death. Now, unless you want to divorce Josh, the other option is his death."

Laura started to cry.

"Now, don't worry, Laura. I know this is a sensitive subject. I am not saying Josh is dead. I am just explaining the legal mechanisms."

"Okay," Laura said. "Sorry. Go ahead."

"Now, if he were truly dead, and we had a death certificate to prove it, we could get full access to all of Josh's money. There is no death certificate, and, in fact, no one can prove that he is dead. But there is another category, called 'presumed dead'. In this category, you get access to half of the funds. All you need to do is file a written statement saying that Josh is presumed dead, and have it signed by yourself and a suitable witness. I can be the suitable witness."

"What if we do nothing at all?

"Then you have to get a job doing something, because you have no money. That won't be easy because your skills from twenty-four-forty-six don't carry over well to this age. So I strongly urge you to declare your husband 'presumed dead'."

"Okay, I guess so," said Laura. She held her head down, still trying to get a grip on this new reality. "So how do we do that?"

"We go downtown to the county courthouse, and explain the situation. They will give us a form to fill out. We have to do this in writing. We fill out the form with our signatures. Then we hand it in. From then, it should just take a few minutes. The clerk gets an approval from a judge, and then hands a copy of the paper back to us. Then we go to the bank, set up an account for you, and move half of the money into your new account."

"Is there any reason to move the money? Can we just take out what I need for living expenses, and let the rest accumulate?"

"Yes, but it is simpler and safer for you to control the money. Then, whenever you need more money, it is very easy for you to make a withdrawal out of your own account. Less trouble for you."

"Okay, now what about the second thing? How do I cut down on my tax burden?"

"My recommendation is that you keep what you need for personal expenses, let's say ten million dollars. You will have to pay taxes on what you take for yourself, so that will knock you down to something like six million five. But six million five is good money to get you going. You can buy and furnish a nice place to live, buy a robot and a new car. You can have plenty of money left for food and utilities, plus recreation and travel.

"Then, all the rest of the money, I recommend that you place it in a basket of municipal bonds. These will earn you a very safe three to five percent per year at close to zero risk. You do not pay taxes on anything that you earn on municipal bonds. So that money will grow and be very safe."

"What about the stock market or real estate?"

"The stock market will, over time, outperform municipal bonds, but the stock market is much more volatile. To invest well in the stock market, you have to have an element of timing. You have to watch that market carefully, and make good decisions about when to get in and when to get out. And the money that you earn in the stock market is taxable.

"As for real estate, that market will appreciate over time at an average of five percent per year. If you invest in a real estate fund, then you can be diversified and minimize the risk. What you make in real estate will be partially taxable. All things considered, I recommend a diverse collection of municipal bond funds. Keep in mind that we don't need to grow your fortune, we just need to protect it from high taxes and from market risk."

"Isn't there any market risk in municipal bonds?"

"Only if the entity issuing the bond goes bankrupt. For example, if New York City wants to issue bonds to fund an upgrade in its subway system, and you buy that bond, you will be paid by New York City no matter what, unless New York City goes bankrupt and can't pay you. That's why you should buy a diverse collection of municipal bonds, so one bankruptcy won't hurt you.

And, as I'm sure you realize, bankruptcies by cities and towns are extremely rare."

"How were Josh's funds invested up to now?"

"Pretty much all of it was in the stock market. In fact, the half of it that you aren't going to touch is in the stock market. Over the long term, like hundreds or thousands of years, the stock market's returns are phenomenal. Over such a long period of time, the ups and downs cancel each other out, and you benefit from the general underlying upswing."

"Okay," Laura finally said. "I guess I'm ready to go to the county courthouse. I assume we will be going together?"

"Yes," said Frank. "We can take my car."

They put on their coats, walked outside, and got into Frank's car. "Take us to the county courthouse," said Frank to the car's computer. "Yes, sir," said the computer, as the car pulled away from the curb and headed down the street. The ride looked familiar to Laura. It was the same way that she went with Angela a few days ago. Soon they were on the freeway, heading toward downtown, then the car exited, and made its way through congested downtown streets. When they got close to the courthouse, the car found a tight parking space along the curb, and expertly maneuvered into the spot. The engine turned off, their seat belts were released, and Frank and Laura got out of the car, and walked the block or so to the courthouse.

They walked up to the second floor, to an office labeled "records". Frank explained the situation to the female clerk, who shoved a form at him, and told him to fill it out and return it to this booth.

"This is for you to fill out, Laura, but I will help you. You don't know your address, and you don't have any other contact information yet. I am writing your address as '429 McNaughton Place', which is where you are staying now. I am also indicating that this address is temporary."

So Frank filled out the form, and showed it to Laura. "You sign here, Laura, and I'll sign below you as the witness."

When they were done with filling out the form, they took it back to the clerk.

The clerk read the form, then stared at Laura. "The astronaut's wife," she said. Laura made no reply, as the woman continued to stare at her.

"Okay," the woman finally said. "I'll go to get approval and be back in a few minutes." Laura and Frank stepped away and sat on a bench, waiting.

"I didn't realize so many people knew about the astronaut's wife," Laura said.

"People don't know you and don't recognize you, but your story is out there and known by just about everyone."

"I don't like that kind of attention," said Laura. "But I guess there's nothing I can do about it."

"Yes, I understand," said Frank. "I hope this clerk knows to keep her mouth shut, because your name and address were on the form."

"Oh jeez," said Laura, shaking her head.

A minute later, the clerk returned and waved at Laura and Frank. They went over to the desk.

"All okay," the clerk said, and handed Laura a certificate on green paper. "I was able to verify your marriage from 2446. Married for thirteen hundred and fifty years. Wow, that has to be a record."

Laura took the green paper without saying a word.

"Now I guess we go to the bank, right, Frank?"

"Yes, Laura."

"And which bank are we going to?"

"Merchant's Bank. That's where Josh has his money. You can open a new account there, and move the money from one place to another within the same bank. Simple."

"So where is this wonderful Merchant's Bank?"

"Down the street. We can walk to it."

The bank was a couple blocks away. They walked along the crowded midday sidewalks, stepping over occasional spots of snow. Frank pointed out the bank, and they walked in.

Frank spoke to the greeter near the entrance, and explained that they needed a banker because they were about to do a large transaction. They were directed through a door, into a long corridor, then into an office with very expensive furnishings. A gray-haired man in a business suit entered the room soon after.

"How can I help you?" he asked.

Frank explained the situation. Laura was happy to let him do the talking.

"Wow!" the man said. "The astronaut's wife. You've become famous, you know."

Laura stared at him blankly without saying a word.

The man proceeded to open a new account for Laura, taking Laura's thumb print in the process. Then he moved half of the money from Josh's account to Laura's new account. He explained that the money could be invested in any number of ways, including stocks, bonds, or exchange-traded-funds. It was all over in about ten minutes. Frank and Laura thanked the man, and they quietly left the bank.

"We still have to figure out how to invest the money," said Laura, stating the obvious.

"Yes, but it will be pretty straightforward. In fact, we have already discussed how to do it. I suggest we go to your house, sit down, and take care of it."

Laura nodded. They walked back to the car, got in, and Frank commanded the car to go to Laura's address. The car sped away expertly, gliding through the city streets, back to the freeway, then down the freeway to Laura's neighborhood.

As they approached Laura's house, they saw a group of about ten people waiting outside on the street. "Oh no," said. "They're after me. They got my address."

"Laura," one of the people called out, and a group of them mobbed the car. "We would like to interview you on television."

"I don't want everyone to know where I live," Laura said, "and I do need to do a few things first. Can you give me an hour or so, and I can meet you someplace, like at your office?"

"Okay," one of the men said, handing Laura a business card with an address and a phone number. Laura took a look at the business card. The name of the guy was Mr. Johnson. Funny that his business card did not include a first name, but that was an unimportant detail.

Slowly, the group dispersed. Then, Laura and Frank entered the house, sat down at the kitchen table, and started looking over the investments. Frank had his personal computer with him, and the process went quickly.

After a few minutes, Frank showed Laura a list of funds he had selected that specialized in municipal bonds. "I want to be solidly invested, but, at the same time, diversified. That's why I selected this group of funds."

Laura looked at the list. Nothing on the list meant anything to her. There were about twenty elements on the list. She nodded her approval, feeling like a dummy, but trusting Frank.

"Now, before we actually buy these things, we need to withdraw ten million dollars, as we discussed, for your personal use. Then we need to prepay three million five in taxes to avoid a penalty later."

"I don't know how to do those things," said Laura.

"That's why I'm here, Laura," said Frank, as he did everything on the computer. "I need to explain that when you buy something with your thumbprint, your net worth will not be trillions of dollars. It will be approximately six million five, because the money you have invested will not count toward your net worth."

"Why is that?" asked Laura.

"Your net worth is calculated using only money that is at your immediate disposal, liquid money as we call it. You can always sell some of your investments if you need more liquid money, but then you should do what I just did to prepay taxes."

"I don't understand what you just did."

"I just typed out the computer session for you. It's all here. Save this piece of paper and then just follow the steps, same as me."

Laura looked at the sheet of paper, a little confused. Frank explained the various steps to Laura, and Laura began to understand.

"You can call me with any questions, Laura. Here is another one of my business cards, but I think you will be fine. In the mean time, let's hope that Josh returns some day."

He headed toward the door, and Laura shook his hand heartily. "It was nice meeting you," she said, "and thank you for all your help."

"You're welcome, Laura. Goodbye for now." He walked out the door toward his car.

30

Laura held Mr. Johnson's business card in her hand as she walked toward her car. She spoke to the car. The car recognized her voice, and unlocked the doors. She got in on the driver's side. She read off the address from the business card, and told the car to go there. The car sped away. Laura sat there, doing absolutely nothing, but looking out the window. It was very strange. She was getting used to the route. Through the neighborhood, onto the freeway to downtown, then exit from the freeway, and through some crowded streets in the downtown area. The car parked itself expertly and told Laura they were at the destination.

"Which one of these buildings do I go in?" Laura asked.

"The one right next to us, just to our right," the car said.

"Okay, thank you," Laura said, and got out, and walked nervously over a few piles of snow, and into the building. She was proud of herself for getting here without the help of Angela. She was starting to figure a few things out for herself.

She walked to a central counter, that she guessed was an information booth. There was a young lady working there. Laura showed her the business card.

"Up the elevator to the second floor, turn left, and walk down the hallway to room 206."

"Thank you," Laura said, feeling a bit ashamed of herself. She should have figured out that room 206 was on the second floor. When she reached the elevator, she was glad to see that it was very similar to what she was used to. She got in the empty elevator, pushed a button for the second floor, rode the elevator up, got off, and walked down the hall. When she saw room 206, she pushed a buzzer-like device by the door handle. Soon, a young woman came and opened the door.

"I am expected here," Laura said, showing the business card.

"Do you have an appointment?" the woman said.

"No, I didn't think I needed one."

"Well, okay, please come in and have a seat. I will see if Mr. Johnson is available to see you."

Laura walked into the office. It was quite large and expensively decorated. There was a row of windows in the back. On the side wall was a row of doors.

In a few minutes, Mr. Johnson emerged from one of the side doors, and came over to Laura. He was a slim man of medium height, probably in his late forties.

"Hello, Laura," he said. "We're so glad you could make it. I need a couple minutes to get ready and gather a few other people. Then we can have a nice chat."

"Okay," said Laura. She settled back in her chair. On the end table next to her chair was a pile of magazines. Laura flipped through them, but didn't find them interesting. One of them was about hockey, another about basketball, one about women's fashions. Laura laid them back down on the table, and patiently waited for Mr. Johnson. She realized she was still wearing her coat. She took it off, and hung it on the chair behind her head. She looked across the room and out the windows. There wasn't much to see – snow-covered buildings and trees with no leaves. She laid her head back and tried to think of what she would say in her interview. But she had no idea what kind of questions they would ask her, so she had no idea what she would say. She wondered if it was a mistake to show up for this interview. She reasoned that, if she didn't come, she might get some bad mention in the press. Or worse, they could keep hounding her for a long time. No, it was best to give them their interview and put this whole thing to rest.

"Okay, Laura, we're ready for you. We can just step in this room here." Laura nodded at Mr. Johnson, then grabbed her coat off the chair and followed him. Mr. Johnson held the door for her, and she walked into the room. There was a group of five people there, three men and two women, all in their thirties and forties, and dressed very well.

"I thought you said this was for television," Laura said. "Where are the cameras?"

"All over the place," said Mr. Johnson, adjusting his tie and pointing around the room.

"I don't see anything," said Laura.

"You can't. You would need a microscope to see them. They are tiny things placed all over the walls and windows."

"Hmmm," said Laura, looking around, confused. "Am I on television right now?"

"No," said Mr. Johnson. "I haven't activated anything yet. But, if you're ready, we can get started now."

"Okay," said Laura. "I'm ready."

Mr. Johnson reached into his shirt pocket, pulled out a small device, and pressed a button on it. "We're on the air," he said.

"Now, Laura, maybe you can start by telling us a little about your life in twenty-four-forty-six."

"I worked in technology," Laura said. "I was a software engineer working on a real time operating system. Other than that, I was unmarried until I met Josh, my current husband. I enjoyed physical exercise, spending some time each day doing swimming or aerobics. I enjoyed doing puzzles, such as crosswords and cryptograms. I belonged to a hiking club, where about twenty of us would meet once a week and take a trip to the country and hike maybe ten miles or so."

"It sounds like you had a fulfilling life, Laura. You were active, and probably quite happy. I'm surprised that you would decide to make this jump to another time."

"Yes, I suppose it sounds like I was happy, and in some ways I was. But I just couldn't get along with my boss at work, my job became miserable. He laid me off, and I knew finding another job would be difficult if not impossible. I didn't have any savings of my own. The world was in an economic downturn then. Jobs were hard to find, especially if you were out of work. So, as you can imagine, I was in real trouble financially, and did not have any way out.

"So, anyways, that's when I met Josh. He was in a similar situation. We had worked at the same company and for the same boss. That boss laid me off and Josh within a few weeks of each other. Josh had been looking for work, and soon realized that finding another job was almost hopeless, so he and I were in similar situations.

"That's when Josh noticed an advertisement for astronauts, and decided to apply for that job. Josh and I fell in love as we contemplated our futures. We got married, Josh decided he wanted to go to outer space, and I decided I would wait for him by freezing myself."

"And what was Josh's mission as an astronaut?"

"He was assigned to explore a planet that was 500 light years away from Earth. The trip to the planet would take 625 years, as measured on Earth, and the return trip would take another 625 years. He was due to return in 1250 years plus whatever time he spent on the planet."

"Do you know how he did at this assignment?"

"I was told by people at the space agency that he performed superbly. He collected an enormous amount of data and videotape."

"So he has been gone for 1350 years. He should have returned after 1250 years. Do you have any idea why he would be 100 years late coming home?"

"Not really. We know that he reached the planet and explored it. If he died, then it must have been an accident on the planet, or a crash of his space ship, or getting lost in outer space on the way home, something like that. Of course, we don't know for sure that he is dead. He may just be far behind schedule. Maybe something was wrong with the propulsion system on his ship, and his return trip is unexpectedly slow. No one knows."

"When Josh left Earth, did the space agency tell you anything about his maybe being late?"

"Yes, they told me that I would be woken up when Josh arrived back on Earth. If he was one hundred years late, they would also wake me up. I guess they thought that, being one hundred years late, he was probably dead."

"What do you think? Do you think Josh is dead?"

"I honestly don't know. I don't know what to think."

"Your life in this new period of time. How are you coping, and have you made any plans for your life?"

"I have only been here a few days, so I am still getting oriented and learning my way around. At some point, I would like to get some training and then go on to a professional career doing something, I don't know what yet. But I would like to make a contribution and to meet some people, and be a part of this new society."

"Now you used to work as a software engineer. Do you think you might want to give that a try again?"

"It is worth exploring, I suppose. But software engineering, even in my day, is a rapidly changing field, and I'm afraid that I am way behind the times in it, no pun intended."

Mr. Johnson smiled. "What are your first impressions of life in thirty-seven-ninety-six?"

"It is not all that different from twenty-four-forty-six. When you read science fiction novels, it fills your mind with a lot of junk science about the future. You start thinking that buildings are 800 stories high, and everyone flies around the city in their own private hovercraft, stuff like that. So, in a sense, it is not as different from twenty-four-forty-six as I had feared. There are some basic differences in lifestyle, like having robots doing most of your work, or giving voice commands to drive your car. In my age, nobody had personal robots, cars were powered by gasoline or electricity, and most cars had to be driven manually."

"What about the political situation today compared with that of your time?"

"I am told that there are no such things as countries any more. In my age, there were over 200 countries in the world, and a lot of them were always fighting. There was an enormous amount of money spent by governments on weaponry to fight against other countries. There were also a lot of economic battles. One country would often boycott goods from another country, or set high tariffs on those goods. In the end, that was a stress on the average person, and nothing ever got accomplished by those wars, whether they were military or economic. I also think that the guaranteed health care of today is a very good thing. It removes a huge stress from families who worry that a major illness could wipe them out financially."

"Do you have any first impressions of the people in your new world?"

"I have only met a small number of them, but everyone so far is very friendly, and very helpful."

"What about day-to-day life in this time compared to twenty-four-forty-six?"

"With robots to do almost all the work for you, you have a lot more leisure time now. Cooking and housecleaning are no longer time-consuming chores. I noticed while riding the monorail that there are a large number of sports facilities. I sense that people use their extra free time to expand themselves, and stay in shape physically. Guaranteed health care removes so much stress from people's lives that I'm sure people must be more relaxed and happier than in my time, but that is just my own supposition."

"In comparing life in twenty-four-forty-six with life today, do you have any thoughts, any little bits of wisdom, any words of advice, anything like that to add?"

"I would say technology is a big key. You want to make sure that efforts to improve technology are in line with efforts to improve the world as a whole, and certainly the lifestyles of people. Technology should keep its goals focused like this."

Mr. Johnson glanced around the room, checking to see if anyone else had questions for Laura. The other people in the room were busy taking notes.

"Laura, thank you so much, that was an excellent interview," Mr. Johnson said, reaching into his pocket for the device to turn off the television cameras. He stepped over and shook Laura's hand. Laura felt happy, but mostly relieved. She had been afraid of this interview, but she had gotten through it.

"Thank you," Laura finally said to Mr. Johnson. "I enjoyed our little chat."

"So did I, Laura. I hope we have another opportunity to talk a little later."

One of the women in the room waved her hand and spoke. "Laura, you have made a huge hit. The responses are overwhelmingly positive. And there are a number of companies that want to offer you a job."

Laura shook her head in disbelief. Yes, the interview went well. Many of the questions she could answer mechanically without much thought. She never expected that she could generate any excitement from this interview. "Wow," was all she could think of saying.

The woman pressed a few buttons and the printer across the room started humming, then printed out two pages. The woman went over and picked up the two pages.

"Laura, this first page is a summary of the responses. As you can see, there were close to a million positive responses, and zero, can you believe it, ZERO negatives. This second page is a list of six companies who would like to offer you a job, along with their contact information's."

Laura shook the hand of the woman, then shook hands with everyone in the room, and especially Mr. Johnson. "I don't know what to say. Thank you all so much. I am so happy."

31

Brandy Jones was a tall blonde lady in her twenties, about Laura's age. She introduced herself to Laura cheerfully.

"Good morning, Laura. My name is Brandy Jones. My title is an occupational therapist, Really, my job is to help you get set up to succeed in this era. You are quite famous, Laura, and I am honored to assist you."

"Nice to meet you," Laura said. "Yes, I suppose I am famous, but I didn't do much to become famous. I slept for a long time, that was what I did."

"You are very modest, Laura. I watched your interview. It was extremely good."

"All I did was tell my story, Brandy. I am still confused why that interview was reviewed so positively."

"You were straightforward, honest, and told your story without any embellishments. And it was a fascinating story. You have experienced a lot, and you told the story honestly. There is a lot to be said for that."

"There are six companies that want to give me a job. I'm excited at the possibility to go to work for a good company, but I want to get your thoughts on what to do about this. If it's okay with you, I'd like to start our session with this discussion."

"Sure, Laura. I assume you have a list of the six companies."

Laura showed her the list. Brandy studied it for some time, then took out her personal computer to do some research. Laura sat silently, watching her.

"It looks like three of these are technology companies, one is an airline, then there is a sporting goods store, and finally a law firm."

"A law firm? Did I hear you right?"

"Yes, Laura. If you go to interview them, you will have to ask them what interested them in you. But I will give you some quick thoughts. First, I'm afraid it will be very difficult for you to work in technology. As you yourself have observed, this has always been a rapidly evolving discipline, particularly the software, where you once worked. You would have to go through a long training period to be productive at one of those companies. Even if you work in a non-technical area such as marketing, sales, strategic planning, or middle management, you will have a lot to learn before you can feel comfortable. Airlines and sporting goods would probably be easier for you to blend in quickly, because those industries don't change so quickly like technology. So you can come up to speed a little easier there. As for the law firm, that is a complete roll of the dice. On the one hand, the legal profession has been slow to change, and it is probably reasonably similar to what it was in your time. On the other hand, you have absolutely no background here, and I don't know how fast you can pick up a new discipline. The bottom line is, I encourage you to interview all these companies, see what interested them in you, and think hard about how comfortable you would be in each environment."

Laura nodded her head in agreement without saying anything. She always hated looking for a job, and she wasn't sure how much she would like it this time. At the very least, it would be a tough decision for her, even if all these companies gave her offers. The dream job was not going to plop into her lap.

"So, Laura, I guess we can start to get you set up. I'm putting together a list of things that you are going to need. You may want to take notes on this." Brandy handed a pen and a pad of paper to Laura.

"First, you need a house of your own. The space agency is nice to let you live here, but within a month or so, you need to move on. I don't think you need a big house. After all, there is only one of you, and maybe two, if Josh makes it back or if you remarry. A two or three bedroom house with two baths ought to be fine for you. But I do recommend that you find your house in a gated community. You are famous now, whether you like it or not, and you do need to worry about crazy people.

"Next you need a car. A simple one, unless you plan on taking elaborate vacations and bringing along lots of luggage.

"Then you need a robot to do chores around the house and drive you around if you need. Then, of course, you need furnishings for your house.

"All that stuff that I just mentioned can be put on hold for a while. You have a month or something like that to find and furnish your new house and buy a new car. You should do your job interviewing as soon as possible, while your fame is still fresh in everyone's minds. So the first things that you need are a good phone, a new watch, and a good personal computer.

"We can get those things by ordering them to be mailed to us. Or, believe it or not, we can use your 3-D printer to create them. But, my recommendation is that we go to some stores and just do some old-fashioned shopping. That way, we can try out the items right there in the store before we buy them. So, Laura, if you're ready, let's go do some shopping."

They got into Brandy's car, and rode through suburban streets to a large shopping area, which sprawled over three blocks. Each of the stores that they visited were large and not very crowded. As they browsed through the various electronic devices, Laura was very impressed. The area of the store devoted to electronic devices was very large, and covered an entire floor by itself. There was a large variety of robots, telephones, personal computers, and programmable devices that Laura didn't recognize.

When the shopping was over in the afternoon, Laura had a new watch, a new phone, and a new personal computer. Laura had successfully bought everything using her thumbprint. She was happy that she figured out how to do it.

They arrived back at the house, and started experimenting with the new equipment. The watch was the easiest. It had a digital display, and was easy to set. The phone wasn't too bad, either. Laura received with the phone an available phone number that she could use. She configured her phone with the new number, and then sifted through an array of configuration parameters, most of which were unimportant. She tried calling Brandy. The call worked, and then she started a list of contacts with Brandy's phone number. Finally was the personal computer. It looked intimidating to Laura, but really was quite simple. Brandy helped her set up a mail account, so she could send and receive messages. Then she learned how to connect to the internet, and how to use the multimedia features. She hooked up her printer, and was able to print out a file in different colors. She practiced using the internet, and was pleasantly surprised at how easy it was.

"Well," Laura said. " I think I'm set up okay. Now can I start getting some job interviews lined up."

"Sounds good," said Brandy. "Remember, I will be happy to help you when it is time for you to buy a house, some furniture, a new car, and a robot." She shook Laura's hand, smiled at her, and headed for the door.

32

Laura was hanging to the side of a sheer granite cliff. The fingers of both hands were gripping small holds in the rock. Her feet were both implanted on tiny ledges below her. She tried to plan her next step up. She could move her right foot over, then move her right hand up a bit to the next hold, but then she would be stuck. She would have no spot for her other hand. Her hands would have to cross over each other. Remember the second rule of rock climbing, she told herself. Three points of contact all the time. Only move one thing at a time. Of course, the first rule was simple. Never look down.

Laura decided there was no better way. So she moved her right foot to the next nub in the rock. Then she moved her right hand up. Then she moved her left hand to the right, crossing over her right hand. Then she moved her left foot to the old spot where her right foot was a few seconds ago. Now she was in trouble. She would have to make a dynamic move. She would have to move both her hands at the same time. She had to hope that her feet were planted firmly on those tiny nubs below her. She wished there was another way, but there wasn't. She saw what she had to do. She kept her feet positioned in place, then swung both her arms around and up, so her right hand found a new spot and her left hand went to the old spot of her right hand. It worked. She didn't know how she had pulled that off. In fact, she didn't know how she was finding this new level of ability. Her previous rock climbing had been totally recreational, messing around on eight foot high boulders. Now she was here free-climbing El Capitan.

She rested a little, then realized that her left hand was bleeding. She must have caught the sharp edge of a rock while she was making her last move. This was not a good thing. There was quite a bit of blood, and blood is wet and slippery. She took a second, eased her left hand off the rock, and sucked the blood off of it. Okay, it was still bleeding, but she should be okay for a while. The next few moves came simply to her. Left foot, right hand, left hand, right foot, and she had advanced a little higher. One last pitch, and the rest would be easy. She took a minute to rest. She caught her breath, then sucked some blood off her left hand, then she was finally ready to move again.

She started with her right foot. As she moved it to the next ledge, she didn't catch the ledge flush, and her foot slid down. She started to panic. Her right foot was hanging in space. Now she had to use a lot of strength in her hands and arms to support herself from above while she swung her right foot back to its old spot. She had to feel around a bit, but eventually she found the spot. She was back where she started. Okay, rest a little, suck the new blood from my left hand, then move my right foot up, she told herself. This time, she was extremely careful and deliberate, and her right foot found its place. Then, one at a time, she moved her hands up to the next catches. Finally, she moved her left foot. There was a nice spot for her left foot, but the problem was that it was far to the side. So her left foot would have to be awkwardly placed, with her left leg parallel to the ground. But there was no other way, so she tried the move. It worked, and she felt her left foot hold, and she felt her left hamstring pull. She hoped it wasn't an injury. But, jeez, she was amazed at the things she was able to do today. She could never move around like this before.

She wanted to suck the blood off her hand, but didn't want to stay in this position for too long. She brought her right foot up and moved her hands to higher holds, and now she could finally move her left foot to a more comfortable spot. Then she was in a spot of rare and wonderful stability, where both hands and both feet were firmly placed. She caught her breath, then carefully moved her left hand over, and sucked off some blood. The rest of the climb would be easy, she told herself. And, comparatively speaking, it was. She made all her moves with extra care and deliberation, not wanting to take any chances when she was so close to the end.

In five short minutes, it was over. She had just free-climbed El Capitan, and was standing triumphantly at the top. Now, finally, she looked down at Yosemite Valley, so far below. She was done. She reached for the medal that was hanging from her neck and pressed it. The vision of Yosemite vanished, and she was standing on the wooden floor. A couple of people walked over to her.

"Well, how did you like it?" one of the men said.

"My God, that was unbelievable," Laura responded, sucking more blood off her hand. Holy cow, her hand was really bleeding. "How did you manage this virtual reality with no helmets, no gloves, nothing?"

"It is augmented virtual reality, combined with artificial intelligence and neural networking. And a lot of help from all the untapped abilities of your brain. By the way, your hand is bleeding."

"I know," said Laura. "I cut it on a rock, but I thought that was all in the virtual arena. How in the world is it still cut?"

"Well, our technology is pretty amazing, Laura," was all the man said.

"And my hamstring feels pulled," Laura said.

"It should be okay in a few weeks, if you're careful with it."

They walked together to the snack room, and sat down for a drink. A nurse came over, put antiseptic on Laura's hand, and bandaged it up.

"We are a games company," the man said. "By the way, I am Marvin, and this is my assistant, Jack. Anyways, we started out as a games company, but now people use us for all kinds of things, like sports training for example. I mean, look at you, a few sessions of this and you could become an expert rock climber."

"What got you interested in me as a possible employee here?"

"Lots of things, Laura. You are an active person, you like the outdoors, and you communicate clearly and straightforwardly. There are several areas of the company where you could fit in and succeed.

"First, we need people to do the low-level programming. This is difficult stuff. You would be writing software in a multi-processor environment. Everything is happening in real time, obviously. So all the processes have to be synchronized so they don't interfere with each other. Then all the processes have to respond immediately to interrupts, which can be tricky. A critical piece of code in one process might have to guard against being interrupted by another process. It's not easy stuff, but you have some background in this kind of software, I believe.

"Second, we need people to invent new scenarios. The scenarios have to be interesting, but they must have some educational or personal growth aspect. Besides what you just experienced, we have scenarios in just about every sport – basketball, hockey, baseball, soccer, American football, deep sea diving, and on and on. But we are always eager to come forth with new ideas.

"Third, we need good sales people, and good spokespeople, who can do a good job representing us to the general public."

"Even though I do have real time operating system experience, and multi-threaded programming experience, I would have an enormous amount of learning to do for your option 1. I can't imagine what software engineering is like in thirty-seven-ninety-six. As for option 2, I'm not sure how much learning there would be for me. I'm hesitant to take on anything where it would take years of study just to become an entry-level person. Your option 3 sounds like something I could do in a shorter period of time, but I just don't know that it matches my interests that well. All I can say right now is that you have a fabulous product and I'm sure a terrific company, but, if it's okay, I need to go off and think some."

"Of course, Laura. Take all the time you need. Here Is my card with my contact information. You can get back to me at any time with questions or thoughts. And it was very nice meeting you, of course."

"Thank you, Marvin."

Laura and Marvin walked through rows of cubicles on their way out of the building. A few people were talking, but most were huddled over workstations, apparently in deep concentration. Most of the men had long hair and beards. The women had long, stringy hair that came to their waists, and most had abundant tattoos. All wore some form of blue jeans with tee shirts. Many of the tee shirts were in need of some laundry.

As Laura exited the building, she thanked Marvin again, and said that she would stay in touch.

33

"Have you ever seen robots play water polo?" Jason asked Laura.

"My goodness, no. I can't imagine that."

"Well, let's go have a look." Jason pointed to the sign hanging above the entrance gate. The sign said "Robotics Sports Tournament."

Jason was a fifty-something man with graying hair tied into a pony tail in the back. He was an upper-level manager at "Cutting Edge Robotics", a rapidly growing high-tech company.

Jason flashed a badge as they walked through the entrance, and they didn't have to pay to get in. They found the water polo arena and took some seats. The game stated with an official throwing a ball into the middle of the pool and blowing a whistle. The players at each end swam madly through the pool to get to the ball first. The player who reached the ball first flipped it back to his teammates and the game was on. Players were sprinting about in all directions, trying to get open. The player with the ball threw it to a teammate, who reached up with one hand to catch it. The game continued on from there.

"These are all robots?" Laura said incredulously.

"They sure are, Laura," replied Jason calmly, as a player took a shot on goal, that was expertly blocked by the opposing goalie.

"They must have very advanced software," Laura commented, stating the obvious.

"Yes," said Jason. "Real-time operating systems forms the basis for the software. They have to react to changing circumstances instantaneously, which they can only do by efficient handling of interrupts. The interrupts are happening all the time. And you have several different instantiations of the operating system. One for each arm, one for each leg, and spinoffs for the hands, fingers, lower legs, and toes. Then there is a master operating system that controls the whole body and sends commands to each of the slave operating systems. It is quite an architecture."

"So the body parts are the slaves, and the brain, for lack of a better word, is the master. Have I got that right?"

"Exactly so, Laura. The interrupt handlers are all in the brain. The brain receives interrupts as things in the field of play happen. The interrupt handlers are all small pieces of code, but they wield a lot of power, because they set flags and parameters for the scheduler, also part of the brain. The scheduler then issues commands to the other body parts, or, more exactly, to the operating systems that govern those body parts."

"What about personal robots that do cooking and housecleaning, like the one I have now?"

"Their software is much simpler," said Jason. "For starters, they don't need to know the rules of water polo. They don't have to throw and catch, and swim. They do have to be ready to defend themselves, but it is very unlikely that someone would attack them. The interrupts that they have to handle are simple ones, like you giving them an order. They have to communicate in basic English, which is a thing in itself. And yes, they all run with real time operating systems, but their implementations are not as complex as the robots you see here playing water polo. They don't have that many interrupts that require their attention."

"It's amazing, Jason. It really is. The science of robotics has come so far. But I'm afraid a lot of this stuff is far beyond my life experience."

"Not really, Laura. You do have a background in real time operating systems. Sure, your background is from a thousand or more years ago, but the basic principles stay the same. What you would need to learn are some details, like a new computer language and a new software architecture. That sounds scary, but it isn't scary. Most new hires have to go through the same learning experience."

"Can we go back to the office, so I can meet with some other people?"

"Sure, Laura." They walked out of the arena onto the snowy sidewalk, then into Jason's car. In a few minutes, they arrived at the office of Cutting Edge Robotics. They walked inside, past a few cubicles, then Jason stopped.

"Sara, I would like to introduce you to Laura. She is applying for a position with us."

Sara stood up from her desk and shook Laura's hand. She was a tall, slim girl, maybe in her thirties, and appeared to be part African-American. She had large earrings dangling from each ear, and some kind of ring that went through her nose. Half of her hair was purple, and the other half was green. She wore baggy green pants, that looked like the old jungle camouflage stuff that Laura remembered from her time. Why in the world would someone be wearing jungle camouflage clothes in this day and time, and working at a robotics company? Laura was taken aback.

"Nice to meet you, Laura," Sara said. "We can go to a conference room and talk so we won't disturb anyone."

"Okay," said Laura. She glanced back at Jason. "Thanks for everything, Jason," she said. "I'm sure we will be talking again soon."

"Yes," said Jason. "Please come back any time."

Sara led the way into a spacious conference room with a large table in the middle and seats for eight people. She took a seat, and so did Laura.

"I'm not really here to grill you," said Sara. "I am more here to answer your questions. So why don't you start off?"

"Okay," said Laura. "I'm trying to understand how long it would take me to become productive here. I do have a background in real time operating systems, but that is it. I don't know anything about programming robots, except the little introduction that I got from Jason."

"Well, it could take anywhere from three months to a year or more, depending on how hard you work at it. What programming languages are you familiar with?"

"I used to program in a language called ORCA. That was quite a while ago, and I doubt that ORCA is still around."

"No, I've never heard of it," said Sara. "But you have probably worked some with device drivers, right?"

"Yes," said Laura." Most of the development in our RTOS was supporting new devices, so naturally I had to get involved with writing device drivers."

"How comfortable are you with that?"

"Fairly comfortable, but I'm afraid that much of what I used to work on is now out of date."

"Can you describe a recent project that you worked on?"

"I was working on a controller to control the tension in the cable on an aircraft carrier."

Sara looked confused.

"Sorry, Sara. In those days, aircraft carriers were large ships that took airplanes out to sea. The airplanes would take off from the deck of the aircraft carrier, do what they needed to do, then come back and land on the deck of the aircraft carrier. The planes had hooks on their undersides that grabbed cables. The cables were strung across the deck of the aircraft carrier. They were used to brake the plane so the plane would be able to stop in time, before running off the end of the deck. Of course, most planes ran on nuclear power, and took off vertically, but a few did not, so we needed that kind of setup.

"An interrupt would be generated when the plane hooked on to the cable, and then the device driver would have to control the tension in the cable to stop the plane in time and not break the cable."

"Yes, I see," said Sara. "What about programming in a quantum state environment?"

"Quantum computing was just catching on in my day. I am familiar with the issues of quantum computing, where an electron can take on eight states instead of two, and all the counting is done in octal rather than binary. But I have not done any programming in that environment."

Sara spoke. "The technology is old, but I think you have enough of a background to jump in and learn. You might be able to come up to speed in a year or less."

"Wow," said Laura. "And what am I doing in the year to come up to speed?"

"Reading manuals, learning our architecture, studying our code, learning our programming language."

"I didn't expect to be so long in a training mode. But I guess I should expect that, since my skill set is so far behind the times."

"You are the same as most new hires, Laura. There is an awful lot to learn. In fact, people who come in without an RTOS background seem never to completely come up to speed. They are always in a learning mode, and somewhat confused, but struggle along and manage to achieve some level of productivity. You have an RTOS background, so you are better off than a lot of those people. By the way, it is not easy to find potential employees with an RTOS background, like you have."

"Okay, well that is somewhat comforting. I have a few more questions, if you don't mind."

"Of course, Laura."

"How many hours per week do you work, on the average?"

"Well, I usually come in about nine in the morning, and leave at ten or eleven at night. I normally take a two hour break around midday to get my exercise and have lunch."

"It sounds like you are working all the time. Not to get personal, but don't you have a husband, a boyfriend, a girlfriend, any other hobbies?"

"Nope. I'm very passionate about what I do. I love my job."

"I certainly admire your level of dedication. I do have one last question."

"Okay, shoot, Laura."

"It seems robots can do just about anything. I saw them playing water polo today. I guess they can cook food, do housecleaning, drive cars, play sports, it seems like they can do anything. Is there anything left for us humans to do? Will robots eventually rule the world?"

"Well, this is a subject for constant discussion in the scientific and political worlds. Lots of people get nervous about the growing abilities of robots.

"Let me start by saying that robots do what their human programmers tell them to do. Of course, they use artificial intelligence to seem extremely intelligent and creative, but they can never be truly creative. Robots are programmed to solve problems in a methodical, algorithmic way. Robots can never compose musical pieces or create works of art. Robots will never be as good as humans in solving problems where creativity is required. For example, a robot can certainly learn to fly an airplane. If the airplane has some mechanical problem in mid-flight, the robot can go through a checklist of items, and try to diagnose the problem in a methodical way. The human being is better at this, however, especially if the problem is a new one that requires some level of creative thought to solve it.

"So, the bottom line, if there is one, is that robots can perform methodical tasks very well and very dependably. Tasks that require a degree of creativity are trouble for the robot, and the human being can do better. Especially for jobs that involve human safety, such as flying an airplane, a robot will never be entrusted to do that."

"Okay, Sara, well I just saw robots playing water polo, and it seems like there is a lot of creativity in that sport."

"I was involved in that project, Laura. What might seem like creative thought by the robot is really nothing more than going through a methodical checklist: Do I have a good shot on goal, is there an open man to pass the ball to, do I have an open lane to swim through, if I pass the ball, can it be intercepted. That is the methodical checklist that the robot water polo player goes through all the time."

"Can a robot perform a surgery or a root canal?"

"Yes, but if something unexpected happens, and the robot is forced to think creatively, then the human is better."

"And there is no way to train the robot to think creatively?"

"The robot makes good use of artificial intelligence. Sometimes, it might seem that the robot is thinking creatively, but in reality, the robot is making use of vast data bases of information to find the best match to its current situation. And, no, a robot will never be able to think in a truly creative way."

"Okay," Laura said. "I think you convinced me, and reassured me. Robotics is certainly an interesting field."

"Any more questions?"

"No, I guess not. Thank you very much for everything, Sara. I enjoyed talking with you."

"Please come by again, Laura, if you have more questions or things to discuss with me."

"Thank you, I will," said Laura, as she grabbed her coat, and headed toward the exit.

34

Bill Hill introduced himself to Laura. He was a senior manager at a company called "Blue Oceans". He was a gray-haired man, probably in his sixties, medium build, and energetic. He wore casual slacks and a sport shirt.

"Nice to meet you, Laura," he said politely. "Have you interviewed other companies yet?"

"Yes," said Laura. "I interviewed a virtual reality company and a robotics company."

"That sounds like a lot of impressive high-tech stuff," said Bill Hill. "I'm afraid we won't be able to offer you the same level of razzle-dazzle here. Our main problem now is providing enough water to the sixty billion people on our planet. Right now, we are still getting most of the water from natural fresh water sources --lakes, rivers, streams, underground springs, and so forth. Ocean water is catching up in usage, thanks in part to our efforts in desalination. Unfortunately, the economics of desalination are against us. For many people, desalinated ocean water doesn't make sense when they can just get their water from another nearby source. Someone living in Chicago or Milwaukee or Cleveland has lots of water in a nearby Great Lake, and doesn't care about desalinated ocean water. But, if we want to save our existing fresh water sources, and, at the same time provide enough water to the world, then we have to take a lot of it from the oceans. It's that simple."

"Can the water from rivers and streams and lakes be used and then recycled?"

"Yes, and we do that as best as we can with highly efficient sewage treatment. But that process is not perfect. Some sewage remains, and some water is lost and cannot be reused. Our best and maybe only chance at an inexhaustible supply of water comes from using the oceans."

They were walking along a corridor on a factory floor. To their right was a network of pipes and tubs. To their left was a collection of what appeared to be monitoring stations and computers.

"There are several ways of desalinating ocean water," Bill Hill continued, "and we have probably tried all of them. Perhaps the most obvious is to boil the seawater. Then the water evaporates, and the salt is sitting by itself. The salt is swept away, the evaporated water is captured and cooled. It condenses, forming rain that can be collected. This method has been in use since the early days of seafaring, when sailors discovered how to do it. Of course, their methods were quite primitive, and they were only able to capture about ten percent of the pure water. On a large scale, this method is economically impractical. The specific heat of water, as you know, is very high. The amount of energy required to raise or lower the temperature of water is considerable. So this method, at first glance, seems way too expensive.

"But the ballgame isn't over yet. From thermodynamics, the boiling point of water decreases as the air pressure decreases. That is why backpackers notice that it is easier to boil water on the top of a mountain than at sea level. That is our first take on desalination."

Bill Hill pointed to the array of tanks on the right side of the corridor. "These tanks, proceeding from right to left, have progressively lower air pressures. As water is pumped into one of these tanks, it becomes easy to boil. Then we get rid of the salt that is left behind, we let the evaporated water condense, and then we have our desalinated water."

"Why do you need a series of tanks? Why can't you just have one tank set at a low pressure?"

"Someday we might be able to do that, but right now, the process is not perfect. We don't get perfectly pure water on the first try. So we take the almost pure water that we get, and send it to the next tank, where it is made even purer, and so forth."

"What are the disadvantages of this approach?"

"There really aren't any. It works, and it produces millions of gallons a day, where it is being used. The world parliament needs to be convinced that this is something worth an investment. If we could somehow make it cheaper, it would be a much better sell. Then the real headache becomes the distribution. For areas close to the ocean, this is not such a big deal. For places like South Dakota, for example, we have to run pipes across the continent to get the water there. Right now, South Dakota gets a lot of its water from the Oglala Aquifer, which is almost dry right now. It's a hell of a problem. We'll need to cover the world with pipelines to get all the water to the people who need it."

"Back in my day, there was some speculation about towing icebergs from the Antarctic to areas that need water."

"Yes. This approach is not feasible at all, unfortunately. Yes, icebergs are made up of fresh water. But icebergs, as you know, lie mostly underwater. As you tow them through the ocean, they will be infected with salt deposits. Plus, most of the iceberg will be melted before it can reach land.

"Another related idea is to freeze ocean water, creating ice, which is salt-free. This would be interesting if it could be made to work. The problem is, salt particles lodge themselves in the middle of ice crystals. This happens at the microscopic level, and is not easy to eliminate, unless you wash the ice with purified water. Then the whole operation has no benefit, because you will use as much water getting rid of the salt as you create by making the ice."

"What other ideas are there?"

"The next method uses electrolysis. Salt, when it is in a water solution, contains ions. It contains the positively charged sodium ion and the negatively charged chlorine ion. The positively charged sodium ions can be attracted to a negatively charged electrode, and the negatively charged chlorine ions can be attracted to a positively charged electrode. The electrodes are placed on the other side of membrane filters, so the sodium and chlorine eventually get separated completely from the water. Then you are left with pure water between the filters."

"Sounds tricky," said Laura.

"It is. The filters have to admit the charged ions but not let the water pass through."

"Any other methods?" asked Laura.

"Yes, but those are the ones worth mentioning, the most promising ones. As you can see, a gigantic remaining issue is transporting the purified water to inland locations. It seems like we need a huge global network of pipelines. That's where we need some outside-the-box thinking."

"Well, Mr. Hill, I like your company and I like what it is doing to help the condition of mankind. Actually, I think my husband, Josh, would do very well here. He is an extremely good problem solver, and has strong backgrounds in physics, thermodynamics, and mathematics. I hope and pray for his safe return. In the mean time, I am not sure how I could contribute here. I'm not strong enough in your technical fields to make meaningful contributions, and I wouldn't know where to start with building pipelines all over the world."

"Well, we like you, Laura, and the whole world likes you. If you come to work here, it might take you a while to get your feet on the ground and start running, just as with all our new hires. So I hope you will consider us seriously."

"I will definitely think about it very seriously. Thank you so much, Mr. Hill."

"Thank you too, Laura, and I am looking forward to hearing from you."

With that, Laura and Bill Hill walked together to the exit door. They shook hands, and Laura walked off.

<h1 style="text-align:center">35</h1>

Laura's next two interviews were with an airline and a sporting goods retailer. Both were interested in Laura as a spokesperson for advertisements. Laura was not interested in either of them. As for her other interviews, none of those jobs interested her, for a variety of reasons. Either the learning curve was too long, her co-workers were too strange, or she didn't have the right background for the job. If it came down to having to choose one of these jobs or staying unemployed, she might decide to stay unemployed and keep looking. Well, there was one interview remaining, the law firm. She might as well give it a try.

She showed up at the appointed place and time, and was introduced to Charles Fink, a senior person in the firm. He invited her to a conference room where they sat and talked.

"Glad to meet you, Laura. I guess I should start by saying that we are interested in smart, educated, motivated people, who are driven to solve environmental problems. That's what we do here. We are a law firm, specializing in environmental law. A good deal of the time, we are hired by the world congress to go after violators of environmental law.

"Environmental law is actually an enormous area right now, with many branches. For example, there is air pollution, water pollution, hazardous waste disposal, wetlands preservation, and preservation of endangered animal species, to name a few. We are all passionate believers in saving the planet, and, even though we are not the engineers who design and fix things, we are critically important whistle-blowers. Without us and people like us, the world could go to hell very quickly."

"That certainly sounds interesting and necessary," said Laura. "But I have no background in law."

"That isn't a requirement," said Charles. "If you join us, we will send you to law school. As an employee of our firm, you will be admitted automatically. You do not have to take an entrance exam. Law school is 6 quarters, or eighteen months of schooling, followed by an exam at the end. The exam is not that tough. Something like 90% of the applicants pass it on their first try. We will support you while you are in law school, picking up all your expenses."

"What if I flunk the exam at the end?"

"You take some time and study your course material, then try again when you are ready. Eventually, you will pass it and become a lawyer. But I honestly cannot imagine you flunking this test. You are a very intelligent woman, and, like I said, the test is not that hard."

"Is there anything for me to do while I am in school, besides studying?"

"Yes, Laura. You will have the title of legal aide, and you will be an employee of our firm. We would like you to sit in on some of our trials as an observer. If you want, you can take on some tasks to assist the legal team. But I want to stress that all this will be voluntary. Your first priority is to get through school and pass the exam at the end."

"Are there any trials going on right now that I can take a quick look at?"

"As a matter of fact, yes. And it is in our building. A Mr. Jeff Cantrell is suing the world congress over a land issue. A few years ago, he bought some land along the coast. He intended to build a luxury resort there. First, he wanted a seawall to keep salt water from the ocean from getting into his hotel. He was denied a permit for the seawall, and he escalated his complaint to the world congress. The world congress also denied him the permit. Occasional rough weather drove the water level up toward his hotel. Mr. Cantrell is complaining that his luxury resort has lost a lot of value because what is normally a sandy beach often becomes an ugly salt water wetland. We are defending the world congress in this action. Our point is that Mr. Cantrell wanted to build his seawall below the high tide mark, thus interfering with nature and the normal functioning of tide pools.

"So, if you would like, let's take a walk down the hall and see a portion of this."

Laura immediately agreed, and they walked to the courtroom.

When they arrived, a scientist was testifying about the average high and low tides in the vicinity of Mr. Cantrell's property. The average high tide mark was quite a bit behind where Mr. Cantrell wanted to build his seawall. In fact, the 95% high tide mark was also behind the proposed seawall site. In other words, at least 95% of all high tides would be blocked by Mr. Cantrell's seawall.

Next, a biologist came to testify about the importance of tide pools in the overall ecosystem. "Tide pools are home to several animal species such as sea anemones, starfish, crabs, mussels, and many more. The diversity of life in a tide pool rivals that in the Amazon rain forest. Many of today's life forms had their original homes millions of years ago in the tide pools, where they started to evolve. In the past, humanity has been much too careless about tide pools and wetlands in general. As a result, there has been a mass extinction of several species and a critical loss to our ecosystem. Among the extinct species have been not only the inhabitants of the tide pools, but animals who feed on those animals. Massive population declines have been seen in some fish, and cormorants, and even seagulls, because of our careless mismanagement of tide pools."

Next came the final arguments. Mr. Cantrell's lawyer spoke first. He said that the numbers and types of extinct or endangered species were greatly exaggerated, and, besides that, there was no proof that depletion of tide pools was the cause of those deaths. He said that the impact of Mr. Cantrell's project on the environment was so miniscule that it was impossible to measure. But the benefit to humanity far outweighed the costs. The luxury hotel with its many amenities including a bright sandy beach was worth the small cost.

Then the lawyer for Charles Fink's firm had his turn. "Mr. Cantrell has many options of where to build his luxury hotel. He doesn't need to build it in the middle of a tide pool. At this point, he could simply sell the land, and move on to a more eco-friendly location. Even if he wants to stay where he is, he could build the hotel on a small hill about 200 yards further from the sea than he is now. His guests could still enjoy a sandy beach. The tide pool might spoil a little bit of the view, but only during extreme high and low tides." In short, he did not recognize Mr. Cantrell's right to interfere with nature to that degree. Building the seawall below the high tide mark shows a blatant disregard for the environment, and should not be allowed.

The judge announced the end of the proceedings, and said that he would return shortly with a decision. He left the courtroom to go into an adjoining chamber. Four other judges followed him.

"What's going on?" Laura asked.

"In this type of trial, where there is a lawsuit involved, a team of five judges determines the outcome. One of those judges is the judge who presided over the case. The other four are chosen randomly before the trial, then observe the trial. At the end, they vote. The presiding judge only votes to break a possible tie."

"And what about criminal cases?"

"When the guilt or innocence of a defendant is at stake, then there is a normal trial by jury, which I guess you have seen before. There are twelve jurors, and they must reach a unanimous decision one way or the other."

"So what happens now? How long will we be here waiting?"

"Usually no longer than half an hour. If you want to take a break and get something to drink, now would be a good time."

"Okay," said Laura. "I'll be back in a few minutes. I don't want to miss the verdict."

Laura walked over to the cafeteria, and got a cookie and some bottled water. Then she sat for a few minutes, eating her snack and reflecting. She had to admit, this was the most interesting job so far. And she had a definite plan for coming up to speed. And, things were not so different from what she was used to. She was comfortable with the people she met so far. They all dressed casually, even the lawyers arguing the case. Mr. Fink seemed easy to get along with, and he would be providing her with free schooling and a path forward where she could become a lawyer. She never thought of herself as a lawyer, but being a lawyer was the best option. Laura felt comfortable with this decision.

She finished her snack and went back to the courtroom. She found Mr. Fink, and sat next to him.

"We're still waiting," he said.

"Well, it's only been a few minutes," commented Laura. She could see that Mr. Fink was nervous as he awaited the judgment.

Laura and Mr. Fink sat in nervous silence for some minutes, waiting for the verdict. Eventually, the five judges entered the courtroom. The presiding judge sat at the desk, pounded the gavel, and spoke.

"We have two votes on the side of the world congress, and one vote on the side of Mr. Cantrell. We have one judge who chose to abstain and did not vote. Therefore, judgment is for the defendant, the world congress, and Mr. Cantrell's suit is denied legitimacy."

With that, the group of five judges together left the courtroom, avoiding any possibility of argument or protest. Mr. Fink made his way through the crowd to congratulate the victorious lawyer, Carl Langdon. The two shook hands and patted each other's backs. Mr. Fink waved to Laura to come join them.

"Carl, I'd like you to meet our hopeful new hire, Laura."

"The same Laura whose husband is lost in space?"

"We don't really know where he is or how he's doing," Laura quickly chimed in. "All we know is that he's late coming back."

Carl smiled, and shook hands with Laura. "Well, we certainly pray for his eventual safe return," he said.

"Thank you so much," said Laura, holding back some tears.

The group of three walked out of the courtroom to the cafeteria for some lunch. "I'm buying," said Mr. Fink.

The two men had steak. Laura had a turkey dinner. It tasted wonderful.

"All the workers here are robots?" Laura asked.

"Of course," said Carl, and Laura felt like she had just asked a stupid question.

"Laura is still experiencing some minor culture shock," said Mr. Fink. "After all, for her this is thirteen hundred years in the future."

"No robots back then?" asked Carl.

"Some robots, and lots of self-driving cars. But not anything like today."

"What was your biggest adjustment when you came to our world in the future, Laura?"

"Well, surprisingly, it's not all that different from where I came from. Science fiction of my day pictured the future as totally bizarre – people flying around the cities in hovercrafts dodging the 200 story buildings and artificial intelligence running the world. It's not like that at all, although technology certainly has advanced a long way. Nuclear energy has emerged as the clean new energy source, fossil fuels have taken a back seat, robots are everywhere, and you pay for a lot of things with your thumbprint. So there definitely are some big differences. But it isn't outright crazy.

"But I do have a question for you guys, if it's okay."

"Sure, Laura," said Mr. Fink. "Anything."

"What about robots taking over the legal profession. Can robots be effective lawyers, and cheaper than humans?"

"Parts of the legal profession are very mechanical, like writing a will, getting a divorce, or selling property, for example," said Fink. "And in those areas, there is a future for the robots. In fact, some of this work is already done by robots. They are somewhat successful at it, and that trend will likely continue. Trial law is another story entirely. Trial lawyers need to be able to read people, figure out what they are thinking, and figure out how to get the most information from them. It is not a mechanical process, nor can it be reduced to one. Trial lawyers often need to think creatively, and this is where robots fail miserably. If something can't be reduced to a programmable algorithm, then a robot just can't do it. Trial law is something that robots will not be able to do in the foreseeable future."

Laura nodded thoughtfully. After a few seconds of silence, Fink finally said, "So what do you think, Laura? Would you like to become a lawyer?"

"Yes," said Laura. "I would like to join your group, if you will have me."

"Okay, Laura, glad to hear it. I'll put an offer letter together and mail it to you. Do you have an address yet?"

"Yes," said Laura, and gave him her address. "But this house actually belongs to the space agency. I still don't have a place of my own."

"No problem, Laura. I'll send it out to this address. When can you start?"

"I need a few weeks to take care of personal business. I need a house, a car, some furniture, probably a robot. Then I can devote my full energy to becoming a lawyer. So, to answer your question, ho about three weeks from today?"

"That would be great, Laura, and we'll be glad to have you." Fink and Carl stood up, and they both shook hands with Laura.

36

Laura moved along quite efficiently with her shopping. There was only one of her, so she bought a small three-bedroom house in a swank gated community. She bought an inexpensive robot to help with cooking, grocery shopping, and housecleaning. She bought a compact car to get around in. Finally, she bought clothes for herself and furniture for the house.

When her shopping was done, and she was settled in at her new house, she stopped by Mr. Fink's office.

"My school doesn't start for another month, Mr. Fink. I need something to do. Can I look in on one of your cases?"

"Well, first of all, Laura, you are now an employee, so you may call me Charlie, instead of Mr. Fink. And, yes, you can actually participate in one of our cases. There is a large outbreak of gastroenteritis in Africa, along the Niger River. The world congress has solicited our help in investigating and remedying the situation. Some violation of environmental law may be the culprit. So, are you ready to fly to Africa, Laura?"

"I would have to get a passport first."

"You won't need one. You are thinking of your own time when there were independent nations dotting the globe. That is not the case anymore."

"Do I need to get shots?"

"Yes, to go to that part of the world, you need to get vaccinated for malaria, yellow fever, cholera, and typhoid. If you agree to making this trip, I will arrange for you to get these shots as soon as possible, probably this afternoon."

"Okay, let's do it."

Charlie Fink grabbed his phone and sent some messages. In a few minutes, he announced that Laura could get her shots at once. He would have one of his drivers take Laura to the health clinic. In a few minutes, an older bald man appeared, and introduced himself as Ernie. He showed Laura to a car, gave an address to the car, and they were off.

The procedure for getting the shots was painless. The staff was expecting Laura, they had her shots ready, and all Laura needed to do was sign something that looked like a consent form. She got four shots, two in each arm, and that was the end of it. She asked about side effects from the shots and was told that there were no side effects. She thanked the clinic, and went back with Ernie to his car.

Ernie was a shy, quiet man, which was fine with Laura. She wasn't sure what she could talk about with Ernie. He seemed like a nice guy, who did menial tasks for the law firm. Laura guessed that Ernie was just doing some work to help fund his retirement, something like that. So Laura, the budding young prospective lawyer, felt awkward in starting a conversation with Ernie. So they drove back to the office in silence.

"Okay, good," said Charlie when they returned. "I've got us set to leave for Africa in two hours."

"What?" said Laura in disbelief. Things happened so fast here. "Wow, I guess I need to hustle and pack my bags."

"Do you have a robot?"

"Yes."

"The robot can pack your bags. Tell the robot that you expect to be gone for two weeks in a sub-tropical climate. The robot will have everything packed for you by the time you drive home."

Laura did as Charlie had advised. When she got home, her bags were neatly packed, and her robot wished her a happy and successful trip.

Laura returned to the office.

"Are you ready?" Charlie asked. "We're just about ready to take off."

"But we have to get to the airport and everything."

"No airport. We leave from here in my private plane. It's parked on the roof."

"Okay," said Laura, swallowing hard. "I guess I'm ready."

She picked up her bags, and followed Charlie up a flight of stairs to the roof. When she stepped outside, the air felt frigid and very windy. She glanced around at the neighboring buildings. This country was her home. Now she was heading off to Africa.

She and Charlie climbed into the plane, which was big enough to carry twenty passengers. Charlie occupied the pilot's seat. Laura sat in the adjacent passenger cabin by a window. Charlie seemed to be going through a pre-flight checklist.

"Okay, here we go," he eventually announced to Laura. The plane lifted off vertically, banked to the right, and sped off to the east, as it continued to climb through broken clouds. There was some turbulence, but not that much. Laura had expected a bumpy takeoff, after seeing how windy it was outside.

In a few minutes, Charlie came into the cabin and sat across the aisle from Laura. "How are you doing so far?" he asked.

"I was expecting more turbulence. After all, it is a very windy day."

"The technology of flight has improved quite a bit since your time, Laura. We use gyroscopic microprocessors in the wings that dampen the turbulence and steady the aircraft. You don't feel much at all. By the way, we're headed for a city called Niamey. It's along the Niger River in an area that is being invaded by the desert. We start our investigation there."

"I know the place," said Laura, and Charlie glanced at her in surprise. "I did some volunteer work there when I graduated from college."

"How did you like it? How did you adapt?"

"I was pleasantly surprised. I was expecting a harsh climate, and very alien customs, tough for a woman. It was not bad at all. In fact, Niamey was a beautiful city of about 2 million people, and I did not see horrible starvation and poverty. I remember there were nice museums, a horse racing track, movie theaters, even a nice theme park."

"Well, brace yourself, Laura. Niamey now has over ten million people. A lot of them live in filthy slums with no running water. All their water comes from the Niger River, and the Niger River is where they dump their waste. The place stinks, literally."

"My God, what happened?"

"A combination of a lot of factors, Laura. Desertification was maybe the biggest. Poor farming and poor land management created desert out of what was once green pasture. Now the only green that you see is right along the river. Go a mile in either direction from the river and you are walking through sand dunes. There are no edible crops anymore."

"Then how do the people eat?"

"Whatever livestock is left provides food for the people. But the livestock have to eat the grass because there is nothing else for them, and the grass goes away. As land management experts around the world will tell you, livestock consumes way more food than it provides. The people would be better off transitioning to a vegetarian diet, and living as best they can off the land."

"And the livestock drink out of the river, I suppose?"

"Yes, and they leave behind the parasite cryptosporidium."

"Huh?"

"Cryptosporidium comes from cattle. It is pretty harmless to cattle, but potentially deadly to humans. My first guess as to what is causing the gastroenteritis is the cryptosporidium parasites from the cattle. The cattle not only drink from the river, but they eat the plants along the sides of the river, and the runoff goes into the river. The people use the river as their only source of drinking water, so there you have it."

"But that is just an educated guess, right? You don't know this for a fact."

"Yes, you are right, Laura. I have seen this before, so it is my first suspicion."

"So what are a couple of lawyers supposed to do about this? And, sorry, I'm using the term loosely because I am not a lawyer yet."

"Well, first, we have to investigate, taking chemical samples of the river water. If we can identify the contaminant in the river, then there are several things that we can do or recommend. First, if clear blame can be assigned to a person or group of persons, then this could be a cause for legal action. Second, if there is anything that we can suggest to give immediate short-term relief to the population, then we should make those suggestions."

"What if we don't find anything?"

"We will definitely find something. A large portion of the population is sick from some kind of contaminant. We need to figure out what is going on, to the best of our ability. If we don't have a definitive final answer, then we make recommendations for further investigation."

"Okay," Laura said, glancing out the window at the night sky. "When will we be arriving?"

"Early morning, local time. Go ahead and get some sleep." Charlie stood up and walked to the cockpit.

<h1 style="text-align:center">37</h1>

A young African man met them at the airport in Niamey. He introduced himself as Obele, and said that he knew the city very well. He spoke fluent English, which was natural. English had been the one official language of the Earth for several hundred years. Obele led them to his car, which was quite old and rusty, but functional. He drove them to their hotel, which was close to the airport. The hotel was a rickety wooden structure with three floors, and several cracked windows. They checked in, left their luggage in the room, then came back out to Obele. Charlie explained that they would like to drive around the city a bit, and then rent a boat to take some chemical samples of the water at various parts of the river. Obele nodded, and then headed off into the city.

The city was as bad or worse than what Charlie had described. There were a few tall buildings in the downtown area, but the rest of the city was a ramshackle, crowded slum. The streets were littered with human waste and other sewage. Naked children ran around playing in the garbage and running through the liquid sewage in the streets. Young kids played games chasing the rats around the piles of garbage. Cars muddled their way through the sewage-filled streets. Many of them were parked in the middle of the street, obstructing traffic, but no one seemed to care.

Laura was shocked. The progress that had been made was on display in America, but Sub-Saharan Africa had been left behind. Obele drove an old car, but at least it was nuclear-powered and had a computer inside. So there were a few modern conveniences like that, but the sanitation was dreadful. They came to a small marina on the shore of the river.

"We can rent a boat here," said Obele, stepping out of the car and heading toward the marina's office. Laura looked out over the river. It was about a mile wide here, and filled with garbage. Ducks and other birds were not there. Obele returned and directed them to a small motorboat. Charlie brought along his measuring equipment and chemical testing gear.

"There's quite a bit of measuring that I want to do," said Charlie. "It will probably take us most of the day. First, I'd like to head north, upstream, past the city limits."

"Okay," said Obele, as he steered the boat into the middle of the river, and angled upstream. They rode for quite some time through muddy, polluted, garbage-filled water. Finally, they passed the edge of the city. Charlie told Obele to go a few miles further upstream where they would start their measurements.

The rest of the day was taken up with measurements along the river. They started far north of the city and headed south, took measurements every two miles until they were far to the south of the city. When they were done for the day, Charlie gave Obele a nice tip, and thanked him effusively. Back at the hotel, Charlie started to analyze the data he had collected. Laura sat by Charlie as he worked tirelessly into the night.

"Cryptosporidium is being generated by something north of the city," Charlie finally commented. "The concentration levels are highest when we are north, upstream from the city. As for the other poisonous pollutants, they are all coming from the city itself. As you have observed, Laura, the sanitation is dreadful. It will be a huge cleanup effort to make this a livable community again. Then we have to remember that Niamey is not the only city in sub-Saharan Africa. The entire region I'm sure has similar issues. But, all that aside for now, tomorrow we need to take another boat ride and find the source of the cryptosporidium."

"Okay," said Laura, and, with that, they both lay down and quickly went to sleep.

They woke up in the morning, had a breakfast of rice cakes and pastry, and Charlie called Oblele for a ride to the marina. Obele came shortly, they hopped into his car, and were off to the marina. The ride upriver went well. Oblele was with them and pointed out occasional landmarks and points of interest. Charlie kept taking measurements that showed increasing concentrations of cryptosporidium.

"We have to be getting closer to the source," Charlie announced. But they kept going upriver, seemingly forever. Measurements every few miles still indicated elevated and increasing levels of cryptosporidium. Finally, they rounded a bend in the river, and there was a group of about one hundred cattle grazing on what little grass there remained along the side of the river. They were also drinking from the river, and some were wading into the river to cool off and wash themselves.

"I think this is it," announced Charlie. "Let's take some more measurements upstream just to make sure, but my guess is we found the problem."

They rode about five miles further upstream, and took measurements. Sure enough, the cryptosporidium readings were down to zero.

Charlie asked Obele to park the boat by a small sandy beach. They all stepped out of the boat and sat on the beach.

"Well, here is where I see things right now," said Charlie. "The city of Niamey has two big problems. One is cryptosporidium. The other is deplorable sanitation. Cryptosporidium comes from the large herd of cattle. These cattle have to be relocated. The problem is, we have to find a place to relocate them where they have a water supply and where they can graze peacefully. We just can't have them poisoning a river that is the main source of drinking water for the city.

"As far as sanitation, you look eager to speak, Laura."

"Yes," said Laura. "First, they need a reliable source of fresh water. Their wells are close to running dry. A good answer is to desalinate ocean water, then use pipelines to get it up to where it is needed. This is very expensive, but I think necessary. Then they need modernized sewage treatment plants, like we have in America. Both these things are expensive but necessary, in my opinion."

"I think we all have to agree with you, Laura. I will write that in my report and make those recommendations. I'm not sure how that will go over with the World Council because of the cost involved, but we do have to make those recommendations. I would just add that we probably need a massive network of pipelines through this part of Africa to provide clean water. So there would have to be a series of studies to evaluate the sanitary conditions throughout all of sub-Saharan Africa to do our planning for clean water."

"Yes," said Laura. "But how do we relocate the herd of cattle?"

"I think the best we can do is report the situation to the local authorities downtown," said Obele. "They will know best where the cattle can be moved."

They got back in the boat, returned to the marina, loaded themselves into Obele's car, and drove downtown. They met the mayor, a friendly man named Mboya, and exchanged business cards. They explained the situation with the cattle upriver from the city. Part of Laura was shocked that the local people could not discover this problem on their own. She didn't know whether to blame it on the lack of good measurement tools, or on downright laziness. The mayor politely thanked them. Then they discussed the sanitation problem. Laura explained the far-reaching idea of desalinating ocean water in the far south and piping the desalinated water to Niamey. But, she presumed that there would be a huge swath of cities in Sub-Saharan Africa that would need the same thing, so they would really need a network of pipelines. It would be an issue for the World Council. The mayor was extremely sympathetic and urged them to talk to the World Council, in person if possible.

When Laura and Charlie left the building, they decided to make a quick jaunt to the World Council Headquarters. The location of the headquarters rotated through many sites, but right now was in Tokyo. The 8000 mile flight would take about 12 hours with a nine hour time difference. Charlie estimated an arrival in Tokyo around 2PM the following afternoon.

Obele drove them to their hotel, where they packed their things, and headed to the airport. Charlie and Laura thanked Oblele, gave him a nice tip, and they boarded the plane, and took off for Tokyo.

Once they had come to their cruising altitude, Charlie messaged the World Council, saying that they were coming, gave an approximate ETA, and requested a meeting. A response came in a couple of minutes, confirming a meeting time for 4PM local time tomorrow. Charlie thanked them and signed off.

The plane headed northeast through the barren and rocky Sahara Desert, just as darkness began to fall as the sun set behind them. Much of the trip would take place at night, so Laura leaned back in her seat and went to sleep.

When Laura woke up, it was daytime and they were flying over the Himalayas. Laura's first impression was that the flight over the mountains was amazingly smooth. She was thankful for the modern turbulence-damping technology on Charlie's plane. Laura stared at the mountains in fascination. They were smothered in snow. Row after row of ridges lined the landscape, like wrinkles in potato chips. The valleys in between were also smothered in snow, but Laura could make out occasional green areas, so-called "snow shadows", where snowfall was blocked by mountains.

Beyond the mountains was the plateau, the Yangtze River valley, and, eventually, the flat farmland and rice fields. Laura expected to see a lot of pollution, but there was actually little or none. It was very clear and sunny with no dust or smoke and no evidence of pollution. The Yangtze River was blue. They continued eastward, with the sinuous Yangtze River sometimes in sight. As the afternoon approached, they flew over the port of Shanghai. Laura expected to see dense clouds of pollution, but, in fact, the air was clean. Shanghai appeared to be a clean, beautiful city that had seemingly solved its massive air pollution problems of centuries ago.

The rest of the flight was over the Yellow Sea, and then the islands of Kyushu and Shiloku, and the Seto Inland Sea. Off to the left, Laura could see the enormous Lake Biwa, and then finally the spectacular Mt. Fuji. By now, the plane was well into its descent toward Tokyo, flying over the scenic, snowy, Japanese countryside.

Charlie phoned in to the World Council and asked permission to land on their premises. He was given approval along with coordinates of a large aircraft parking lot that the World Council owned and used. Minutes later they were on the ground. Laura stepped out of the plane and stretched her legs in the cool, invigorating Japanese air. She took a quick look around, and saw many tall, modern buildings. Tokyo seemed to her a very modern, clean, beautiful city. The streets were clean and free of litter. After coming from the stench of Niamey, the contrast was striking.

They walked into the main entrance of the World Council offices. The lobby was extraordinarily ornate. Large statues and busts decorated the perimeter. There was a gift shop and a jewelry store. Laura felt like she needed to be more dressed up to come here. People mulling around the lobby were dressed in exquisite and expensive clothes. Laura, having just come from Niamey, and then a long plane ride, was dressed for comfort, not for show. She was wearing a tee shirt, blue jeans, and tennis shoes, that had gotten dirty from the dust and mud in Niamey. She felt very out of place. Charlie seemed to sense her discomfort, and touched her hand lightly. "It's okay," he said. "The World Council is anxious to hear of our research and recommendations. They don't care how we're dressed. Come on, let's grab something to eat before we head upstairs." Charlie pointed to a long hallway, branching off into a food court. They went into a cafeteria-style area, where Laura ordered Miso soup and chicken teriyaki. She wasn't sure what Charlie ordered. It looked to her like unrecognizable slush.

As they were eating, Charlie asked, "Do you think you can talk about the possible water desalination project and network of pipelines?"

"Sure," said Laura. "I would be honored."

"Good," said Charlie, shoveling a spoonful of mush into his mouth. "I can talk about the outbreak of cryptosporidium. But I have to say, your part is tougher."

"Why is that?"

"Because nobody is going to like the runaway costs of the pipeline network. Don't let that bother you. Just go through the facts and present your proposal, even though it cannot be finalized yet."

"Okay," said Laura.

They finished their food, and Charlie messaged the man they were supposed to meet with. He said that someone would be coming to the food court to show them the way.

A young man dressed in an expensive suit came by to meet them. Laura and Charlie must have been easy to find, because at 3 PM they were the only customers in the food court. He introduced himself as Iwate, and proceeded to escort them to the elevators, and then to the seventh floor to meet Mr. Omura.

Mr. Omura was a tall, thin man, who appeared to be vigorously healthy. He motioned them to sit on a couch, while he sat at a large desk, facing them. He spoke impeccable English, and asked how their trip was. Charlie explained that it was a long flight from Niamey, but they had managed to sleep through most of it. Omura commented that he had heard of Laura and her experience, coming from the year 2446. He asked her how she was coping with the culture shock. Laura explained that it was more of a culture adaptation than a culture shock. "Things are certainly different now than in my previous day," Laura said, "but not shockingly different, and I am quickly adjusting."

Omura leaned back in his seat, folded his hands on the top of his head, and asked about Niamey. Charlie began by explaining the outbreak of cryptosporidium, and how they had determined it was from a large herd of cattle upstream from the city.

"The challenge is in relocating the cattle," Charlie went on to explain. "We don't know who owns the cattle, if anyone. They may have just been abandoned. Then, of course, wherever we move them, the cattle need drinking water and grazing land. Now they are poisoning the Niger River, which, unfortunately, is the only source of drinking water for the city of Niamey."

"How many cattle are there?" asked Omura.

"About two hundred, give or take."

"That is a problem," Omura said. "Can the local authorities help?"

"We hope so," said Charlie. "We have already met with them about this problem."

"What did they say?"

"Not much, unfortunately. Just that they would look into it and think about it."

"Do you have a contact there?"

"Yes," said Charlie, as he handed over Mboya's business card. "This man is the mayor of Niamey."

"I see," said Omura, fingering the card. "I will call him directly, and we will work something out. In the worst case, we will airlift the cattle out of the area, but we have to do something to save the population."

"Laura has something she would like to talk about," said Charlie, to break a silence. "It might even be a long-term solution to this issue."

"Okay," said Omura. "I'm very interested, Laura. What do you have?"

"Well, first, I'd like to show you some video that I took of the conditions there."

Laura grabbed her phone, pressed a few buttons, and showed Omura the video. For a few minutes, Omura looked at human waste in the streets, naked children playing in the sewage, cars and houses covered in filth.

"They have a serious sanitation issue," said Laura.

"Yes," said Omura. "As do a number of large cities in that part of the world. Nairobi, Addis Ababa, Khartoum, Ouagadoogoo. It is a problem of worldwide concern."

"I don't want to be out of place here, but it seems they need a rework of their sewers and sanitation systems. They need some state-of-the-art sewage treatment plants."

"I think we all agree," said Omura. "The thing is, we don't have an infinite amount of money, and all this over a large swath of Africa is expensive as hell."

"I'm afraid it gets worse," said Laura, smiling. "The drinking water that they get from the Niger River is clearly not safe. So, how do we get them healthy drinking water? Well, the obvious quick answer is we pull water from the river and siphon it through a network of filters, then pass it on to the city. This approach has some problems. First, the Niger River will eventually run dry with so much water going to the city. In fact, this is an issue now even, since the river is the only source of drinking water for ten million people. But siphoning the water through a filter system will use up even more water from the river.

"A second approach is to desalinate ocean water, and pump it up to Niamey. The technology to do this is there. The only concern is the cost of piping it so far."

"Yes," said Omura. "Desalinating ocean water is already used to supply fresh water to many parts of the world, notably some major metropolitan areas, like Karachi, Mumbai, Kolkata, Mecca, Tel Aviv, and on and on. The thing is, those places are all fairly close to the ocean and the cost of piping the water is manageable. In the case of Niamey, the water would have to be pumped a large distance with a considerable elevation gain."

"I would remind your honor, Omura, that we probably have the same problem throughout all of Sub-Sharan Africa. I doubt that Niamey is a special case. There is also Timbuktu, N'djamena, Khartoum, Ouagadoogoo. So if we build a pipeline for Niamey, that could be the start of a network of pipelines that could supply all of Sub-Saharan Africa."

"You make a good point, Laura," said Omura, rubbing his palm across his chin. "It's expensive but it may be our only option. We need to do a cost study and see if we can shoehorn this into the budget. Of course, my fear is that the idea will not be approved, and the people in Sub-Saharan Africa will not see any change soon."

"On humanitarian grounds, there can be nothing to dispute," said Laura. "The living conditions there are not suitable for human beings."

"That is certainly true," said Omura. "Your video is quite graphic. I will do my best to make your case."

"What about sewage treatment plants?"

"Yes," said Omura. "I already have that in my notes. I can get a cost estimate for that, but the sewage treatment and the fresh drinking water are two issues that are linked together."

"Well, thank you for taking the time to see us," said Charlie, taking his cue from a long silence.

"You're very welcome," said Omura. "I'm impressed with your work on the cryptosporidium outbreak, and with your ideas for fresh water. "

They stood up and shook hands. Omura gave a pleasant wave of his hand, and they were gone. Charlie and Laura rode the elevator back down to the first floor, grabbed a quick snack at the food court, and got on their plane. It would be a long flight across the Pacific. It dawned on Laura that this last leg of her trip would complete her circumnavigation of the world.

38

Laura started school a few days after she got back home. She quickly realized that school would be a very difficult challenge. She was a thousand plus years behind the times. Everyone in law school was extremely bright. The instructors spoke at an advanced level and often were not good at expressing themselves clearly. Laura would usually come out of a lecture with her head spinning, and realizing that she had not grasped a single concept in the last hour. She kept reminding herself that she was highly motivated and disciplined, and she could close the gap between herself and the other students. It was just a matter of working hard and staying focused. But self-doubts still lingered. Could she really do this? Was Charlie being too optimistic about how easy this would be for her?

Her first courses covered the basics of law. There were courses in contract law, property law, torts, and introductory environmental law, her chosen profession. She fell into a routine of going to class in the morning, exercising and having lunch at midday, then going to class in the afternoon, then coming home and doing homework and studying. She found herself going to bed later and later, and getting up earlier and earlier. She knew she was cheating herself on sleep. But there seemed to be no choice. She needed the time to study, or she wasn't going to make it.

One day after her morning class, a girl approached her.

"Hi," she said. "My name is Debra, and I guess you are Laura. I'm hungry. Want to go to lunch?"

Laura was somewhat taken aback, but she agreed, and they went to a cafeteria style restaurant that featured vegetarian dishes. They filled their plates and sat down.

"I've heard about you," said Debra. "Whether you know it or not, you are quite famous."

"Yes," said Laura. "I am slowly figuring that out. But I didn't do anything to become famous. My husband is somewhere lost in outer space, or at least late in returning. That's why I am famous."

"You are overly humble," said Debra. "Maybe you didn't do anything courageous or provocative, but the way you are handling the situation is admirable."

Laura shrugged. "I don't know. I am doing what I have to do to get by in this new time, far in the future for me."

"How are you doing so far in your courses?"

"They are very hard for me. I am studying really hard, trying to keep up."

"I think it's hard for all of us," said Debra.

"Are you married?" asked Laura.

"No, and probably fortunately. The married students seem to be having the hardest time in law school. Trying to get through law school, and being a good wife and mother, seems next to impossible. I don't know how the married students can manage at all. I admire them for just being here."

"So how are you doing with your classes, Debra?"

"I don't know because we haven't had any tests yet. It's hard, I have to agree with you."

"Can you offer me any advice on how to study, how to pass all my classes, anything at all?"

"Funny you should ask," said Debra. "I'm trying to form a study group. Would you like to be a part of it?"

"Sure, I guess. What is a study group?"

"I'm thinking of a small group, four people, maybe five. Each person specializes in one subject. When we meet, each person goes through the key points for the week in his or her subject. So we all benefit from each person giving a good summary. Then we go off on our own and do our homework, but using what we have learned in the study group."

"I want environmental law," said Laura.

"So I take it you want to be in it. It seems like you can have environmental law. So far the group is you, me, and one other lady, Tammy. Tammy wants to do property. Myself, I'm thinking about contracts, but, as the group leader, I have to stay flexible."

"Great. So when do we meet?"

"Well, I guess we could start meeting, but we need more people to really get going. I was thinking about Wednesday evenings at 7PM. How does that sound?"

"Okay," said Laura. So the first meeting is day after tomorrow. See you then."

39

There were four people who showed up Wednesday for the study group. Besides Laura, Debra, and Tamara, there was a new lady named Carla. They all got introduced to each other and chatted a little.

When they got down to business, they each took turns to present their material to the others. Laura went first and talked about the case of the piping plover, an endangered species of bird that nests on the dunes of a remote beach along the Pacific. Recently, a profit-hungry corporation opened the beach up to dune buggies and other off-road vehicles. The habitat and nesting grounds of the piping plover were being endangered. To Laura, the case seemed straightforward. The beach needed to be closed off to vehicle traffic to protect an endangered species. The corporation argued that there was a lot of revenue being generated by the permits to use vehicles on the beach. Much of this revenue was being pumped into the local economy, and much of it was being paid in taxes. And the beach offered tremendous recreational value to the tourists. The fate of the piping plover on this particular beach was insignificant when weighed against the benefits. The piping plover had many habitats and nesting places, not just this one beach. Laura concluded by saying that the endangered species needed to be protected, and that idea trumped the opposing arguments.

The others agreed with her, but generated a lot of discussion. They asked where the beach was located, what the piping plover's preferred climate was, and how many other beaches were suitable for the bird. Laura wasn't able to answer all the questions. Many times, she just had to say that she would have to look into it.

Next, Tamara talked about a case in property law. One person was suing another, claiming that part of his land had been taken from him. When he bought his land, he had paid for it based on its measured area. The person had neighbors on either side of him. Something was suspicious, because the person could not possibly own as much land as he had bought without infringing on the land of the neighbors. So what can be done? Tamara suggested an independent expert should measure the land that the person now owned. The expert should also measure the land of the neighbors. From this data, there would be a number of possibilities. If the neighbors had more land than they bought, then some of it should go to the original plaintiff. The tricky part comes if the neighbors had the correct amount of land, and the plaintiff was short. Here, Tamara argued, the plaintiff should sue the person who sold him the land in the first place, and get monetary compensation for the missing land.

Laura thought that Tamara's recommendation was logical. But, as the girls argued about it, it was obvious that the case was not simple at all. Had the land gone up in value since the plaintiff bought it? If so, how should the plaintiff be compensated? Then, in the case where the plaintiff could claim a piece of the land from his neighbors, a bunch of new questions arose. What if he still didn't have enough land? Could he take the land from a neighbor, and then the neighbor now didn't have all his land? Then the neighbor could sue the other neighbor next to him, and the process could go on forever. That didn't seem right, but as Laura was beginning to appreciate, law was an incredibly complicated area of study.

Then Debra spoke on a case from contract law. A woman had gone to a plastic surgeon to get the size of her nose reduced. When the surgery was completed, the size was reduced, but there were several unsightly scars in and around the nose. The woman was suing the medical clinic that did the work. The tricky question was calculating the right amount to sue for. Debra suggested bringing in an unbiased outside expert to examine the damage. If the scars could heal in time, then the woman should be compensated for the lost amount of time while the scars were healing. If the scars could be surgically repaired, then the defendant clinic would have to bear the cost of this surgery. If the scars would not heal on their own, and no reconstructive surgery was possible, then the woman should sue for permanent damage to her appearance. This last case was the most complicated. Was the woman's career affected by the damage to her appearance? In that case, the amount of the suit would be significant, but it could be estimated. If there was no impact from her career, she could still sue on the basis of changes to her appearance. For this, Debra recommended researching similar past cases to help determine a fair amount to sue.

Finally, Carla spoke about a case involving torts. A motorist put his car in manual mode, disabling the computer. Why he did this is an open question.

But, while in manual mode, he struck a bicyclist, breaking his leg and giving him a serious concussion and likely brain damage. But the bicyclist was breaking the law for not wearing a helmet. The question became the degree of liability of the motorist. Was the motorist liable for all of the injuries, or just for the non-head injuries? Carla argued that, even if the bicyclist were wearing a helmet, his head struck the ground with such force that he would still probably suffer a serious concussion. Also, when the motorist went into manual mode, he was implicitly assuming responsibility for any damage and injury that might happen as a result. Therefore, Carla argued, the motorist should be held fully liable for all injuries. Much group discussion followed. The main question was determining how much brain damage could be avoided if the bicyclist was wearing a helmet. This was not an easy question at all, and could only be estimated by laboratory testing with dummies. Carla suggested that some studies may have already been done to determine this exact point, and it was just a matter of doing the research and legwork. In the end, the motorist's liability would be the bicycle, the non-head injuries to the victims, and the portion of the head injuries which would result, whether or not the victim was wearing a helmet. Everyone agreed with this, and decided it was time to dismiss the meeting. It was now a little after 10PM. The meeting had lasted just about three hours.

Laura was exhausted as she walked home. The study group had helped her tremendously. She was beginning to appreciate the law, and how complicated things were when the law was involved. There were always two sides to each case, no matter how simple things seemed at first glance.

She saw Debra in class the next day, and told her how the study group had really helped her, and that she appreciated Debra's efforts in starting it up. Debra modestly replied that the study group was as good as the people in it, and she was nothing more than an organizer and catalyst. She asked Laura out to lunch again, and Laura quickly agreed.

They talked the whole time at lunch about their classes and about the study group. Debra complimented Laura on her contributions in the meeting. Laura was very touched by the praise.

"So you're planning to stay with the study group, Laura?" Debra asked.

"Of course. It's been a big help to me already. I'm in unless you guys throw me out."

"Don't worry, Laura. That isn't going to happen."

"When are the first tests coming up?" Laura asked.

"All of the beginning students are taking the same classes. So there will be one comprehensive exam, not four individual exams. The big exam will probably be in a couple of weeks. Then three weeks or so after that is the midterm exam. Another few weeks after that is one more exam, and then the big final exam at the end of the quarter."

There were two more meetings of the study group before the first exam.

The class average on the first exam was 82. Debra scored 90, Tamara 87, Carla 86, and Laura 83, one point over average. Laura was ecstatic. It looked like she was going to get through this after all.

40

Laura gradually gained confidence as the quarter forged on. She did okay in the midterms and pretty well in the next set of tests. For the final, the four girls in the study group banded together to study in seclusion for a week before the exam. They met at Laura's house because it was the most spacious. Classes were suspended during the so-called "dead week" leading up to the final exams, so the group was free to spend the whole day at Laura's house studying. They met every day around 9AM, took an afternoon lunch break, then met again for several hours into the evening. By now, the group of four had become close friends.

Debra gave her opinion of the final exam. "The final exam, unfortunately, will be very tough," she said, grimly. "I have an older brother who went through law school, and he passed off some wisdom to me. They try to flunk out the marginal students early. If a bunch of students aren't keeping up, they don't want to string them along for a long time. They want to get rid of them quickly. They look at this as the humanitarian approach. Don't let some poor student struggle for a long time, holding on to a false belief that she or he can make it through law school."

"We have six quarters to get through," said Laura, pointing out what everyone else was already thinking. "So does that mean the finals get easier as we go along?"

"Yes," said Debra. "Of course, at the end of all this is the real exam, the exam that you have to pass to become a lawyer. That is supposed to be pretty tough. But the toughest of all the exams is the one that we are about to take this week."

"What kind of questions will we get on this exam?" asked Laura.

"Mostly open-ended ones," said Debra. "They will give you a bunch of fictitious cases, and ask you to take one side or the other, and make an argument. They might ask one or two specific questions about points of law, but the main emphasis will be on case studies."

"How do we study for something like that?" asked Laura.

"I suggest going through all the case files that we have, reading and understanding the arguments on both sides, and getting a general idea of how lawyers view these things. Chances are, a few of the cases that show up on the final exam will be similar to ones that we have looked at."

"That sounds exactly like what we have been doing," commented Laura. "I guess we just keep on going with it."

"Yes," said Debra, and everyone silently nodded in agreement.

So that is exactly what they did. For hours on end, they plodded through reams of case files, making sure that they understood the arguments on each side before they moved on.

"This is going to take forever," said Laura, as the enormity of the task started to sink in.

"It is a daunting job," Debra agreed. "Let's do the best we can. Obviously, we don't have time to go through everything."

They were getting through about 50 cases per day, which meant that at the end of one week they would have 350 cases examined. That wasn't even half of the number that was in the case book.

But onward they plodded, their brains getting more and more tired with each passing day. At the end of each day, they had a ritual of sitting in a circle, holding hands, and saying a short prayer for their success on the exam. Laura had to admit that it was an excellent idea. It kept the group together as a team. Petty arguments that sprouted up during each day's sessions were quickly forgotten, as they were reminded of their ultimate goal. Everyone was interested in Laura's ordeal with her husband seemingly lost in space. Laura was getting tired of so many people asking about this, but she politely responded to all her colleagues, reminding herself that these were the best friends she had right now.

Laura sent a quick message to Charlie that evening, saying that she was preparing for the final exam at the end of the first quarter. She explained that law school was a real challenge for her, but she was cautiously optimistic that she could make it through. Charlie answered her almost immediately. He repeated his offer that she could come by any time to observe some of the cases in action, but he understood that Laura was under a great deal of pressure to pass her exams, and her first priority was to make it through school and become a lawyer. Laura thanked him profusely for his understanding, and assured him that she was doing the very best she could to do exactly that. Silently, she wondered how anyone in law school could possibly have time for anything else.

The next day during her midday break, she went outside to do her par course. That was a set of calisthenics stations in the park. You jogged between stations. By each station was a sign describing an exercise. There were pushups, sit-ups, squat thrusts, pull-ups, hand walks on parallel bars, vaults over uneven bars, balance beam walks, and many others that weren't as tough. It was a good workout for Laura, that took close to an hour. With that plus a shower and lunch, she would spend her full two hour break.

When Laura completed her par course, she noticed a trim, middle-aged man standing, catching his breath.

"Hi," Laura said, half-smiling. "Are you just getting through with the course?"

"About five minutes ago," he said. "I push too hard on these things. I run instead of jog, and I do the highest level on each exercise."

"Wow, that's impressive," Laura said, wiping some sweat from her forehead. The weather had warmed up with summer approaching. "My name's Laura," she ventured, tentatively. "I'm a law student right now."

"I'm Vince," the man said. "Do you come here often?"

"This is my favorite workout during midday break. Probably about three days a week, something like that."

"How are you liking law school?"

"I'm working my ass off trying to keep up. I don't even think about whether I like it or not."

"Well, I hope we meet again, Laura," the man said, smiling, as he headed back to his car.

"See you later," Laura replied. "Nice meeting you."

Vince got in his car and drove off. Laura, took her shower, had lunch, then rejoined her friends for the long afternoon session.

For the next few days, Laura returned to the par course at the same time, wondering if she would run into Vince again. Sure enough, she did see him two days later, and two days before her exam.

"Hello, Laura," Vince said. "Are you ready to start your routine now?"

"Yes," said Laura, doing a few easy stretches.

"I've already gone one around," Vince said. "But I wouldn't mind doing a second lap with you. What do you say?"

"Sure," said Laura. "Just don't go too fast for me."

"I don't think that'll be a problem," said Vince. With that, they started jogging to the first station, a hamstring stretch. As the course wore on, Laura realized that Vince was in amazing shape. He was completing all the exercises easily, and at the maximum level. He was jogging easily between stations, but Laura was running to keep up. When they were done, Laura's arms and legs were exhausted, her heart was pounding hard, and she was very out of breath.

"Wow, that was a tough workout," Laura said between taking gasps of air. "I'm not used to pushing myself this hard."

"Well, you did very well, Laura. Let's do this again sometime."

"Sure," said Laura. "But I have an important test in law school day after tomorrow. Then I have a week off. How is your schedule for next week?"

"Next week is fine. How about Monday about this same time?"

"Okay, sounds good to me. I'll plan on seeing you Monday."

Laura took her shower and had lunch. She realized that she enjoyed being with Vince. It wasn't just that he pushed her on her exercises. It was a lot of things. For one, he had nothing to do with law school, or with job interviews, or any of that. He and Laura were spending free time together and enjoying each other's company. Laura also noticed that he never mentioned a peep about her as being famous. Maybe he didn't know or didn't recognize her, or maybe he just didn't want to make her uncomfortable.

Whatever the reason, she enjoyed being with someone who didn't always bring that up.

When she got back home to the study group, she was a little early, and no one else was there yet, except Debra.

"How was your lunch period, Laura?" she asked.

"Okay, I guess. I did meet an interesting man on the par course."

"Interesting man, eh? What was he like?"

"Well, he's about forty years old, and in very good shape. He's a good guy, very easy to talk with. Other than that, I know nothing about him. I don't know if he's single or married, or if he has kids, if he goes to church, heck I don't even know if he has a job."

Debra smiled. "Sounds interesting," she said. "Just be careful. Not that you're anywhere close to this, but boyfriends can be a real distraction to the law student."

"Yes," said Laura. "I realize that. And you're right, he's nowhere close to being my boyfriend."

Soon the rest of the group arrived for the study session, which went well into the night. Around midnight, Debra announced that tomorrow would be a day off. It was the day before the test, and it was more important to go into the test with a fresh brain than to do some extra time cramming.

They finished the session with the usual saying of a prayer together while sitting in a circle and holding hands. Laura spent the next day relaxing. She skipped her exercise, and just watched some television and did some reading. She ate some nice meals that her robot prepared for her. When she went to bed, she was relaxed and fell asleep quickly.

On the day of the exam, Laura woke up at her usual time, had the robot fix her a nice breakfast, and walked the few blocks to the school and the exam room. She took her usual seat, turned on her computer, and nervously waited. In a few minutes, the proctor arrived and gave instructions for how to access the exam.

41

The first case was about an employee who had worked for a company for twenty years, and was laid off with two weeks of severance pay. The employee wanted to sue the company for more severance. The company said that they were in accordance with the law, and there was no legal requirement to offer a larger severance package. Laura argued that the employee had every right to sue. He had given up a good part of his life, and many years of prime earning potential to work for the company. His termination came as a total surprise. He was given no warning at all, nor did he have any clue that a layoff was coming. He did not commit any acts of bad behavior such as insubordination or sexual harassment, and his work over the years was consistently rated as average to good. The company claimed that it was legally obligated to provide one month of severance pay for every year of employment, but only if the layoff involved ten or more people. Laura argued that this was an unjust law, and that the employee should try to find a way to circumvent it. She concluded that the employee deserved twenty months of severance at minimum, and that he had every right to sue.

The next case involved a man living along the Nile River delta. Years ago, he had captured a baby crocodile, and moved it into his house, where he kept it as a pet. The crocodile had since grown to be twelve feet long, and was getting restless in his pent-up surroundings. One day, the crocodile broke out of his "prison", and was wandering the streets of the town. He came upon a dog, who was barking at him, and he viciously bit the dog, requiring the dog to spend time in a veterinary hospital. The dog recovered from its wounds but will suffer some permanent damage to internal organs. One of the man's neighbors, realizing that the crocodile was a threat to the neighborhood, owned a gun, and used it to kill the crocodile. Problematically, the Nile crocodile is recognized by the World Council as an endangered species, so killing one is against the law and carries a harsh punishment. The dog's owner was suing the crocodile's owner for damages suffered by the dog. The crocodile owner was suing the crocodile's killer for improper death, in particular death to an endangered species.

Laura argued that the endangered species status was meant to ban the hunting of crocodiles. This was not a case of hunting. It was a case of self-defense of the community. Laura also argued that the crocodile's owner was totally at fault here for allowing a predatory, carnivorous beast to be set free to roam the inhabited streets of a town. Laura also argued that he was at fault for removing the crocodile from its natural habitat and caging it. In summary, the crocodile's owner should pay for the damages to the dog, and should receive no compensation at all for the death of his crocodile.

The third case involved two companies, located next to each other on the street. Company A had a row of trees that extended along the length of its property and close to its border with Company B. Company B had an issue with its water being shut off. Upon inspection, Company B suspected that roots from Company A's trees had ruptured the pipes supplying water to Company B. They submitted underground photos of tree roots adjacent to the pipe and to the point of fracture in the pipe. Company B wanted Company A's trees cut down, and wanted to sue Company A for loss of business for two days while its water supply was cut off. Company B was a large, well-established company, and loss of business for two days would amount to a considerable sum of money.

Laura took the side of Company A. Her first point was that there was no proof that roots had fractured the pipe. The pipe was made out of plastic, and the fracture may have been the result of material fatigue. In fact, Laura doubted that tree roots would have the power to fracture a pipe. She posited that a human being banging a secure pipe with full force from a tree root would probably not even fracture the pipe, although this was her speculation. She supposed that the pipe had fractured on its own, and then the tree root had moved to the general vicinity of the pipe. She also noted that, in the underground photos, the tree roots were not in direct contact with the pipe. The pipe was made out of cheap plastic material and was several years old, making it especially susceptible to material fatigue rupture. Furthermore, Company B had some trees in the general vicinity of the fracture, and it was certainly possible that roots from Company B's trees were observed in the underground photos. Laura concluded that Company A was not at fault, and Company B should upgrade its pipes to steel.

The fourth case was about a middle-aged widowed man, the former son-in-law of a wealthy lady. When the lady passed away, she conspicuously left the son-in-law out of her will. The son-in-law was angered. He had done much to support the lady and her daughter over several years. He had juggled his personal life so he and his wife could live close by the mother-in-law, and be able to respond to any of her needs. The man's wife, the daughter of the woman, was also deceased. The mother-in-law left all her assets to immediate family, like brothers, aunts, and so forth. The son-in-law claimed that these people had little stake to an inheritance, as they had done nothing to support the mother-in-law over the years. The son-in-law, on the other hand, had re-arranged his life and the life of his wife, going to considerable personal expense to support the mother-in-law. He was suing for a considerable fraction of the estate.

Laura took the side of the mother-in-law. She asserted that the mother-in-law had total control of her estate, and she had every right to allocate assets in her will however she wished. Unless she could be found to be of unsound mind when she made up her will, her wishes had to be honored.

That was the end. Laura had finished her test. She checked the time, and was surprised to see that there were only five minutes remaining in her time limit. She seemed to be zipping through everything, and was hoping to have some leftover time to review her answers. As it was, she just decided to call it quits, and declare herself done with the test. She took a deep breath, turned off her computer, stood up, and walked out.

The cutoff for the test was a complicated thing. For a candidate to continue with legal training, three conditions had to be met. First, the candidate had to achieve a score of 65 or better, out of 100, on this test. Second, a weighted average of marks from this test and previous tests this quarter had to be greater than 65. Third, that weighted average could not be in the bottom 20% of the class. This complicated set of rules insured that 20% of the class or more would fail. If a person failed, there was still a chance that a compassionate professor would plead to have the student re-instated in the program, although this was a rare occurrence. The tabulation was done by computer, and the results would be released soon after the final exams were all completed and graded. In a few hours, Laura would know how she did.

Her friends in the study group had gathered at Laura's house, which had come to be the de facto meeting place. They started talking about the test and how they answered each of the questions. Laura was getting nervous because it seemed like her friends had thought much deeper into the scenarios than Laura had. They all seemed to agree that the test itself was not that hard, but it would probably be graded hard. To score over 90, you would have to think about lots of arguments and counter-arguments for each case. Laura listened to this discussion, becoming more and more worried that her straightforward, rather simplistic answers might not be good enough to earn a good grade.

"Well, enough of this," Debra said, possibly noticing Laura's increasing uneasiness. "How about we have some lunch?"

"I can have my robot whip up something here," Laura offered. The others in the group nodded in agreement.

They all had a pleasant lunch together and talked about random topics, none related to law school.

The little party was about to break up around 6 in the afternoon, when Carla noticed that the results had been posted. They all logged on with their phones to check. Laura was the slowest to check, as she was filled with dread. As it turned out, Laura was fine. She scored 76, so she passed, but maybe not with flying colors. Debra scored 93, and Carla and Tamara got 90 and 88 respectively. Laura was accepted into the next quarter of law school. She breathed a huge sigh of relief. But there was a bit of a sour taste in her mouth, as she realized she was far worse than the rest of the study group. Debra came and congratulated her, and went on to say that Laura was a valued member of the study group who made important contributions to the group's efforts. Laura thanked Debra and gave her a hug. Debra said that she hoped Laura would continue with the study group next quarter. Laura said that she would. As it turned out, they all would be taking the same classes next quarter – continuations of environmental law, property law, and contract law, and a first course in criminal law. The group all said their good-byes, and then went off, leaving Laura alone in the house with her robot. Laura felt like she needed to talk to someone, so she talked to the robot.

"Well, I passed my test, and I am promoted to the next quarter of law school. But the other girls in my study group scored much higher than I did."

The robot surprised Laura by actually responding, and responding wisely. "Laura, you don't need to compare yourself to others. You are pursuing your own goal, and you just took another step toward achieving that goal. You have also proved yourself a very capable woman. You have every reason to be pleased with yourself."

"Thank you, Miss Robot. I did not expect you to answer me, and I am happy to hear your bits of wisdom on this. That reminds me, I still have not given you a name. Do you have any suggestions, anything that you would like to be called?"

"Elsa," said the robot. "I would like to be called Elsa."

"Okay, Elsa. You are not only my devoted robot, you are a valuable friend. I am grateful for my friendship with you."

"Thank you," said Elsa.

With that, Laura went to her bedroom, lay down, and fell asleep quickly. It had been a long, tiring day.

42

After spending a quiet, restful weekend, Laura went out to meet Vince on Monday. They did a par course together, then went to a fancy restaurant for lunch. Vince had chosen the restaurant, and had told Laura that he would pay for the lunch. He encouraged Laura to have whatever she wanted. Laura decided to not overdo it, and had a veggie sandwich and some pie for dessert. Vince had a bigger meal, saying that he hoped Laura wouldn't mind. Laura assured him it was okay.

Laura took the lead, and told Vince that she had passed her first big test in law school. Vince was very impressed, and congratulated her.

"So you've got, what, five more quarters to go, Laura?"

Laura nodded. "Sometimes I doubt that I will make it. Getting through this first quarter took every ounce of strength that I had."

"But it gets easier after the first quarter, doesn't it?"

"I don't know that it gets easier. I think maybe the grading is a little easier. They grade tough for the first quarter, thinking that if someone isn't going to make it, then they want to get rid of that person early, before too much time and money is wasted."

"That's encouraging," said Vince. "Do you have any stats? Like, if you make it through the first quarter, what are your chances of becoming a lawyer?"

"I don't know," said Laura. "But the general scuttlebutt is that once you pass that hurdle in your first quarter, then you will probably make it and become a lawyer."

"Sounds good, Laura. I'm sure you will do fine, and eventually become an excellent lawyer. But I want to know more about you. What were you doing before law school?"

"Wow," said Laura. "That is a long story, if ever there was one." And she poured out her life story to Vince, starting when she was working in technology with Josh, and they both were laid off. She talked about the quick marriage to Josh, and how she had been cryogenically sleeping for 1300 or more years. And she talked about Josh, being somewhere in outer space, and over 100 years late in arriving back.

Vince stared in astonishment. "My God, Laura, so your real time is like twenty-four hundred and something?"

"Yes," said Laura. "Twenty-four-forty-six." She couldn't believe Vince had never heard this story before. She thought everyone in the world knew about her.

"Holy gadzooks," said Vince, slapping himself on the forehead. "How are you adjusting to your new world?"

"Well, surprisingly, it isn't all that much different from the world I left. There are differences for sure, but it isn't that much of a culture shock. For example, automobile technology has definitely improved, everyone has their own robot, everything is driven by clean nuclear power, computers are much faster, everyone speaks English, there are no countries any more, you buy things with your thumb print. But, when you get down to it, so what? You get used to those things pretty fast.

"Most science fiction of my day depicted the future in wildly phantasmagoric ways. Like everyone scooting around in their own private jets, buildings reaching to the sky, space ships going around the universe, junk like that. Of course, those kinds of visions for the future leave a lot of questions unanswered. Like, where do they get the energy to propel all these private jets? How can you go zipping around the galaxy at speeds faster than light? How do you support a growing population, where does the food and energy come from? What about the growing problem of human waste, air pollution, water pollution, and so forth? How do you avoid a massive world war with everyone competing for scarce resources?"

"So you came to the future and decided on becoming a lawyer. With a background in technology, why would you want to go into law?"

"Technology has changed so much since my day. My background in it is over one thousand years old, and it would take me years to catch up. Law, on the other hand, has certainly changed, and the political world has changed, but that kind of change is manageable for me. I can learn law in this new era, and learn it in a reasonable amount of time. Law school only takes eighteen months. I'm studying hard, and I am starting to feel like I really can do it."

"That's great, Laura. You are definitely making the most of your trip to the future."

"And what about you, Vince? I don't know much about you at all, except that you are quite good on the par course."

"Right now I am a history professor. So, naturally, I am very interested in your life before your trip to the future."

"Wow!" said Laura. "I never would have guessed. I guess you have a lot of questions for me and I have a lot of questions for you. But, to start, can you summarize history between 2446 and today. I know almost nothing about what happened while I was asleep."

"Well, amazingly, World War Three never happened, but tensions throughout the world were high. There was a lot of "saber rattling" as it is called. A lot of cyber warfare and smuggling of dirty nukes. We were lucky to avoid a devastating world war. The situation was scary enough that countries agreed to a meeting in Zurich, to discuss possible ways forward. The conference lasted ten years. Progress was slow, but the ideas were shocking. The biggest idea was to get rid of individual countries. There would be one central government to run the Earth. All individual countries would cease to exist. There would be no government-sponsored religions. The ideas from the Zurich Accord were at first unpopular and controversial, but gradually became accepted.

"Other than that, space exploration has advanced. The World Council has made it a priority to find habitable planets in the galaxy that human beings could live on. It's a good long-term strategy. To save the human race, you need to spread out among several planets. A disaster hitting the Earth could wipe us all out, and that would be the end of humanity. Better to make homes on a number of planets. A disaster on any one of them wouldn't spell the end of us. So, many expeditions were sent out, like your husband's trip, to do reconnaissance on other worlds. Things are moving along. We have already identified five livable planets, and have set up colonies on them. It is logistically difficult, however, to terraform an alien world. We are using robots to do this terraforming after initial reconnaissance by humans. This is much simpler than using thousands of human colonists, but is still tricky. The robots need a lot of intelligence programmed into them to accomplish the tough tasks of terraforming and defending themselves against alien life forms. Once the robots complete the initial terraforming, human colonists can take over from there."

"Sounds like you are not only a history person, but a science guy as well. You have certainly been keeping up with modern science to know all what you know."

"Well, history is my passion, and what's happening now in science is part of history. So I try to keep up. I think of it as part of my passion."

Laura and Vince continued to talk into the afternoon, and agreed to meet again later in the week. Laura explained that she had one week off from school before starting up again, and once school started, she wouldn't have much time at all. Vince understood. He gave her a little hug, and they said goodbye for now.

Laura watched Vince leave and felt sad. They were both married, so nothing was ever going to happen. But Vince was a terrific friend. Laura could talk forever with him.

Then Laura sent a quick message to Charlie, saying that she had passed her final exam for the quarter. She mentioned that she had a week off, and may drop by the office and maybe observe part of a case. Charlie responded quickly, congratulating her, and welcoming her to stop by whenever she could.

43

Time flew by. Laura and her study group stayed together and continued to do well on all the tests. Whenever Laura had time, she would stop and visit Charlie, and observe one of the trials in action. She still saw Vince a few days a week. They would usually do a par course together, then have lunch. Vince was a nice soul mate. He would talk some about his own life, but mostly listen to Laura, showing a genuine interest in her law school. Laura continued to get passing grades on all her tests. Charlie, Vince, and her study group were all cheering for her, and she felt like she had a real group of friends.

The sixth and final quarter of law school was a series of moot courts. The students had to interrogate witnesses, and argue their cases before a panel of judges. The idea was to simulate a real courtroom as closely as possible. Laura was uncomfortable on the first moot court, and probably performed poorly. But, as time went by, she gained some experience, got more comfortable, and believed she had become a respectable lawyer. She received passing grades in all her courses and all her moot courts. Things were going well for Laura. She soon graduated from law school along with her study-mates. They all took a day and celebrated with some hiking and lots of food. But, besides getting through law school, there was still the exam from the World Council that Laura had to pass before finally becoming a lawyer.

So, after the one day of celebrating, they got back to their routine of group-study for hours each day. Laura was exhausted from doing so much of this, but the exhaustion had an optimistic edge to it. Now Laura truly believed she could become a lawyer. There was just one more test to pass, and, supposedly, this test was not as tough as some that she had been through already.

When it was finally time for the last test, Laura entered it well-prepared. It was different from her earlier tests. The earlier tests were very open-ended. A scenario was explained, and Laura was free to choose one side or the other and make her case. In this final test, scenarios were given, but specific questions were asked. What law was broken? How serious should the punishment be? What were the mitigating circumstances, if any?

Laura did okay on this final test, and passed with a score of 85. Debra scored 97, but Laura had actually scored higher than her other two study-mates. But the important thing was that she passed. She soon received her diploma, which authorized her to become a lawyer. After celebrating with her friends for a few days, she proudly marched into Charlie's office, and showed him the diploma, which she had gotten framed. Charlie was overjoyed, and so were the rest of the people in the office. They had all come to know Laura by now, and had been quite supportive of her.

"Now that you are a lawyer," Charlie said, "we would like you to try your first case." Charlie handed her a notebook, and a reference to some computer files for her to read in preparation. "The trial starts day after tomorrow," Charlie stated matter-of-factly.

Wow, Laura was overwhelmed. She had thought that she could enjoy more time of celebration and praise. She did not expect to have the responsibilities hit her so quickly.

"Well, I'll do my best," she said simply. "And thanks, Charlie." Charlie nodded, and walked with her to her new office, which contained a nice desk with a computer and printer, and some elegant leather chairs.

"We're here if you need us," said Charlie, as he walked out.

After spending a few minutes getting used to her new computer, Laura located the files on the case and began her work. The case seemed relatively straightforward. The World Council was charging Thomas Alfino with illegally storing toxic wastes on his property. Mr. Alfino said that the waste was stored in a remote area of his property so that no plants, animals, or humans would come into contact with it. In the trial, Laura was asked to take the prosecution's side, charging that Mr. Alfino had broken the law.

Laura called on an expert to map Mr. Alfino's property, and locate where the toxic waste had been buried. It was quite a significant amount that was placed five feet underground, and was adjacent to some tree roots.

It turned out that Alfino was operating a waste disposal site, where anybody could, for a fee, come and dispose of hazardous waste. Of course, this was illegal. During the trial, Laura found Alfino guilty on several counts.

First, he was accepting toxic waste from his customers, and never reporting that he was doing this. Second, he was not submitting to regular inspections. Third, he had no written documentation of the waste material that he was storing. Finally, he was not taking adequate measures to protect the public from the waste. The waste, in fact, was sitting underground, having never been treated or neutralized. Alfino had to pay a large fine, and was forced to shut his facility down.

Officials from the World Council congratulated Laura on the verdict. Charlie and several others in Laura's firm also congratulated her. True, it was not a difficult case. Nonetheless, Laura had performed at a very high level. Laura was elated. She had handled her first case as a lawyer. And she had won.

44

Josh woke up to the sound of soft music. The computer spoke to him, as Josh struggled to climb out of bed.

"We are almost here, Josh. Almost back to Earth."

"I'm very relieved," said Josh. "I was nervous about the directions I gave you when we were lost out there."

"Your directions were not perfect, but were good enough, Josh. When we were getting close, there was only one star system nearby, and I steered toward it. As I got closer, I recognized the sun, and then Jupiter with the big red spot, and then Saturn with the rings. This has to be the right place."

Josh got out of bed, and noticed the welcome pull of gravity. "I guess you are decelerating at one g," he commented needlessly.

"Yes," said the computer.

Josh grabbed the portable telescope and looked out the massive window. He could definitely make out the sun, Jupiter, and Saturn, but he couldn't yet find the Earth. He decided to pee out the rest of his gel, then take a shower and change his clothes. He would come and look for the Earth a little later.

He took a long trip to the bathroom, peeing out whatever he could, then took a welcome shower and got into some nice comfortable clothes. Then he was back to peeing. He went back and forth to the bathroom for close to an hour before he couldn't pee any more. Then he walked back to the viewing window. It was there. There was no mistaking it -- the huge blue oceans, the sprawling continents, patches of green, brown, and white. It was his Earth. It looked the same as it did in his day, over one thousand years ago. There was no trace of a devastating nuclear holocaust or a climate disaster. Josh studied it for a long time, unable to tear his eyes away. The Earth looked fine. He was enormously relieved that his planet was still healthy and normal.

But what would his life be like in this new world? Would he still be able to get a job? Were his skills completely obsolete? And what about Laura? Was she still around? Maybe she had become an old lady. Or maybe she was long since dead. Did she still love him?

Tears welled up in his eyes as he realized over one thousand years had gone by on the Earth since he was last here. He kept staring at the Earth, which was visibly growing larger.

"We should be in range for messaging now," the computer said, after a few more minutes. "You can just speak into this microphone when you're ready. It will automatically transmit to our home station on Earth."

"Okay," said Josh. He could feel the sweat collect on his hands as he made his way clumsily to the microphone.

"Hello," he began. "My name is Josh. I am requesting permission to land. I am with the United States Space Program."

The receiver came to life. "You are with the what?"

"The United States Space Program," Josh repeated, enunciating his words slowly and carefully.

"There is no such thing as the United States Space Program." There was a long pause. Josh didn't know what to say. "Oh, wait a minute, I'm checking here. Do you remember what year you left Earth?"

"Twenty-four forty-six," Josh said.

"Yes, I see now. Back then there was something called the United States Space Program. Now it's the Planet Earth Space Program. Wow, you have been gone an awfully long time."

"Yes," said Josh, wiping some sweat from his forehead. "Now I would like clearance to land."

"I can give you clearance in a minute, Josh. Please hold on."

Josh waited for what seemed an interminably long time. Finally, his receiver crackled back to life.

"Sorry for the delay, Josh. Yes, you are cleared to land. We are messaging you a vector."

"Thank you," said Josh.

"I received their vector, Josh," said the computer. "I can take it from here. You can relax and enjoy the view."

Minutes later, they landed, and Josh prepared to exit the plane. He thought maybe there would be some kind of welcoming committee. But there wasn't such a thing. Instead, there were two armed security guards. They weren't happy or smiling. As Josh walked off the ship, he was instructed to follow them.

45

Laura was relaxing in the parlor, when there came a knock on her door. When she went to answer it, she was met by two police women.

"Is your husband named Josh?" one of them asked.

"Yes," said Laura guardedly, not knowing what to expect next.

"Josh has made it back to Earth. He landed an hour or so ago. He's being held in jail."

"Jail? What? What in the world for?" Laura was stupefied.

"We can take you to where he is being held. But I can't tell you anything about what crimes he committed."

"Okay," said Laura, quickly straightening herself up. She didn't know whether to be overjoyed that Josh was back okay, or frightened that he was in jail.

Laura rode in the car with the two police women. The ride was very tense. Laura had no idea what to talk to these women about. She just wanted to see Josh and to learn why he was in jail.

The jail was an old building, painted a dull gray. Laura looked the place over, already feeling dread. The women led Laura through the main entrance. Laura had to submit to a quick body search to make sure she was not bringing in a concealed weapon. Then they went through a series of long hallways, finally coming to a large conference room. Laura was told to take a seat.

A few minutes later, Josh was led into the room, looking tired and haggard. He had a prominent stubble from not having shaved in a few days. Laura ran up to him and threw her arms around him.

"Oh Josh, I can't believe it's really you," she cried. Josh could not hug Laura back because his arms were constrained, but a torrent of tears was pouring from his face. He looked very confused. He probably couldn't work out where he was, or why he was being held in jail.

"I love you so much, Laura. And I'm so sorry to put you through this. I don't know what I did, I really don't."

Laura saw an officer standing in the room, and she asked him what Josh's crime was. The officer explained that he had committed mass murder, killing a large group of intelligent alien life forms. He was in violation of the Endangered Species Act, which had been enlarged some time ago to include alien life.

"Josh, I am a lawyer now. I can get you out of this, or at least give it my very best shot. But first we have a lot of catching up to do. Tell me about your trip."

Josh told Laura everything. He told her about taking the ice core samples, and exploring the planet, going underwater, being attacked by the giant squid, finding the space ship full of crocodile people, how the crocodile had killed Missy, and how Josh had brought her back to life.

"Who is Missy?" Laura interrupted.

"Missy is the computer that controls the rover. The rover is what we took when we were exploring the planet. We were lucky we could save Missy. Otherwise, we would have been marooned on the planet.

"The crocodile people came from another planet. I guess they sent their hardened criminals there in exile. The life forms on the planet were plant-eaters, and had no defense against the crocodile monsters. The crocodiles were twenty-five feet tall standing upright, and could run at thirty miles per hour. We came upon a scene that was horrific, where a herd of crocodile monsters was butchering a group of indigenous animals. I couldn't stand to see it. We flew around in the rover and killed the crocodile invaders. I think there must have been like sixty of them. That is the mass murder that they are talking about."

Then Josh went on to describe the trip to the crocodile planet, and how Josh was captured and had to fight in an ancient Roman style amphitheater against a crocodile monster. It was a fight to the death. Josh killed the crocodile monster, and was awarded his freedom.

"My God!" was all Laura could say, as she buried her head in her hands, imagining the horror that Josh had experienced.

Laura reached for her phone and messaged Charlie. "Charlie, my husband has made it back from his expedition. Unfortunately, he is being charged with a crime for something he did on another planet. I want to defend him."

Then Laura started to describe for Josh life in the year 3798. She told him that things were different but that he could get used to things very fast, as Laura did. Josh listened to all this, nodding politely, but it was obvious that he was consumed with worry about his situation.

Soon Charlie messaged back. "Wow, Laura, great news. This will be exciting for you and for the firm. We should get a lot of media attention, which is always nice. You handle the case, but don't hesitate to ask if you need help."

Laura turned her attention back to Josh. "Josh, that was my boss at the law firm. I will be defending you. I swear, I will do everything in my power to get you out of this mess. I want to go home and study the data, the videos that you captured, and whatever I can get from the ship's logs. Let's talk again tomorrow, Josh. And I love you so much, Josh. I will do my absolute best for you."

"I know you will, Laura. And I love you too. More than you can imagine." Laura hugged Josh around his neck, and kissed him on the lips. Then she waved to the security guard to show her the way out. As she left, she and Josh were both crying.

The next day was Sunday, and Laura came back about the same time to see Josh. When he entered the room, she ran over and kissed him. Then she led him to the table in the center. They sat down, facing each other.

"Josh, I have studied your case for most of last night. You are innocent. We will plead 'not guilty'. I have looked through all your videos, including the fight in the arena with the crocodile, which was recorded from your phone. You had every right to do what you did. You were not breaking any law. We will win this thing. I will make sure to set you free.

"So here's the thing. Tomorrow, I will meet you here. We will go to court and enter your plea of 'not guilty.' Then the judge will set a date for the start of trial, probably in a few days. The verdict will be determined by a regular jury of twelve people.

"So, other than that, how are you doing?"

"I guess okay," said Josh. "It's nice to see you. I just wish that our reunion could be happier, and less full of worry."

"Don't worry, Josh. I may be fairly new at this, but I am a good lawyer. I will get you out of this mess, and then we can have a nice life together."

"I love you" was all that Josh could say, as tears flowed down his cheeks.

"I love you too, Josh," Laura said, brushing her hand against his cheek.

The next day, Monday, Laura picked up Josh and they went to court. The whole thing lasted five or ten minutes. Laura declared that Josh was pleading 'not guilty'. The judge set the trial date for Wednesday, two days from now. The first thing that would happen in the trial would be jury selection.

Then Laura and Josh left the courthouse. Laura had her arm around Josh. They got into a car, and went back to the jail. Laura dropped Josh off with a flurry of kisses, and then walked out, with tears streaking down her face.

46

The jury selection went from Wednesday through Friday. Laura was looking for jurors who understood science and who could relate to Josh and what he had experienced. Beyond that, she just wanted jurors who could be sensitive and deep-thinking, who could understand Josh's position when he murdered 68 crocodiles. The prosecution was looking for uneducated, simple people, who would be swayed by the video of Josh's mass murder, and never think any deeper than that. In the end, the twelve-member jury was a mixture of those two kinds of people. When the jury selection was completed on Friday afternoon, the judge dismissed the court, and announced that the trial would begin on Monday morning.

On Monday, the prosecution started out in a fury. First, they showed the video of Josh murdering 68 crocodiles along the shore of a lake. The prosecutor made the point that this was clear evidence that Josh had committed mass murder of intelligent beings on another planet, and was therefore in clear violation of the Interplanetary Endangered Species Act. Next they called to the stand a professor of criminal law, and asked if he thought the mass murder was justified because of self-defense, or some other reason.

"No," the witness said. "There is no way to justify this mass murder by calling it self-defense."

"Your witness," said the prosecutor, yielding to Laura.

Laura patted Josh on the hand. "It's okay," she whispered. "We've got this."

"Now professor, can you tell me when the Interplanetary Endangered Species Act went into law?" said Laura, standing.

"That's ancient history," said the professor. "I cannot give you an exact date."

"It was thirty-four-fifteen," said Laura. "I looked it up. Here is the reference document that I would like to enter as a defense exhibit with the court. It is an entry in the Galactic Encyclopedia, most recent edition." She handed the printed page to the judge, who nodded his head, and set it aside.

Laura continued. "Now, Professor, you and the prosecutor have correctly pointed out that self-defense is a legitimate and legal reason to break the law. By the law, I am of course referring to the Interplanetary Endangered Species Act. Are you aware of any other allowable reason to break this law?"

"Not offhand. I guess there are excusable reasons, analogous to a murder of a human being. For example, if the violator was criminally insane and could not control his thoughts or actions, that would be one case."

"Well, professor, I have here the exact text of the Interplanetary Endangered Species Act. You may have a look." Laura handed him the printed pages.

"You will notice, Professor, that the manual entitled 'Guidelines for Interacting With Alien Life Forms' is listed in the body of the law. Why is that, Professor?"

"I don't know."

"Well, a little farther down, the law states acceptable reasons for not obeying it. One of the reasons is self-defense. Another reason is that by following the law, you would violate one of the principles set forth in 'Guidelines for Interacting with Alien Life Forms'."

The professor studied the printed pages for a few seconds, and shrugged. Laura took them from him.

"Your honor, I would next like to enter this in evidence, the full body of the Interplanetary Endangered Species Act." She handed the text to the judge, who admitted it as evidence.

"No more questions," said Laura.

The judge glanced over to the prosecutor. "No more questions," he stated simply. Then he added, "The prosecution rests."

Laura breathed a sigh of relief. Apparently, the prosecution's case was based entirely on the video of Josh committing the murders on the planet.

"The defense may call its first witness," said the judge.

"Thank you," said Laura. "The defense calls Mr. Arthur Maxwell."

Mr. Maxwell stepped forward, took his oath, and sat down.

"Now, Mr. Maxwell, you are a theoretical physicist employed at the Planet Earth Space Program, is that right?"

"Yes, that's right."

"And you have a number of advanced degrees in physics, including a Ph.D. from Sorbonne, is that right?"

"Yes."

"And you have a clear understanding of the General Theory of Relativity."

"Yes, of course."

"Can you provide us with an explanation of time dilation, as it applies to an object moving at a velocity that is significant compared to the speed of light?"

"Yes. If we imagine two clocks, one attached to the fast-moving object, and the other at rest, the clock attached to the fast-moving object will move slower than the clock that is at rest."

"Objection," yelled the prosecutor. "What is the relevance of this testimony?"

"Your honor, I am trying to establish the time that Josh was on the planet, as measured by a clock here on Earth. It is a vital part of my defense."

"Okay, I will overrule the objection. You may continue questioning."

"Can you give us the formula, Mr. Maxwell, for relating the two clocks?"

"Yes. What I refer to as the factor is the quantity the square root of one minus v squared over c squared. The variable v is the object's velocity, and the constant c is the speed of light. When we know the clock on Earth, and we want information about the clock on a space ship, say, then we multiply by the factor. Going the other way, we divide by the factor."

"Thank you, Mr. Maxwell. I will call you back shortly. But first, I need to call another witness. I call the ship's computer."

"Objection," yelled the prosecutor, standing up and waving his arms. "You can't call a computer as a witness. The council is making a mockery of this trial."

"Your honor, the computer is the most accurate, most reliable source of data regarding the ship's flight. The computer is incapable of telling a lie."

"Okay, I will allow the witness."

The computer, which weighed about twenty pounds, was carried in by the bailiff and placed on the witness stand.

The computer was asked to take the oath, which was a bit comical because the computer did not have a hand to touch the Bible or another hand to reach up and solemnly swear. But the judge approved the computer's oath. Then Laura began her questioning.

"Now, Mr. Computer, if I may call you that, do you recall the flight leaving Earth for the target planet?"

"Yes, of course. My memory is very good." At this, most of the courtroom broke out into a chuckle.

"How long did the trip take, and what was your average speed?"

"According to the clock on the ship, the trip took 375 years. The average speed was 80% of the speed of light."

"How accurate are those numbers?"

"375 years is accurate to within 0.2 years. 80% of the speed of light is accurate to within 0.1 percent."

Laura recalled Mr. Maxwell. "Mr. Maxwell, as you heard the testimony, the ship was traveling at 80% of the speed of light, and the clock on the ship measured 375 years. Can you help us figure out how much time elapsed on the Earth?"

"Yes. I will take you through the calculation if you don't mind. V over c is 80% or 0.8. Then v squared over c squared is 0.8 squared or 0.64. One minus 0.64 is 0.36. Finally, the square root of 0.36 is 0.6, and this gives the factor. Since we are going from ship time to Earth time, we divide 375 years by 0.6, and get 625 years, the time observed from Earth for Josh to make his outbound flight."

"Your honor, here is the flight plan for that outbound flight. As it states, the flight was begun in the year twenty-four-forty-six. So Josh arrived at the destination planet 625 years thereafter, or in the year thirty-seventy-one.

"Now he certainly did not stay on the planet for over several years, but the computer can help us figure out when he left. So I call the computer back to the stand.

"Now, Mr. Computer, the return trip to Earth was complicated because you got lost, correct?"

"Yes," said the computer.

"And why did you get lost?"

"The star Betelgeuse was a key navigational point for me. But I could not find it when we left for Earth. Betelgeuse is a red giant star, and I locked onto another red giant, Aldebaran. As a result, we were off in the wrong direction for quite some time. When I realized I was lost, I woke up Josh. Josh used his knowledge of astronomy and mathematics to point me toward Earth."

"And why couldn't you find Betelgeuse?"

"In the time we were gone, it had exploded in a supernova. It just disappeared. It wasn't there any more."

"Well, you eventually arrived at Earth in the year 3798. If you started your trip around 3071, then your return trip took seven hundred and twenty-seven years. Normally it would have taken 625 years, so you were late by one hundred and two years."

"Yes, you are correct."

"And how long did the return trip take, according to the clock on the ship?"

"Four hundred and thirty six point three years."

"And your average speed was, again, 80% of the speed of light?"

"Yes."

"Okay, now I need Mr. Maxwell again."

Maxwell came to the witness stand, and took his seat.

"Mr. Maxwell, the return trip took 436.3 years as measured on the ship's clock. The average speed was 80% of the speed of light. Can you help us figure out how many years that would be for the Earth?"

"Sure," said Maxwell. "Since the speed is still the same, our factor of zero point six hasn't changed. We need to divide 436.3 by 0.6 to get the time elapsed on Earth." Maxwell took out his calculator and punched in the numbers. "Here we are. Seven hundred and twenty-seven point one seven years."

"Which is exactly what we had estimated before, so this validates our estimate. I think now we can say positively that Josh was on the planet during the year 3071. We can say that he committed the mass murder in the year 3071. We also know that the Interplanetary Endangered Species Act was put into law in the year 3415. So he is being accused of breaking a law that didn't exist yet.

May I continue tomorrow, your honor?"

"Yes. Court is adjourned until tomorrow."

Laura and Josh walked out of the courtroom together. Laura glanced at the prosecutor's team on the way out. They looked confused and frustrated.

"Don't worry, Josh. We got this," Laura said, and she kissed Josh on the lips.

47

When Laura and Josh arrived at the courthouse the next day, they were startled to see a mob of people greeting them on the steps outside and cheering. Many held up large signs that said "JOSH IS A HERO", "JOSH IS NOT A MURDERER", "WAY TO GO LAURA", and so on. It was clear that the public was completely behind Josh and Laura. Laura and Josh smiled politely as they continued to walk purposefully up the steps. They still had work to do.

Laura and Josh took their seats in the courtroom. Laura looked over at the prosecution's table. The men looked deflated, uninterested, just wanting things to end. The judge entered the room and indicated that Laura was still conducting her defense.

"You may call your next witness," the judge said, looking at Laura.

"I call the defendant, Josh, to the stand." There was a murmur that swept through the spectators. It was unusual to call a defendant to testify. Josh took the oath and then sat in the witness chair.

"Now Josh," Laura began. "How did you first get interested in Planet Earth Space Program?"

"I responded to a newspaper advertisement. I was immediately interested because I love the idea of exploring outer space. By the way, in those ancient times it was called the United States Space Program." A few spectators chuckled at the reference to ancient times.

"When you first became interested in space exploration, did you imagine yourself killing alien life forms?"

"No, not at all. I was an explorer, not a warrior. I was to gather information, not to fight."

"Okay, Josh, let's fast forward to your first encounter with the Crocodile Monsters. Excuse me, I use the term 'monsters' because these creatures were gigantic -- they were 25 feet long, and walked upright, so they were taller than a two-story building. And they could run at 25 or 30 miles per hour."

"Yes, that is correct. I have also referred to them as monsters. They scared the living shit out of me." The spectators laughed at this. "I first saw them when we were in the rover underwater. By chance, we found an alien space ship crashed into rocks below the surface of the ocean. The passengers of this space ship were all crocodile monsters, including the pilot."

At this point, Laura showed the video that was captured by the rover. It showed the rover approach the crashed ship. Then it showed the crocodile who was piloting the ship.

"So here you have discovered the alien ship. What theories about the crocodile monsters did you form at this time?"

"Well, first, the crocodile monsters were not of this world. Second, they must have only planned a one-way trip, because they did not leave themselves enough fuel for a return trip."

"So then you towed the space ship to a safe location where you could further analyze it."

"Yes, we were able to find a remote island, which served as a good base for doing our research."

"And what else were you able to find?"

"We saw there were many crocodile monsters tied up in chains in the ship's hold. They were all dead. We found that the space ship used liquid fuel. It had a large fuel tank that was almost, but not totally, dry. From the size of the fuel tank, we were able to estimate the volume of fuel that the ship had used to make its trip. Then, we were able to make a rough guess as to how far away was the crocodile's home planet. Of course, we could also see the obvious, that the crocodile monsters had developed an advanced technology that gave them the capability for interplanetary travel."

"Now, just as an aside, if the crocodile monsters had such an advanced technology, why couldn't we detect this on the Earth?"

"Well, the crocodile planet is 500 light years from Earth. So, for us to detect anything in 2446, a signal would have to be sent 500 years previously, in the year 1946. We did not detect a signal from the crocodile planet in 2446, and we would have if they had the technology in 1946. We can conclude that the technology on the crocodile planet was developed after 1946."

"So then how were you able to identify the crocodile planet?"

"With a telescope, we studied the night sky, where we could separate the planets from the stars. There weren't many planets at all. But we could identify which planets were within range of the crocodile planet's space ship capabilities. As it turned out, there was really only one candidate planet. So we undertook a journey to explore it."

"And when you got to the crocodile planet, what happened?"

"First, we had to evade a number of attacks from a nearby space station, which fired a type of plasma energy ray at us. After several such firings, we judged that, in self-defense, we needed to destroy the space station. And we did. After that, we faced an attack by surface-to-air missiles. One of them struck the ship, damaging the engine, and forcing us to crash land on the planet.

"Then I was taken prisoner by the crocodile monsters, and escorted to a huge arena, where I was forced to engage in a fight-to-the-death with one of the monsters."

"We actually have a video of that fight. Josh captured it on his phone."

"Objection!" yelled the prosecutor. "This is not relevant."

"It is a display of the savagery of the crocodile monster's society. The jury should observe this."

"How long is the video?" asked the judge.

"About ten minutes, your honor."

"Okay, I will allow the video. You may proceed, counselor."

Laura started the video, which began as Josh was entering the huge arena, and crocodile spectators were jeering him. The video continued, showing the entire fight between Josh and the crocodile monster. When Josh covered himself with feces, many in the audience had to look away. Laura explained that this was to disguise Josh's smell, which was how the monster could locate him. At the end, the spectator crocodiles stood and raised their arms in the air, acknowledging Josh as the winner.

Laura wasn't exactly sure if the video had the desired effect. Some were inspired by Josh's cleverness and bravery, others were disgusted by the brutality.

"And what did you learn from this experience, Josh?"

"The crocodile monsters, although a very technologically sophisticated people, are quite barbaric, and place a low value on life."

"Yes, I think we would all have to agree with that assessment.

"Your witness," Laura said, waving her hand at the prosecutor. The prosecutor only sat, feeling rather dumbfounded, as he saw his case was clearly a lost cause.

"No questions," he finally said in a deadpan voice.

"Your honor, I would like to call 'Missy', the computer on the rover."

"What more testimony do you expect from this so-called Missy?"

"Your honor, Missy was with Josh the whole time while Josh was firing on the crocodile people. Her testimony is important in proving his innocence."

"Very well, I will allow the witness."

The prosecutor didn't bother to object, probably knowing that the judge would overrule it as he did with the other computer.

Missy was sworn in and then Laura began her questioning.

"First of all, Missy, can you explain where you got that name?"

"Yes. Josh, having interacted with the ship's computer on the outbound flight, was used to a male voice. He naturally started addressing me as 'Mr. Computer.' When he heard my voice, he apologized, and starting saying 'Miss Computer', which somehow got shortened to 'Missy'. "

"Now, Missy, can you explain your duties on this mission."

"Yes. On this mission, there were two ships -- there was the main ship, capable of traveling interstellar distances at fast velocities. Then there was the rover, a smaller ship that was used for traveling around on a single planet. I was the computer who operated the rover."

"When you were underwater, and discovered the crocodile's space ship, you were using the rover for that?"

"Yes."

"And the rover was capable of traveling large distances across the planet?"

"Yes, we traversed pretty much the entire planet with the rover."

"And what was your relationship to Josh?"

"Josh was the commander. I followed his commands."

"Was it within your power to refuse to follow a command by Josh?"

"Yes. If I believed that Josh was telling me to do something morally or legally wrong, I could refuse to obey."

"Did such a situation ever occur?"

"No."

"What was your general opinion of Josh as a commander?"

"Superior. He had excellent judgment, and he succeeded in his assigned mission of exploring the planet, and collecting necessary data."

"Is it true that Josh once saved your life?"

"In a way, yes. A crocodile monster attacked me, disabled the rover, and destroyed some of my critical circuitry. Josh got me back aboard the main ship, where the robots there were able to patch me up."

"Now let's talk about the incident where Josh murdered the herd of crocodiles. The prosecution has already shown us the video of Josh's actions. But they left out the few minutes that preceded that battle."

Laura then showed the video of unspeakable carnage as the crocodile monsters were mercilessly killing the plant-eating animals that were native to the planet.

"Now, Missy, after watching this new video, what do you think was Josh's intent when he murdered the group of crocodile monsters?"

"I believe it was to save the wildlife that was native to the planet. The crocodile monsters were not native to the planet. They could outrun the animals on the planet, and they could easily kill them. Josh thought it was important to save the native animals."

"Did he tell you that?"

"Yes."

"Did he also say that he would like to declare war on the crocodile monsters?"

"Yes."

"How did you respond to this?"

"I told Josh that I agreed with him."

Laura now turned to the judge and spoke.

"The defense rests, your honor."

"Does the prosecution wish to cross-examine the witness?"

"No, your honor," said the prosecutor.

"Okay," the judge said. "It is now time for closing arguments. The prosecution may go forward."

But the prosecutor sat motionless and defeated.

Then Laura stepped forward and spoke.

"There are several points that need to be made here. Point number one – defending the animals native to a planet is a prime directive according to the manual 'Guidelines for Dealing with Alien Life Forms.' The text of the Interplanetary Endangered Species Act allows an exception for activities that conform to the specifications set forth in the Guidelines. In the Guidelines, I am displaying the critical lines of text that specify that the prime directive is to protect the native life on the planet."

The text appeared on the display screen.

"Now, continuing on," said Laura, "point number two is that war is another excuse for ignoring the Interplanetary Endangered Species Act. When Josh fired on the crocodiles, he was in a state of war with them. He had told Missy that we should be in war, and Missy had agreed. According to the Guidelines, this places them legally at war. Here is the relevant text from the Guidelines."

Laura displayed this new text on the display screen.

"And then there is the issue of timing. Josh spent his time on the planet during the year 3071 as measured on Earth. But the Interplanetary Endangered Species Act did not become law until 3415, as measured on Earth. Even without the previously mentioned points, Josh cannot be accused of breaking a law that doesn't exist yet.

"With all these considerations in mind, we move that the charges against Josh be dropped."

The judge pondered for a second, then spoke. "I hereby declare that the charges against Josh are dropped. The reasons are what the counselor has just explained. The case is very clear. There is no need for a jury to debate this. Josh, you are free to go."

The bailiff removed Josh's restraints. He and Laura passionately kissed, and then walked out of the courtroom, arm-in-arm. As they stepped outside, they were met by a huge crowd of thousands of people, cheering wildly. A man with a microphone approached Laura.

"Laura, what is your reaction to the verdict?"

"Josh displayed courage and bravery throughout his ordeal. He should be regarded as a hero. The prosecution saw a chance to defame him, but there was clearly no basis to their accusation."

Josh and Laura walked to their car, and settled into the back seat, while Laura gave verbal directions to her house. The car sped off through the city streets. Josh and Laura, very much in love, began to plan the rest of their lives together.

EPILOG

Following Laura's impressive win in defending Josh, she was immediately promoted to partner in the firm. She was a very famous person. Wherever she went, people recognized her and often asked for autographs.

Josh's fate was similar. He became very famous, his picture appearing on the covers of magazines, and his face recognizable to everyone. He accepted a job at the Planet Earth Space Program as Vice President of Planetary Exploration and Colonization. His job allowed him a lot of time to spend on research.

In a few years, Josh and Laura quit their jobs and moved to Polynesia, where they remained blissfully happy.

Laura's study mates – Debra, Tamara, and Carla – founded their own law firm, specializing in contract law. It was quite successful.

Vince remained a good family friend.

Charles Fink continued in his job as senior partner in the law firm, and remained a close family friend to Laura and Josh.

Gronk became leader of his clan, and undertook an ambitious project to build sturdy ships, capable of exploring the world.

The crocodile monsters suffered through a series of long, destructive wars, which brought great harm to their world, and wiped out a large portion of their population. Their program of interplanetary travel came to a stop as their population declined and their supply of resources diminished.